Yakuza, Go Home!

More Mark Shigata Mysteries by Anne Wingate

Death by Deception
The Eye of Anna
The Buzzards Must Also Be Fed
Exception to Murder

Yakuza, Go Home!

A Mark Shigata Mystery

Anne Wingate

Walker and Company
New York

First published in the United States of America in 1993
by Walker Publishing Company, Inc.

Published simultaneously in Canada by Thomas Allen & Son
Canada, Limited, Markham, Ontario

Library of Congress Cataloging-in-Publication Data
Wingate, Anne
Yakuza, go home! : a Mark Shigata mystery / Anne Wingate.
p. cm.
ISBN 0-8027-3226-7
I. Title.
PS3573.I5316Y3 1993
813'.54—dc20 92-43523
CIP

Printed in the United States of America
2 4 6 8 10 9 7 5 3 1

To Alice

Who is more of a sister than my sister is

Author's Note

SOMETIMES, IN REAL LIFE as in fiction, the mystery the investigator faces is not one of whodunit, but rather one of "What can I do about it?" And there are other real-life situations the public rarely knows about—the friends injured or killed, the threats to the investigator's family.

I have watched television with a pistol on the end table and cooked with a pistol on the counter because of believable threats against my children. I have taken photographs and fingerprints, collected evidence and talked with witnesses with the blood of my friends on my hands and shoes, and seen the man who shot them go free.

For me, those days are past. But for my brothers and sisters in law enforcement, it goes on. This book tries to capture some of what it's like.

Obviously I could not have written this book without doing a certain amount of research on the Yakuza. But here, as in all other books, I wish to emphasize that all characters and situations are made up. I intend no reference to any real family or individual, Yakuza or otherwise, and if I have used any person's real name, it is accidental.

▽

Acknowledgments

SPECIAL THANKS TO THE FOLLOWING:

The Salt Lake City Public Library, especially Judith, David, Patty, and Rebecca in the Rose Park Branch. When I call them, hysterical, at three o'clock in the afternoon needing a book yesterday, they almost always have it located and either there or en route by tomorrow.

The University of Utah Library, for having bought so many books nobody but me seems to need.

The San Francisco office of the Federal Bureau of Investigation. My husband points out to me that my books always trash the FBI and I always call the FBI for information. That's because local police are rarely extremely fond of the FBI, but the FBI agents in general remain ladies and gentlemen anyway.

Various other branches of the United States Justice Department on whom I have called for information.

Defense attorney Robert Breeze of Salt Lake City, for providing legal opinions that U.S. Justice Department employees are forbidden to give out over the phone for hypothetical cases.

Assorted relatives, friends, and neighbors, especially including Alice Schiesswohl, Kathy Lethco, Eleanor Page, Joe and Virginia Stencel, Jeff and Liz Adams, Naomi Wingate, and Verda Mae Christensen for providing rides when I was stranded and encouragement when I was depressed.

My youngest daughter, Alicia Lynn Wingate, for raking leaves, washing dishes, and going to the store and the library.

And, as usual, my husband, T. Russell Wingate, for being on call twenty-four hours a day for looking up map locations and describing neighborhoods in San Francisco, where he used to drive a taxi and I have never been, and for thinking up names, descriptions, plot developments, Max Kerensky, and E. P. Honshu.

Yakuza, Go Home!

▽

Prologue

"YOU LOST HIM." The voice wasn't loud, wasn't harsh. It didn't have to be.

The other two men knew better than to try to offer excuses. They stood, more or less at attention, and listened.

"Where did you lose him? When? How long ago?"

"He was in Mexico," one man offered.

The *oyabun* snorted. "Mexico! Is that the best you can do? You know how big Mexico is?"

The other two men spoke together:

"It was just one day—"

"He was supposed to be setting up a factory in Nuevo Laredo—" He stumbled over the foreign word.

"Setting up a factory in Nuevo Laredo, right," the *oyabun* said. He didn't stumble over the word. But by now, to him, very few languages were foreign. "Setting up a factory in Nuevo Laredo. And you thought that would take all his time. And you didn't watch him."

"We watched him—"

"It's a controlled border—" Once again the two men spoke together, growing desperation outpacing the defensiveness in their voices.

"It's a controlled border an American doesn't need a passport or visa to cross. You ought to know that; you're *Americans* yourselves. His wife is American." The unmistakable scorn in the *oyabun*'s voice totally ignored the fact that he, too, was legally a citizen of the United States. "You didn't watch him well enough. If you'd really watched him you wouldn't have lost him."

That was unanswerable, and after a moment, the *oyabun* went on. "Now find him. And when you do—" His contemptuous gesture was meaningful; he didn't need to add, "Delete him." But he added it anyway, then rephrased. "Delete them."

"Them? But—"

"Them. Delete them."

"But the boy—" This time the *kabun*'s voice was shocked.

"What do I care about the boy? Delete them."

"But the family—"

"They've left the family. I've got other family, loyal family. I don't need them. Find them and delete them and bring me proof." The *oyabun* paused for a moment to see if there were any more objections. Satisfied there would be none, he pointedly returned to his reading.

The two men slunk out as silently as whipped curs.

▽

1

IN SOME PLACES, FORTY-SIX degrees at noon on a Tuesday (or any other day, for that matter) in January wouldn't be considered cold. Bayport, Texas—fourteen miles north of the place where I-45 dead-ends into the Gulf of Mexico at the south end of Galveston Island, with a raw (if officially subtropical) wind blowing right off the Gulf and colliding with the Arctic blast that had started out from Siberia and curled down west of Alaska, entering the North American continent around northern California—wasn't one of those places. It was cold. Cold as a witch's never-mind-what and a whole lot wetter, with the semiwarm moisture from the Gulf and the cold moisture that came overland from the Pacific colliding over southeast Texas to produce rain, and rain, and more rain.

Normally, here, it wouldn't be very wet this time of year. Normally the January jet stream flows west to east through the center of the North American continent. But sometimes, for complicated and still poorly understood reasons involving unusually heated currents near the coast of South America, the North American jet stream splits. Half of it flows north, into Canada and the extreme northern United States, and half of it flows south, bringing unseasonal, unusually heavy rain to the southern United States and northern Mexico, including the normally bone-dry Sonoran desert. The central part of the North American continent gets droughts, and the southern and coastal areas are likely to flood.

The weather forecasters had been explaining the whole

thing on television, pointing at the satellite photographs. The explanations didn't do anything to change the general nastiness of the weather.

Captain Al Quinn, who'd been off duty Sunday and Monday, so today was his Monday, looked outside miserably, adjusted the collar of his raincoat (which wasn't going to do much good; he knew because he'd already been out in it most of the morning), opened the front door of the police station, and held it as Chief Mark Shigata—whose Monday had been on Sunday when the flooding really got started—stepped over the pile of sandbags. He followed Shigata and let the door shut. The sandbags weren't as effective as everybody wished they were, and the inside of the police station was two or three inches deep in most places. The street was a wide flowing river, and the sidewalks were shallower but just as fast-flowing. The Bronco was made as much for off-road use as street use. Unlike the police sedans, it could still reach much of the town—not all, of course; Shigata, in some desperation, now had two officers patrolling in outboard motorboats, the way they did during hurricane mop-ups.

But the Bronco's engine and transmission, as well as its door, were above the flood on Main Street.

Nevertheless, both men were knee-deep heading for the Bronco. Quinn slid briefly on leaves that had been dry when they fell in the street, that had fallen too late to be swept up even the last time the city crew came around to rake leaves. Now they were slick, invisibly slick under the torrent. Shigata reached out to steady him.

Quinn caught his balance, landing his right hand heavily on the hood of the Bronco, and swore, briefly and comprehensively. "El Niño," he finished bitterly. "Think you're going to get flooded out?"

"No doubt of it," Shigata answered. "I've been watching the water. The garden's a foot deep, and so is the front yard. I figure it'll be in the door in about another day."

"So where's your family going?"

"Fourth floor of the Holiday Inn, Galveston," Shigata

tures. But those pictures *do not* go to a newspaper, here or in Siberia. They go to the police department and nowhere else. Got me?"

"Yes—"

"And don't touch anything, not anything at all, understand?"

"Yes—"

"I mean it!" Then Hansen ran back to the car, ignoring the ambulance that was entering the parking lot, and grabbed the mike. "Car Three to Car One!"

"Go ahead, Car Three."

"Chief, I'm at Bartlett's, and we've got a double homicide up here!"

"What's the room number?" Shigata asked quickly.

"Twenty-three."

"A man and woman? Japanese?"

"A man and a woman, but that's all I can tell right now. Chief, this one's nasty."

"Ten-four," Shigata said. "Headquarters, call the medical examiner's office. And you better call Galveston and get a full crime scene crew up here."

"Ten-four, don't you want to look at it first?"

"I don't need to look at this one to know what I need. I'm en route."

Shigata's voice, Hansen thought as he returned to direct Kerensky's no-longer-necessary photography, sounded odd. But maybe it was the weather.

Or maybe it wasn't, he thought moments later.

Shigata came in fast and then stopped. "What the hell is this civilian doing here?"

"Chief, this is Max Kerensky," Hansen said. "He's a journalism student from Siberia, now attending the University of Texas and interning on the Galveston paper. I let him ride with me tonight. And he has a camera—I was going to have him take pictures, until I found out you were calling Galveston. But I let him take a few anyway. Max, this is Chief Shigata."

"Hello," Kerensky said. "You would prefer that I leave?"

"I would prefer that you keep your hands to yourself."

"Pardon?"

"He means don't touch anything," Hansen said.

"I already promised I would not touch anything," Kerensky said. "You would prefer—?"

"Hush," Hansen said, and he watched silently as Shigata, without touching anything, examined the bodies.

"This one's Phyllis Yamagata Omori," he said to Hansen, over his shoulder. "American national, born in San Francisco." Phyllis had been stabbed once, and from all he could tell right now he'd say it was directly through the heart. "This other's Isoruko Omori. Japanese national, employed in Mexico."

"Chief, you knew them?" Hansen asked as Quinn crowded into the room with them.

"He's my cousin." Shigata was working at keeping emotion out of his voice. He wasn't doing a very good job of it.

Rocky Omori had fought hard. That was evident from the defense wounds on his hands, defense wounds where knives had cut to the bone as he used his hands to shield his face and torso from the blades. But he'd been outnumbered, and at some point they'd stopped him from fighting anymore. Stopped him, tied him, and gagged him. But they hadn't killed him fast.

Phyllis's body was almost cold to the touch. But Rocky's was still warm.

If Lissa had tried to bring Daniel to them, she might have walked right in on them.

If Hansen had come to Bartlett's first instead of last, he might have been there in time to keep Rocky alive—though by then Rocky might not have wanted to stay alive.

If wishes were horses—

"He wanted to be a samurai," Shigata said, turning blindly toward Quinn. "Damn it. Damn it. Damn it—and damn Buddy Yamagata."

said. "I made reservations yesterday afternoon."

"How come Galveston? Bartlett's isn't flooded yet, and at least they'd still be in town."

"Bartlett's isn't flooded *yet*," Shigata said.

"Oh. Yeah."

"Where's your family?" Shigata asked. The Quinn house was on lower ground than his; it would have flooded over the weekend, and he'd been too busy to check on the Quinns, who were very good at taking care of themselves anyway. He knew they weren't at Bartlett's Motel or the Holiday Inn; Johnny was married and Mark, who would have been seventeen, was dead, but that still left ten children at home. Ten children, and Al and Nguyen. The Quinns couldn't afford motel bills. They could be in the high school gym, with a lot of other evacuees, but somehow Shigata doubted that they were.

"Nguyen and the little ones went to stay with Johnny and Mei Ling. That's high ground."

Shigata nodded. Normally he wouldn't know where his officers' adult married offspring lived, but Johnny and Mei Ling's neighborhood had been one of the centers of a recent murder investigation. The little ones were Wayne, five; Susie, four; and Alice, three. Sometimes Jeff, seven, was included; sometimes he wasn't. This time he apparently wasn't, as Quinn added, "Janie and Mary and Jeff and the twins went to stay with Hoa, on the boat." He chuckled grimly. "If this keeps up much longer, we may *all* want to go stay with Hoa on the boat. But for now Steve and Ed are camping out at the house, to salvage what they can. You heard anything from Hansen?"

Shigata, now inside the Bronco, waited for Quinn to join him and then shook his head. "Uh-uh. I told him yesterday he could take off today to try to get his books to high ground."

"His books?"

"Well, I said his furniture," Shigata answered, "but you know Hansen."

"Yeah. I know Hansen."

Anybody who knew police sergeant Steve Hansen, Ph.D., knew that given a choice of saving his furniture or saving his books, the furniture came dead last, after his books, his son, his weapons, his recently acquired dog, and his clothes—probably in that order.

"He told me then," Shigata added, "that he'd sent Todd to Tyler to stay with his aunt."

"Todd's aunt or Hansen's aunt?"

"Todd's aunt. Sorry."

"I pity the aunt," Quinn said. Todd Hansen, now seventeen, had done nothing at all to make himself liked by anybody nor, Shigata and Quinn suspected, was he likely to begin making himself liked in the next few days. "One thing about it," Quinn said, "at least the crooks are too busy trying to salvage their own stuff to start in looting."

"I wouldn't count on it," Shigata said. Then he swore, as the ignition whirred fruitlessly.

"It was working when I parked it," Quinn said.

"Obviously," Shigata answered. "When's the last time you dried out the distributor cap?" The Bronco could drive through puddles most cars couldn't navigate, but the water splashed up, hit the inside top of the hood, and splashed back down. And car parts—especially distributors—aren't made to be waterproof.

"About two hours ago."

"I'll get it this time."

"I might as well," Quinn said. "I'm wet anyway." He grabbed a shop rag from a pile of them on the backseat, popped the hood, and climbed out into the rain.

"You know who you look like in that raincoat?" Jack Horan asked, sliding a plate in front of Quinn.

"No, who do I look like?"

"Columbo, that's who, you know on TV, that Los Angeles cop that always sneaks up on people? I mean with his questions, you know, he's always about to leave and then he says

something like, 'Oh, one more thing.' That one. You ever watch him?"

"Sometimes," Quinn said. "But how do I look like him?"

"You know that rumpled raincoat he always wears, like it can be the fourth year of a three-year drought and Columbo's always in that rumpled raincoat?"

Shigata, who'd already been served, put his hand over his face to hide his smile. Short, stocky Al Quinn, with a rumpled gray civilian raincoat over his police uniform, did indeed bear a certain resemblance to the fictional Columbo. But he didn't seem too happy to have it pointed out.

"I figure I can stay open two or three more days before the kitchen floods out," Horan said, straddling a chair with his chin on the back. "That's if the water doesn't start rising faster and the customers keep coming in. Sorry I took so long. What with cooking, waiting, and busing tables—"

"No problem," Shigata said, cutting roast beef. By now he was used to southern truck-stop chow. But he'd given up trying to like collards, and his plate contained sliced tomato, coleslaw, and mashed potatoes besides the roast beef. "We're glad to have an excuse to relax a minute. Where's Milly?"

"Home trying to get everything off the floor. Last time it was this bad we got six inches in the house."

"You need more sandbags?" Quinn asked around a mouthful of collards. "We got plenty."

"Don't do no good," Horan said. "Here or at home. There's always that little trickle of water that gets in anyway, and I got too much electrical stuff on the floor. Last time this happened I swore I'd have all the plug-ins moved to the ceiling, but of course when the water went down I forgot about it. You folks want some pie? I've got chocolate, coconut, and pecan."

"Haven't got time," Shigata said. "We're trying to get people to evacuate while they can still do it by car instead of boat, and some people are harder to convince than others."

Horan chuckled. "Yeah, I've noticed that. But as long as I can keep the kitchen open I'll be here. I'd rather wade to work than try to tell the bank how come I can't make the mortgage payment this month."

"I hear that," Quinn said, talking with his mouth full.

When they got back to the station, Shigata had a visitor. And for a while, even the flooding was shoved to the back of his mind.

"I didn't know I had a cousin in Japan," Shigata said. "Well, I mean, I suppose I guess I did, but—"

"But you didn't ever have any reason to think about it," Isoruko "Rocky" Omori replied. Shorter than Shigata and stockier, he was sitting across from Shigata's desk, looking somewhat more relaxed than the chief felt.

"Well—that too. But you know about my father?"

Omori leaned back comfortably. "I have heard of your father." His tone implied that he had heard nothing good of him.

"He—he sort of hated Japan."

"That's one of the things I have heard. That, and that he hardly ever allowed you to see either his own family or your mother's family, both of whom now reside in California. So you certainly would never have been told that about the same time your parents were married, your mother's older brother married a Japanese girl and returned to live in Japan and was . . . fighting for the emperor at the same time your father was fighting for the president."

"My father wasn't fighting for the president," Shigata said. "He detested Roosevelt, and he had every reason to. He was fighting for his country and his honor."

"Especially his honor, from what I've heard," Omori said. "Such as it was. Of course honor is important, but I don't understand how he could defend a country that put him and his family in concentration camps."

Shigata was silent for a moment; that was, and always had been, a major sore point with him. He had been born in one of those camps, a dry dusty place called Topaz tucked into Utah's western desert well out of sight of the rest of the citizenry. Then he said, "It wasn't always like that, before the war or since. It's just—fear and rage can make normally decent people do strange things."

"Fear and rage, and a knowledge of who is *really* superior," Omori said.

Shigata couldn't help laughing at that. "You ever study any anthropology?"

"Anthropology? No, why should I?"

"Because if you had, you'd know that every primitive people at one time had a name meaning 'The People,' implying that *we*—whoever *we* might happen to be—are the real people, and nobody else is quite real, or quite human, at all. Rocky, every race and culture on the face of the earth is quite certain it is superior to every other race and culture. Me, I don't think any race and culture is superior. Some individual human beings are superior, but it has nothing to do with race and culture. No, it was rage and fear, especially after an unwarranted sneak attack, and the prejudice that results from rage and fear. That's all."

"I know about fear and rage," Omori admitted, abruptly changing the subject. "But anyway, that was a long time ago, and *I* didn't bomb Pearl Harbor."

"I never said you did. All I said was, you look young to be my cousin—"

"Cousins here are determined by ages? In my country they are determined by relationships."

"But you know what I mean. I'm pushing fifty. And you're—what? Thirty?"

"Almost thirty. But I have older brothers and sisters. I thought you might question," Omori said, "so I brought"—he began to spread a document out on the table—"this. A chart of family relationships."

"A family tree?" Shigata looked at it. "I can't read that."

"You don't read—"

"I don't read or speak Japanese."

Omori folded the chart back up. "I should have guessed. So it is fortunate that I speak English."

"Excellent English. It's hard to believe—"

"That I was born not too far from Tokyo? Ah, but I was, and lived there until I was twenty-two. But all schools in Japan teach English now. And I did get a graduate degree in international business from UCLA—where you went to law school, your mother told me. It is a shame that this visit is not getting off to a good start. Perhaps you could telephone my aunt—your mother. She will assure you I truly am her errant nephew."

"I believe you," Shigata said. "And why errant?" *I know part of it. But what are you going to tell me? And how much of it will be true?*

"That," Omori replied, looking far less lighthearted than he sounded, "I will explain later. If I decide to. If you decide I am indeed your cousin."

"I said I believe you," Shigata said. "It's just—unexpected. Especially right now. I'm sort of—sort of in the middle of things."

"With a flood. It could be worse."

"I'm sure it could."

"You could have an earthquake. Or a *tsunami*—and don't tell me you don't know what *that* means."

"Tidal wave, yes," Shigata said. "A flood's enough, thanks. Well—what brings you here?"

"I wanted to meet you and your wife and daughter. I wanted my wife and son to meet you and your wife and daughter. I wanted you and your wife and daughter to meet me and my wife and son, who are staying at a nearby motel while you and I—deliberate."

It should have been casual, except for the things that told Shigata it wasn't. Except for a slight stiltedness that could have been the result of imperfect command of the language, it sounded casual—almost—but not quite. There was something going on in Omori's mind besides a desire to create more family ties, but Shigata wasn't going to find it out by asking questions now. So the best thing he could do now was pretend to accept this as the family visit it pretended to be. "Well," he said, "well, let me call my wife."

American-born but genetically Japanese Phyllis Omori was talking with blond Lissa Shigata in the kitchen over the dishes they were putting away, and sixteen-year-old Gail Shigata had taken four-year-old Daniel Omori to put him to bed in the guest room. She was still in there fifteen minutes later, and Shigata could hear her voice rising occasionally as she pretended to be Goldilocks and all three bears in sequence. Daniel was still giggling, but the giggles now had a decidedly sleepy note.

"And you still want to know why I came here," Omori said, very quietly, after a quick glance at the closed kitchen door.

"I would like to know, yes," Shigata answered. "And don't tell me you were suddenly overwhelmed by the desire to meet your American cousins, because I don't believe it."

Omori leaned forward, his voice lowered even further. "Daniel has dual citizenship," he said. "He was born in this country. We—Phyllis and I—have decided we would prefer him to grow up with American citizenship."

"The way the law works, he'll have to decide that himself when he comes of age." *I'll play it your way,* Shigata thought. *I know some of what you're not telling me, but not enough that I want to let you know I know it. Not yet.*

And this doesn't jibe very well with your claims of Japanese superiority. But I won't ask you to explain your reasons. Not until I find out what you're going to tell me, and then I may not have to.

Then Shigata fixed his mind on his cousin, who was answering what Shigata had said. "True. But—that which is not perceived as an option is not a true option. Do you understand me?"

"Yes, of course. If he returns to Japan and grows up there he'll almost certainly—"

"That's not all of it. But—"

"But," Shigata interrupted, "surely you and Phyllis can decide where you live. I mean, Phyllis is an American citizen, so—"

"But we travel a lot, you see. We fly a lot. We drive a lot. We are, perhaps, at higher risk than many people. And we would like to select a fit guardian for Daniel, in the event that—you understand?"

"I understand, but surely—"

"There is no one else. Phyllis and I have discussed the matter. You are our only hope. My other relatives in the United States—they are good people, all of them. But perhaps, perhaps, a little too traditional."

"Then Phyllis—"

"No," Omori said forcefully. Then he took a deep breath. "Have you ever heard of Buddy Yamagata?" He paused.

To Shigata, it was as if an icy wind from the past had swept through his small, comfortable living room. He'd expected something like that. But not that name. Not *that* name.

"Perhaps there is no reason why you should," Omori went on, "but—"

"But I was once an FBI agent and I was once stationed in San Francisco. Yes. I've heard of Buddy Yamagata. Heroin, *shabu*—amphetamines—forced prostitution, loan-sharking, money laundering, large-scale gambling—"

"And murder," Omori finished. "Especially murder. Murder for hire, murder to serve as an example for someone who might think of . . . defecting. Yakuza. Like the Cosa Nostra in some ways, not in others. Gangsters playing at being samurai. The organized crime of my homeland and, like other organized crime, exported everywhere to which it can be exported. There are, perhaps, three thousand Yakuza 'families.' Not half of them operate outside Japan. Many of them, perhaps most of them, both in and out of Japan, continue to follow the code."

"What code is that?" Shigata asked.

"*Giri-ninjo.* Moral debt, empathy for the disadvantaged. Never harming *katagi no shu,* the innocent, the citizens under the sun. But Buddy Yamagata is a law unto himself. He forgets the code; he models himself on the Mafia while demanding the due of an *oyabun* of his *kabun*."

"Meaning?" *Yes, I know. But how much are you going to tell me?*

"*Oyabun*—in Mafia terms, think of the Godfather. *Kabun,* child—the underling owes the *oyabun* the respect and absolute obedience a child owes its father. Buddy Yamagata plays it both ways. I say he patterns himself after the Mafia; perhaps, because I myself know nothing of the Mafia, perhaps it would be more just to say that he patterns himself after the Mafia movies. And he is an American citizen, which means that he cannot be deported."

"I understand that," Shigata said. "Believe me, I understand that. But what does he have to do with—"

"With me? With my wife and my child? You are right to ask. I was not thinking of such problems when I married Phyllis Yamagata."

"Buddy's—?" *And that, I did not guess—could not have guessed.*

"Daughter. Yes. Buddy Yamagata is my father-in-law. Daniel's grandfather. Do you understand now?"

"Do you think you're in danger, then?" Shigata asked quietly, as Phyllis and Lissa returned to the living room in the midst of a different conversation.

"Practically everything important is in a storage shed on high ground," Lissa was saying. "The attic gets so hot we don't dare put anything there. And of course all the neighbors are gone already, we're the only ones in a three-street radius still here."

"I'm surprised you're still here at all. And the furniture—"

"Well, considering Mark's position, we really have to stay as long as we can," Lissa explained. "And the furniture's so old—we decided we were due for new furniture anyway, so if necessary we'll just replace it. And of course it may not get here at all, though it may get here sooner, and deeper, than we'd expected. I mean, floods are always so unpredictable."

"Not as unpredictable as earthquakes," Phyllis said. "Is it true you don't have them here?"

"That's true. Of course we have hurricanes, which can be just as destructive."

"But at least you have a few days of warning of hurricanes," Phyllis said. She looked around at the men. "Did we interrupt something?"

Shigata glanced at Omori and then said, "I had just asked the reason for the urgency about appointing a potential guardian for Daniel. Do you feel you're in any danger?"

"Oh, no," Omori said heartily, after a quick—almost furtive—look at Phyllis. "No more than anybody else who travels extensively. It is just, it is well to be prepared. So—are you willing to serve as guardian for my son, if the need should arise?"

Shigata looked at Lissa. She nodded. "Yes, of course," she said, "Phyllis and I had already talked about it in the kitchen, but I don't see any reason why the need should arise."

"You concur?" Omori asked Shigata.

"I concur."

Omori rose. "Then it is settled. Phyllis and I have already made out wills to that effect, but we have not signed them. If there are people in your police station who can act as witnesses, we can get them signed tonight, and then—"

"But what's the hurry?" Lissa asked.

"Ah, I am putting together a factory in Nuevo Laredo," Omori said. "It will manufacture small electronic parts. But I must keep close watch as the building is being prepared. I should not have left even for these few days, but I did wish to conclude this business. We will be driving back to Mexico tomorrow. You will keep the wills, Mark, and I will see to it that you are notified if there is a need. And now I regret, after your daughter has spent so much time getting Daniel to sleep, we must wake him and—"

"Awww," said Gail, who had just reentered the living room. "Can't he stay here tonight? You can come back and get him in the morning."

"I don't think—" Omori began.

"But he's my *cousin,*" Gail wailed, "and I don't even *know* him, and he's the only cousin I've got that I've met, and at least he can stay here *tonight!*"

"Well—"

"Do let him stay," Lissa urged gently. "The way it's raining, it would be a shame to take him out this late."

"Surely it would be all right." Phyllis had a soft voice, and during the evening she had addressed almost everything she said to Lissa, rarely speaking directly to Shigata or even to her own husband. Even now, under the water beating on the roof, she was almost inaudible.

"I wish I could talk you into staying too," Lissa added wistfully. "We hardly ever have guests."

"I could sleep on the couch," Gail said eagerly. "You could have my bed."

"Ah, but we already have a bed, at the motel," Omori said firmly, "and I will not be responsible for putting a lady out of her own room. But Daniel—he sleeps late in the morning. We can be back before he wakes. Yes, let's let him stay here tonight."

"Mark," Lissa called.

Shigata, on his way to the Bronco to lead the Omoris to the police station, turned. Then, seeing the look on her face, he returned to the front door, car keys in hand. "What is it?"

"Mark, she's frightened."

Shigata glanced at the sedan, but its doors were shut already, and under the pounding rain Lissa's voice wouldn't carry two feet. "Frightened of what?"

"She won't tell me. But she told me, in the kitchen, what Rocky was going to ask. And she said—Mark, she said, 'Be sure Daniel knows I loved him.' I think she thinks somebody's going to try to kill her."

"She may be right," Shigata said. "Lissa, I should have told you before we agreed. If the situation is what I think it is, even agreeing to take Daniel could put us—all of us—in danger. Do you still want to—"

"I know something about being frightened," Lissa interrupted. "No matter what happens, we can't turn that child away. We can't—I can't—tell Phyllis we won't take him."

"I knew you'd say that," Shigata said, "but I'm not sure you understand—"

"I understand enough." She tried to laugh. "You taught me to shoot. And I have a gun, now. You gave it to me."

"But sometimes a gun isn't enough, Lissa. Sometimes a hundred guns, and a hundred people to fire them, aren't enough."

"If they aren't, they aren't. Nobody has to win. But if you don't even fight—I didn't fight for too long. I'll never not fight again. You can finish explaining when you get back tonight, after Gail is asleep."

Shigata kissed her, quickly, lightly, then splashed through the night to the Bronco with the light bar on its roof.

"Mark," Omori said later, sitting in the car under a streetlight, after Phyllis had dashed into the motel room, "I lied to you tonight."

"I thought you did," Shigata said. "I saw your hand. Putting that together with what little you did say—"

"My hand? Oh. Yes, of course, you would notice that." Omori raised his hand and looked at it, the last joint of the little finger of his right hand gone—a Yakuza apology for minor past failure and promise of future loyalty. "It was because Phyllis came back into the room, you understand."

"Yes. How deeply into the Yakuza were you?"

"Too deeply to be allowed to leave. The Yakuza sometimes will allow people to leave, if they are true underlings, just seeing to it that person is accepted into no other *kai*. But Buddy Yamagata allows no one to leave."

"And you were no underling."

Rocky looked directly at Shigata and smiled briefly. "No. I was not."

"But you left."

"I left. Phyllis agreed, when I told her I wanted to. She—we—did not want Daniel to grow up thinking—you understand. And she does not know the danger. She has not been allowed to know. No one has told her. Her father would not. To her, her father was only her father, strict but loving; I am not certain she even knows how he lives. Oh, she knows he is Yakuza, of course, but I am not certain she fully understands what Yakuza means—especially to him. I—could not tell her. Mark, please understand. I did not learn this life from my family. I was no *bosozoku,* juvenile delinquent, and my family is not Yakuza, they did not teach me to be Yakuza. Not . . . deliberately. But my father taught me to honor the emperor, to worship the emperor. No one worships the emperor now; the emperor has said he is not divine. But my father taught me to worship the emperor. And in Japan it is different—the Yakuza have offices in the town, regular office hours, even business cards. In many towns they are the only moneylenders, even if their interest rate does approach and sometimes exceed a hundred percent. In many small towns the police could not keep order without the aid of the Yakuza."

He grinned. "At least that was how it was then. There has been a government crackdown in Japan. They think they will be able to stop gangsterism, which is what they have begun now to call the Yakuza."

"Accurately," Shigata said softly.

Rocky stared at him for a moment, then said, "Yes. Accurately. The crackdown will not work, of course. They may succeed in driving it a little underground for a short time, that is all. But there will always be more hooligans wanting power, drawn into the Yakuza for that reason. And there are always the Yakuza movies, hundreds of them, and in almost all the movies the Yakuza are the heroes, like the Robin Hood of your legend, so there will always be more confused idealists like me. It is easy for a Japanese child to learn to like the Yakuza, unless his family is more careful than my family was to teach him the truth. It is hard to learn what it is really like—particularly when you learn too late. When I—when the Yakuza recruited me—I thought I was helping the emperor. I thought I was honoring the emperor, upholding the tradition of the samurai warrior, helping the common people who had no one else to turn to. I did not—I did not know. Not then. By the time I knew—"

"You were in too deep to get out."

"Yes. It is very strange, to think of it—you drink a drop of *sake* at a Shinto shrine and do not know then that you will never draw another breath of freedom. My degree in international business—my country exports automobiles. And electronics. Much legal business is done. Most of it is simply good business. We do have excellent production skills. Some of it—" He smiled faintly. "You bombed the hell out of our factories."

"*I* didn't," Shigata said.

"True. Just as I did not bomb Pearl Harbor. But we had to rebuild everything."

"Not everything," Shigata said. "Maybe forty percent. The majority of the factories were untouched."

Rocky looked briefly surprised. Then he grinned. "Oh yes, you have studied history. All right, maybe forty percent of our factories were damaged or destroyed. But when we rebuilt, we rebuilt everything. And when we rebuilt them, we made them modern. As modern as we could. And we have kept on making them more and more modern. We have good factories and good equipment, and our workers are loyal and work hard. We do good work."

"I know that."

"So most of what my country exports, we are just doing good business. But—"

"But not all," Shigata finished for him. "And for the Yakuza, legitimate business may be used to conceal the other kind."

"And my family—that is, my *kai*, my organization—in Japan lent me to Buddy Yamagata. I am not sure they knew as much about him as I know now. But by the time I knew it was too late."

"Rocky, when you came to me today, before I mentioned it, did you know I used to be an FBI agent?"

"I knew. Mark, they are going to kill Phyllis and me. Me because I am a traitor to the organization, because I disobeyed direct orders and walked out, because I took Phyllis away. Phyllis because—when the time came to make a choice—she chose her husband and not her father. She knew then she would never see her family again. But that they will kill us—she does not know that. I know that. They are hunting us now. It was always only a matter of time before Buddy looked our way. I always knew that, from the time I left. But I did not know how long it would take. Buddy has many matters to keep him busy. I hoped we would have time to raise our child. But Buddy has looked our way now, he has remembered us, and the order has been given. I have a friend—he will not try to save us, he cannot, for his own friends would pay the forfeit—but he cared enough to tell me when the order was given. I'll tell you who he is—he might be able to help you, someday, if you don't ask too much of him. E. P. Honshu—that's his stage name. He's a singer, an"—Rocky grinned briefly—"an Elvis impersonator. His real name is Bobby Yamagata. Well, Wataru Yamagata, but he called himself Bobby before he became E. P. Honshu. Buddy's brother. He's not as stupid as he seems, and he is a man of goodwill, but not strong. Not strong, and not to be depended upon. I doubt—I truly doubt that Phyllis and I will live another week. But he—Buddy, I mean now—will not harm Daniel. He will not harm Daniel because Daniel is his grandson and he will think that after I am dead and after Phyllis is dead he—because legally, you understand, he has never committed a crime."

"Believe me, I know that," Shigata said.

"Then you know that legally he is a perfectly upstanding citizen. And he thinks that after Phyllis and I are dead, he will get Daniel. Get Daniel, and raise Daniel his way, to inherit his empire. But with these wills, you should be able to keep Daniel. It might come to a court fight. Probably it will. Anybody can fight in a courtroom. But Buddy will fight in other ways too. Could your mother's family, gentle people, growers of lettuce and cantaloupes, keep Daniel safe? No. I do not think so. I do not know whether anybody can. You are a lawyer. You can fight in a courtroom. And you are"—he smiled faintly—"a cop. A very tough cop. I have heard that. I have heard that you are a man who does not count the cost. I do not know if anybody can keep Daniel out of Buddy Yamagata's hands. But if anybody can, it is you."

"Do you want to tell me the rest of it now?" Shigata asked.

Omori took a deep breath. "It would take too long. The rest of it is on tape recordings in my safe-deposit box in the Bank of America. The one on California Street, in San Francisco. In my will, I have left all my assets to you. You will be able to get in, if you can reach the box before Buddy does. And if you can—if you can get the tape recordings, if you can get them to your Justice Department, then—then, I think you will be able to keep Daniel safe. And yourself and your family as well."

He opened the car door, stepped out into the rain, and added, "Keep him safe, my cousin. For that, I hold you to answer to our ancestors."

▽

2

IT WAS GAIL WHO discovered the water in the house when she got up at 2:00 A.M. to go to the bathroom. She was on her way to wake Shigata when the phone began to ring. She didn't answer it.

"Daddy?" she yelled from the hall. "Daddy?"

"Are you up?" he mumbled. "Then answer the phone. Tell them I'll get to it in just a sec." Because it went without saying that calls at that hour were for him.

"I'm scared to," she said, and this time he heard the note of near panic in her voice. "I'm standing in water." By that time Shigata had gotten out of bed only to discover that he, too, was standing in water.

"Is it okay to answer a phone when the water's like this?"

"I don't know," he answered, "so let's not try. Go on back to bed. For now anyway."

"I was going to go to the bathroom."

"Then go ahead. But don't try to turn on the light, there or anywhere else. Use that flashlight I gave you. And don't try to flush," he added hastily.

The phone was still ringing. Prudently, Shigata sat back down on the bed and drew his feet up out of the flood, then leaned precariously across the open space to grab the phone that was sitting on the dresser. "Shigata," he said.

There was so much static that it was hard to understand, but he could tell it was the department. "I'll get to the radio," he said. "Stand by a couple of minutes." He hoped they could understand him, because right then the phone went dead.

By now Lissa, too, was up. "Gail," she called, "get Daniel up, and both of you get dressed. We're going to Galveston."

"Everything's all wet in my room," Gail protested.

"Everything's all wet everywhere."

"I mean my clothes."

"That's your fault for throwing them on the floor. You're bound to have *something* dry hanging in the closet."

"Nothing I want to wear."

"This is a bad time for vanity. Put on something you don't want to wear, and let's go. We've got dry suitcases in the trunk of the car, but if we don't get out of here in a hurry we won't be able to. Get dressed *now.* I'll get Daniel."

Shigata, in a dry shirt and jacket, slacks that were wet above the ankles, and wet boots, was already on his way out to the Bronco, which didn't start. "Lissa!" he yelled. "Can you come hold the flashlight for me?"

No answer.

He splashed back to the house through the rain that wouldn't stop falling. "Lissa!"

Lissa, in slacks and a somewhat oversized sweatshirt, her blond hair down in her eyes, came out of the bathroom in wet and odoriferous sneakers. "I should have known not to try to flush."

"You certainly should," he replied, "but there's no use worrying about it now. There's nothing you can do about the house now. Come hold the flashlight for me. I've got to dry out my distributor again. Then we'd better check yours. This is one of the times I wish you drove something like what I've got, instead of—"

"A Pontiac is a pretty well built car," she objected mildly. "And anyway it's in the garage."

That was true. Belatedly worrying about the police chief's car being too visible on the street, Shigata—with the assistance of Hansen and Quinn—had spent a couple of weeks worth of off-duty time building a closable garage, only to find out that he'd miscalculated its height. Lissa's Pontiac would fit in it; the Bronco wouldn't.

"I was going to get Daniel up," Lissa added.

"Let Gail do that. I need your help now."

She followed him with the flashlight as he resumed the earlier discussion. "Your Pontiac is a damn well built car. But it's low to the ground, and that's what I'm talking about, in this weather. I mean, it isn't in the garage when it's on the road."

Even with the flashlight, it took close to fifteen minutes to dry a sufficient quantity of mechanical parts for Shigata to start the Bronco so that he could use its radio, and by then he'd run its battery down so far he had to jumpstart it from the Pontiac. Sometime in the middle of that Gail, in sandals and miniskirt unsuited to the weather, topped by a slightly more suitable hooded sweatshirt, came out with Daniel, still asleep, wrapped in a blanket. She laid him in the backseat of the red Pontiac and returned to the house, emerging the second time with the clothes Daniel had taken off to go to bed and a large gray plastic cat carrier with a very loudly unhappy occupant. A third trip produced cat food and a litter box; in a fourth trip she brought out a boom box and a cassette holder.

After waiting long enough to be sure the Bronco wasn't going to die and have to be jumped again, Lissa took off. Shigata said into the radio, "Car One to headquarters."

"I've been trying to raise you." Eve Booth's voice. The head dispatcher, she had just turned twenty-three.

"Yeah, well, I couldn't get the car started and I didn't dare try to use the radio until I did because of the battery. What's going on? Stand by," he said quickly, noticing Lissa had reentered the driveway. She parked beside him, her car pointing in the opposite direction from his, her window open beside his closed one. He rolled his down. "What is it?"

"Should I take Daniel to Rocky and Phyllis, or—"

"There's no need for that. Just take him with you. I'll let them know where he is. They'll probably have to leave Bartlett's before the night is over anyhow and move to the gym or to Galveston."

"Okay."

"Gail," he added, "see to it that Daniel's seat belt is fastened. And yours too."

"They both are." Her voice was slightly sulky. She did not like to be nagged about seat belts. That was one of the reasons Shigata nagged.

The Pontiac was gone. Shigata returned his attention to the radio. "Car One to headquarters. Now, let me know what's going on."

"The water rose faster than it was supposed to."

"So I noticed. It's in my house. What do you want me to do about it?"

"I don't know, but Barlow said call you."

After Chief Shigata, Captain Quinn, and Sergeant Hansen, the next most experienced officer in the department was Corporal Ted Barlow, now twenty-four, whose own experience was to some extent augmented by that of his father. Special Agent Jim Barlow, in charge of the FBI office in Houston, had once been Shigata's supervisor; their close friendship had deteriorated sharply when Shigata left the FBI exactly six months before he would have been eligible for retirement to take over as chief of a department that had fewer than twenty-five sworn officers and rarely kept an honest chief longer than a year.

So far Shigata had held on more than two years. He expected to stay as long as Jolene Robinson remained mayor and Bob Crowley remained city manager. If Robinson lost the next election and her successor fired Crowley, it was anybody's guess what would happen next.

But the next election was about two years off, and Robinson and Crowley were both in their second terms. It looked good.

"Barlow said to call me," he repeated. "Did he say why?"

"He said call the whole department in. He said if we didn't get everybody in the low-lying parts of town awake and out now there might be some we wouldn't be able to save by morning, at least not without calling in the National Guard, and they're already pretty busy."

"Is it that bad?" Shigata asked, astonished. He'd expected his house, in a little bit of a dip in the road, would flood earlier than most of the rest of the town that wasn't already flooded.

"Barlow says so. So do Ames and Gonzales. And they're all that are on duty right now besides me."

Paul Ames and Susa Gonzales weren't extremely experienced officers. But they both had lived in Bayport all their lives, and they both kept their head in crises.

"If it's that bad, then Barlow's right. I'm on my way."

"Chief? There's a reporter here."

"So?" He was driving toward the police station as he spoke. Then he braked, as fast as he could without risking locking the brakes and going into a skid. The road directly ahead of him was impassable. "It's going to take longer than I thought to get there," he said. "The eight hundred block of Alamo looks four feet deep."

"All units, avoid the eight hundred block of Alamo," Booth said. "Car One says you can't get through it. Chief, this reporter, he's a Russian."

"He's what?"

"He says he's a reporter for the Galveston paper, but Chief, he's a Russian. I mean a *real* Russian from Russia. Or Siberia. Is Siberia part of Russia?"

"Unless it seceded since the last time I watched the news it is, and I think I'd have heard that it was planning to. I'll talk to him when I get there."

"Sergeant Hansen just walked in. You want—"

"Yeah, let him talk with your Russian."

"Max Kerensky?" Hansen, who had arrived in uniform, said. He paused, jiggling car keys in his hand. "Any kin to *the* Kerensky?"

"*The* Kerensky?"

"Yeah, the one that ran Russia before the Bolsheviks took over."

Max Kerensky looked about twenty-two. At five six, he

looked short to six-foot-four Hansen, but then just about everybody did; he was a little chubby, with a round face and an infectious grin that, at the moment, had been replaced by an expression of puzzlement. "The man that ran Russia before the Bolshevik Revolution was the czar." His English was perfect, with a very slight British accent.

"No, after the czar was deposed in the First Revolution of March 1917—February by the old calendar that Russia was still using then—there was a fellow named Alexander Feodorovich Kerensky, a writer, who held several brief offices in the provisional government and then became prime minister until the November 1917 revolution. Then Kerensky took off to Paris to live in exile and go on writing. I forget when he died."

Kerensky continued to look puzzled. "I have never heard of this man. Or a revolution in March *or* February. And the czar abdicated. Later he was killed, but first he abdicated. I was named for a writer, but it was the writer Maxim Gorky. My father was a writer and he wanted me to be a writer. Do you say you know more Russian history than I do?"

"It would appear that way," Hansen said blandly. "Since I *have* heard of the March revolution and Alexander Kerensky. Obviously you wouldn't know whether you're related to him or not."

Kerensky grinned. "I suppose that I am not. My hometown is not Paris but Omsk. That is in Siberia."

"Yeah, on the—Irtysh River? Or the Ob? You could still be related. Just because he got to Paris doesn't mean all his relatives did. And Siberia—"

"Siberia," Kerensky said, "is beautiful. It is very foolish to think of it as a place of exile. It worked as a place of exile only because the old government kept gulags there, and frightened people with the gulags and it is true that the gulags were very bad. It is true too that my father was sent to a gulag by the evil old government and while he was there he got scurvy and all his teeth fell out, and my mother and sister went to live near the gulag—all this was before I was born—but when my father was released we stayed in Siberia because we wanted to. If people knew what it was really like they would fight to live there. Great forests and plains, wide rivers, much oil and other minerals. The taiga. No one else has the taiga, only Siberia. In the winter, beautiful deep snow. It is a great place for fishing and hunting or just for looking at nature. There are many wild animals, reindeer in great herds eating the summer grass, bears and other large animals, and small creatures like sables and otters which are extinct or live only in captivity in many places. If there were any mammoths left alive they would live in Siberia. Where I live the land is fertile. In the summer the tomatoes grow as big as basketballs. There are of course problems with food distribution, but that is because we were governed for so long by greedy fools. It takes time for a country to recover from such things. But these problems will be solved. Omsk is a great city, the second largest in Siberia. It is on the Irtysh River, which flows into the Ob, and in the winter when it freezes we can ice-skate where the river is smooth until the snow is too deep. You are well informed, but perhaps not well enough."

By now Hansen had his hands in the air, laughing. "I surrender! I surrender! Clearly Siberia is heaven on earth, the Texas of Russia, only I don't want to go there today. I try to be well informed, but this time I must have missed the boat." He looked down at the keys he continued to jiggle. "And speaking of boats, right now I'm supposed to be out waking people up while we can still do it *without* a boat. I just came in to get keys to a police car. So I'll have to let you tell me more about Siberia later."

"I want to go with you," Kerensky said rapidly as Hansen headed for the front door.

Hansen paused and turned. "You what?"

"I am journalism—I am *a* journalism student at the University of Texas, after I took my first two years at the university in Moscow, and I am interning at the Galveston newspaper, but I am also sending material to my hometown paper in Omsk, the free newspaper you understand, but they are all free now because my country is free, and I want to write about the flood and how it is treated and what the police do in this country to help people." He picked up the camera case he'd laid on the table. "And I want to take pictures, to show people how it is here. It is very important. Please let me ride with you. Or"—the grin slowly faded out—"do you have to have permission? I should have thought of that, and I know your chief will be here soon, but—"

Hansen looked at him and made a quick decision he probably wasn't authorized to make. "Come on," he said. "We've got work to do."

"The Russian left with Hansen," Booth told Shigata, still sounding very uneasy.

Shigata couldn't help chuckling. "Eve, the Russians aren't our enemies. The Russian people never were, just their damn-fool government which they finally managed to get rid of. If this Russian is a young journalist, then he was almost certainly on the right side. Quit worrying. He's not going to hijack our police car. Now tell me what's going on. Who's where? What parts of town have we reached and what parts do we still have to get to?"

The streetlights were out, and the only interruption to the deep darkness was the headlights of the police car. Overhead, tree branches waved in the wind and rain, and the only sound was the unceasing beat of the rain and the splash of people wading through the flood.

Hansen scrambled back into the marked sedan as Kerensky, who had crawled through a high bedroom window to remove two children, got into the other side. By now both men were effectively drenched, although Hansen had managed to protect his pistol and Kerensky his camera. From the backseat, Guadalupe Martinez said, "If you had not come we would have drowned in the night."

"I doubt that," Hansen said. "But you'd have gotten mighty wet. Everybody in?"

Martinez, clutching her baby and a large orange cat, counted heads. "Everybody is in."

"Next stop, high school." The high school had been built on the highest ground in Bayport; it was all of twenty feet above sea level. It had never flooded in hurricanes, and there were reasonable hopes that El Niño couldn't flood it either.

The gym was getting fuller and fuller; this time, as Martinez, her cat, and her five children headed through the rain toward the lights, Kerensky asked, "Is there time for us to go inside a minute? I would like to take some pictures. And—uh—I need—uh—"

"We'd better make time," Hansen replied. "If I don't get some coffee soon I won't be fit to drive."

"You sound educated," Kerensky asked, back in the car. "May I put this in the glove box?"

"May you put what in the glove box?"

"This roll of film. I have changed film, after I took pictures of the children playing on the stage and the women serving the free coffee and hot chocolate and doughnuts. I do not want to keep the film in my pocket because my pocket is wet. And the new film, I need to put it there too."

"Yeah, put the film in the glove box."

Kerensky obeyed and then asked, "You have studied history?"

"I have a Ph.D.," Hansen admitted. "But it's in English, not history. The history is just because I like to read."

"About Russia?"

"About everything."

Kerensky frowned and stared at Hansen through the near darkness. "But you have a Ph.D. and you are a police officer? Are you then a political dissident, so they would not let you teach at a university?"

Hansen laughed. "No. It doesn't work that way in this country. I guess some of the universities would consider me a political dissident, because I don't agree with what they call political correctness, but I'm a cop because that's what I want to be. If I wanted to teach I'm sure I could find a university that would take me." Actually he wasn't a hundred percent certain of that; political correctness in academia seemed to weigh more heavily than he was admitting. But he saw no sense in disillusioning Kerensky this early.

Kerensky's expression was unreadable. "My father had a Ph.D.," he said. "They let him get a Ph.D. because they thought he was a party loyal. They let him study in Paris, even. But then they found out he was not. They sent him to the gulag as a dissident and when they let him go free they made him drill for oil. They would not let him write and they would not let him teach. But he wrote anyway, and he taught me. This political correctness, who controls it?"

"It's just sort of a matter of group opinion," Hansen said. "Nobody really controls it. If a majority of the educational leaders agree to something then somebody who doesn't agree isn't politically correct, but that's just opinion. It's not anybody's official policy. The official policy is academic freedom. That means everybody is allowed to think whatever he or she wants to think. So don't worry about it. I'd like to hear more about you."

An hour later, he was regretting that invitation. Kerensky's enthusiasm might have been contagious at another time, but Hansen was twenty years older and a whole lot tireder. By the time he stopped the car in front of Bartlett's Motel, now completely dark in the rising water, he knew that Kerensky's father was dead but his mother and sister still lived in Omsk, that he'd begun college in Moscow and decided to transfer to a college in Texas after first seeing the Lone Star flag where it flew above a drilling rig in a joint U.S.-Russian oil venture in Siberia, that he'd talked the American part of that oil venture into providing him with a scholarship and the use of a car, that he loved the United States and especially Texas about as much as he did Russia and especially Siberia, that he had eaten pizza on the barricades in front of Yeltsin's White House during the Three-Day Coup, and that he didn't know how to stop talking. Hansen was beginning to wish he could put a cork in Kerensky's mouth long enough to stop some of the joyful burbling.

"Car Three to headquarters, ten-six at Barlett's," Hansen said into the radio. "Stay put just a minute," he added to Kerensky and swung the car door open. A moment later, flashlight shining into the open door of the motel, he shouted, "Radio for an ambulance!"

"How?" Kerensky yelled. "I don't know how!"

Hansen dashed back to the car and grabbed the microphone. "Car Three to headquarters, get me an ambulance, ten-eighteen, no, make that ten-thirty-nine." Ten-eighteen means lights and sirens and as fast as reasonably possible; ten-thirty-nine means floorboard it.

In this weather, Hansen realized as soon as he'd said it, nobody was going to floorboard for any reason. Not unless he was suicidally inclined. "Cancel the ten-thirty-nine," he said. "But make it ten-eighteen."

"Ten-four, Car Three," Booth said. After a moment's silence she said, "Ambulance is en route. Car Three, what do you have?"

"It looks like an electrocution," Hansen said. "Ed Bartlett. I think he was trying to unplug his outside lights."

"What is your condition?" Booth asked quickly.

"I'm fine. Everything's off around here now. The lights must have shorted out. But Ed doesn't look good."

"Is he breathing?"

"That's affirmative; he was lying on his back in about four inches of water. I got him out of the water, up on the couch in his office. But he's unconscious and badly burned. There's nothing else I can do here. Max and I are going to go try to roust out anybody that's staying in the motel."

"Who's Max?"

"The reporter who's riding with me, remember? Stand by." He laid the mike down on the seat. "Come on, Max, let's see who we can wake up."

Kerensky, camera strap around his neck, glanced once, wistfully, at the office, where a story wasn't being covered, then followed Hansen.

Not many people want to drive into a flood area. Cars or trucks were parked in front of only four of Bartlett's cabins. Hansen knocked at the door of the first. Silence. He knocked again, louder.

"What the hell do you want?" a male voice yelled from inside. "Can't you see it's the frappin' middle of the night?"

"Police," Hansen called. "Water's coming in. You've got to get out of here."

"I've got to what?" Then the man must have put his feet on the floor, because the next words were a muttered, "Oh, shit."

"I've got an idea," Hansen said more to himself than to Kerensky. He dashed back to the car, reached in, and threw switches. Suddenly his siren filled the night, with the rotating red, white, and blue lights coloring the rain.

Within seconds three more doors had opened, as people—a man whose camper full of fishing gear was in front of his motel door, a woman who seemed to belong with a L'eggs delivery van, an unexpected long-haul trucker whose eighteen-wheeler Hansen belatedly noticed parked across the street—woke up to find out what was going on and then, as their feet touched the water, found out. But the fifth door, the one with a late-model station wagon with a Mexican license plate in front of it, remained shut.

Hansen knocked on it.

Yelled.

Yelled again, and knocked harder.

Tried to open the door.

And then, reluctantly, applied his foot to the door directly at the lock. The door burst open, just as Kerensky's camera strobe flashed on Hansen kicking the door in. Hansen turned on his flashlight, and Kerensky followed him in. And then Kerensky exclaimed loudly, in Russian, and Hansen said, "Oh, shit!" He grabbed Kerensky's arm. "Back up," he said. "Out of here. Now."

"But I can take pictures," Kerensky objected.

Hansen paused. Then he said, "All right. You take pic-

▽

3

"CHIEF?" QUINN SAID.

Shigata, still kneeling in the cold water on the floor beside Rocky Omori, turned. "Yeah?"

"You want me to call in and put a lookout on this Buddy Yamagata?"

Shigata grinned briefly, humorlessly. "Buddy Yamagata hasn't left San Francisco. If he were accused of this he'd say we were crazy, and he'd produce as many witnesses as anybody would need to say he was at home when this crime was committed. And he almost certainly was."

"Yakuza?" Hansen guessed.

Shigata nodded. Quinn, who had never heard of the Yakuza, looked puzzled.

"Japanese Mafia," Hansen told him.

Shigata focused his eyes on Kerensky, who was standing behind the others, almost in the doorway. "You the Russian journalist?" he asked.

"Journalism student, yes, sir."

"They have any organized crime in Russia?"

After a brief pause, probably to figure out that a statement ending in a rising tone is a question, Kerensky said, "In the past, the Party took care of that."

There was a temporary silence while the double meaning of the answer was assimilated, then Hansen laughed delightedly and even Shigata grinned.

Kerensky added, "Now, I don't know. I think there is. But I don't know how organized. Nothing in Russia is very organized, right now. We are so used to being told from the top what to do that having to figure out all of it for ourselves is very confusing. But much Western aid that is supposed to be distributed through the state winds up in open-air markets. I think that is organized crime."

"You can stick around," Shigata said. "But don't go around repeating everything you hear at a crime scene. Especially this one."

"Yes, sir," Kerensky said, sounding vaguely bewildered.

"I've got to find a phone that works," Shigata said. "Steve, Al, how's the rescue effort going?"

"It's going," Quinn said.

"Al, you stick around here. Steve, hit the road."

"Right," Hansen said, and Shigata headed out the door as Quinn bent to take a closer look at the body on the floor.

Following Shigata, Hansen paused and asked, "Kerensky, you coming with me, or staying here with Quinn?"

Kerensky looked undecided. Then he asked, "Is okay if I stay here? My readers at home would like to know how crime is treated in America."

"The chief said it's okay," Hansen said, "so I guess it is."

He splashed back to his sedan and took off; Shigata, in the Bronco, was already gone, as was the ambulance carrying Ed Bartlett. Only Quinn's police sedan remained, its siren silent now but its lights coloring the night so that the Galveston units, when they could find a way off I-45 that would lead them into the town rather than into a mudhole, would know where to go.

The phone booth in front of Jack Horan's café still had lights on. Shigata parked beside it and scrambled out. There was still a dial tone, though no telling for how long.

Lissa answered sleepily. "Mark? It's five-thirty in the morning, is something wrong?"

"Yes. Did you write down Daniel's name when you registered?"

"No—" She sounded a little more alert. "Should I have?"

"Did anybody see you take him in?"

"I don't think so. I left the kids in the car while I registered. Why?"

"The Yakuza got Rocky and Phyllis sometime during the night." Over her horrified, startled exclamation, he went on talking. "Lissa, keep Daniel hidden. Don't try to go down to the restaurant. When you order from room service, don't order for him. Order two large meals for you and Gail, and share. Don't let anybody know he's there. Make sure—"

"What about the maids, when they come in to clean?"

"Oh, shit, I didn't think of that. I guess—"

"I can tell them—I'll think of something to tell them," Lissa said. "I'll make them just hand in fresh towels and stuff and Gail and I can handle it from there. Mark, I don't know how long—"

"I don't know how long either," he said. "Just do the best you can. If anybody calls you and asks questions, or calls and doesn't say anything, or tries to get in, call the Galveston PD first and let them know it's urgent, and then call me. If you can't reach me—"

"I know. Call dispatch. What am I going to tell—"

"Don't tell Daniel anything, except that he's staying with us right now. I'll explain it to him later. Let Gail know, but do it when Daniel can't hear you. Did you take that pistol with you, or leave it at home?"

"I brought it with me, but—"

"Keep it with you, and make sure Daniel doesn't get hold of it. Take care, sweetheart."

"Yes—you too—"

He returned to the Bronco and sat in it, silent, for a moment, surprised by the depth of his grief for a man and woman he had known for less than one day. Probably part of it was because there were so few people to whom he could claim kinship, and fewer still for whom he could feel any degree of kinship. He tended to blame that on his father, but his father was long dead; surely some of the blame of it must belong to himself.

But there was more than that. Perhaps he was only now recognizing an essential gallantry in Rocky Omori, as he remembered Rocky sitting in the Bronco last night talking to him, laughing, while knowing as he had to know what his death would be like. Shigata didn't possess that kind of gallantry; he could endure, but he couldn't laugh.

Perhaps he respected Rocky for making those tapes that were locked in his safe-deposit box.

And there was more. . . . He hadn't told Rocky, would never have told Rocky no matter how long Rocky had lived, but Mark Shigata knew Buddy Yamagata. Knew him, and feared him with a gut-wrenching cold-sweat terror that had nothing at all to do with pain or death.

Sitting in the Bronco in the darkness and the rain, he spoke aloud. "Rocky, I wish I could swear on our ancestors that I'd get Yamagata for this. But I can't. I'm not Shinto and I don't know how to talk to ancestors—and I'm not man enough to stop Buddy Yamagata. But you can understand that. All I can promise is what I've already promised—that if I can keep Daniel safe I will."

Rocky had characterized Shigata as a man who didn't count the cost. Shigata had tried to be that kind of man, as Rocky had been himself. Shigata had endured enough pain in his life that he didn't want to think of dying the way Rocky died, but that wasn't the reason he wouldn't try to write a permanent halt to the American Yakuza leader. No, the reason was far simpler: it was his certain knowledge that no one man could stop Yamagata. Shigata would go after him, yes, but he'd try to go after him with all the weight of the United States Department of Justice. And if that wasn't enough it wasn't enough.

But—last time he had tangled with Yamagata he'd wound up being transferred out of San Francisco, and they said it was for the good of the Bureau, and nobody admitted, at least not out loud, that it was for the good of Mark Shigata, because Shigata couldn't handle Yamagata. And now he was going back to San Francisco, going back alone without the

Bureau behind him, to take on Yamagata again.

Maybe we're both samurai, Rocky, he thought, *or maybe we're both damn fools.*

His throat aching, his eyes burning with unshed tears, Shigata started the car and drove back to Bartlett's, to find the Galveston crime scene truck already there, extension cords running from the generator on the truck through the windows, and floodlights on tables and windowsills at the end of the extension cords, so that the motel room was probably better lighted than it would have been if the electricity had not been off.

"Phil, will you look at this?" Sergeant Donna Gentry said. "I've never seen tattoos like this in my life!"

Investigator Phil Conroe took another picture and then paused. The tattoos—easy enough to see where they weren't obliterated by knife wounds, because the body was wearing nothing but the shreds of what had once been boxer shorts—ended abruptly at a well-demarcated line at the neck, halfway between the knee and the ankle, and halfway between the elbow and wrist. Other than that, they were full-body, an elaborate repeated design in multiple shades of purple, blue, and red that took in feathers, birds, dragons, flowers, and undefinable arabesques. "Chief?" Conroe called. "Did you see this?"

"I saw it." Shigata was standing well back, out of the way, until the photographs had been taken and the bodies moved, which come to think of it wasn't going to happen until somebody from the medical examiner's office arrived. Then he was going to tear the room apart, because if he couldn't find the key to the safe-deposit box, he could forget about Buddy Yamagata.

The key, he was dismally aware, might be in Mexico. Might be in California. Might be in Japan.

But somehow, he had a hunch Rocky wouldn't have traveled far without it.

Of course the key might have been taken by whoever had tortured Rocky to death. But he didn't think it had.

"Why would anybody—" Conroe started to ask.

"He was Yakuza," Shigata said, suspecting he was going to get tired of saying it.

Conroe's expression said he'd never heard of the Yakuza. It was Gentry who turned, startled. "I thought you said he was your cousin."

"He was my cousin. He was also Yakuza. Look, I just met him yesterday, okay? Just because my mother was his father's sister doesn't mean we had to be just alike."

"Sorry," Gentry said, "didn't mean to—"

"I know you didn't," Shigata said. "But I'm . . . a little on edge."

Gentry looked back at the body. "Gee, I can't imagine why something like this would have you on edge. I never even saw the dude alive, and *I'm* a little on edge myself."

The door opened again, and Shigata swung around to look. "Kerensky," he said, "let the man by."

"Oh. Sorry." Max Kerensky moved to one side, and medical examiner's investigator Joel Moran waded into the room.

He looked first at Phyllis, then at Rocky, and his eyes widened. "You needed me to say that's dead? Guess what, they're dead." Automatically he glanced at his watch, because the death certificate would show the time at which death was formally pronounced. Then he asked, "How come they took their ears?"

"Legally, Joel, legally," Gentry said. "The state doesn't figure we dumb cops know for sure whether somebody's dead or not. It takes somebody smart like you to say so, if it's too cold and wet for a reallio-trulio doctor to come out. And we figure they took their ears to prove they were dead. And it's Shigata's cousin, okay?"

Moran shifted his gaze to Shigata. "Shee-yit."

"That's one way of putting it," Shigata said.

"Hey, man, I'm sorry—"

"It's a crime scene," Shigata said. "Treat it as a crime scene." He sat suddenly, hard, on a chair beside the window as Kerensky wandered past him and out the door.

* * *

The murderers had taken the time to shower and put on clean clothes before they left the motel to the incoming water. Now they were sitting in a back corner booth of a Denney's in Galveston, arguing as quietly as possible.

Like Shigata, Benjamin "Boat" Marubyashi and Kenji Ishi didn't speak Japanese.

Like Omori, they had learned of the code of the Yakuza before they swore fealty to Buddy Yamagata.

Unlike Shigata and Omori, they did count the cost.

And going back to Buddy Yamagata with two ears, when they were supposed to have three, might cost more than they were prepared to pay. Boat was a big man, in terms of size: plenty big enough to take a shy, gentle woman; to take a short, stocky, and very tough man. He had minded killing the woman, at least a little, because he'd known her for twenty-five years, since she was just past toddler age. Like many Yakuza recruits, he'd started out washing cars and pulling weeds and baby-sitting kids until the higher-ups knew how well he would take orders, and one of the kids he'd baby-sat was Phyllis Yamagata.

He hadn't minded killing the man, because the man had come over from Japan, cocky and arrogant because he was real Japanese and real Yakuza, old-style tattoos and everything. Old-style Yakuza *and* educated. What a combination.

He hadn't minded killing the man, even the way they'd done it. It wasn't like he was some sort of freak like Ishi, who liked killing and even torture as long as it wasn't kids. Ishi was a small man, short and slim and neat-looking and mean as a coral snake; if he didn't like you he'd rather chew you to death than kill you fast. Boat told himself he didn't *like* that kind of thing, but he didn't mind it. That was part of the point of being Yakuza, you were supposed to be tough enough to dish it out *or* take it. Well, he figured he was. But he wasn't in any hurry to find out what it would be like to be on the receiving end.

He didn't want to kill the kid. That wasn't right, that

wasn't the code. But disobeying orders wasn't the code either. And going back and admitting you hadn't finished the job you were sent out to do—that could get very costly.

"We gotta find him, Ken," Marubyashi said to Ishi. "The *oyabun* said—"

"The *oyabun* said 'What do I care about the kid?' That's what he said," Ishi repeated stubbornly.

"Right, and then he said to delete him. That means kill him. Look, man, do *you* want to go back and tell the *oyabun*—"

"We can't find him. If we can't find him we can't find him and if we can't find him we sure as hell can't kill him."

"So you want to be the one to tell him that?"

"Hell, no," Ishi admitted finally. "But what are we gonna do?"

"Think, man. They had the kid yesterday. We know that. We saw them check in at Bartlett's about ten o'clock yesterday morning, and they had the kid with them. So where could they have lost him in eleven hours?"

"Maybe they just had him in a different room. I toldja we should have checked—"

"Right, check every room in the motel and wake everybody up. I mean, that was why we gagged Omori, so he wouldn't wake anybody up if he got to yelling. We're not s'posed to kill anybody unnecessarily. Anyway, they wouldn't have had him in another room. He's just four years old."

"If he was in another room it would have been right next door—"

"He wasn't in another room," Marubyashi said savagely. "They left him somewhere. I'm betting that's what they came to this penny-ante town for, to leave the kid somewhere."

"But all the kid's clothes were in their room—"

"Right, and they just had two suitcases, so the kid's clothes were mixed in with theirs. So maybe they'd left the kid but they weren't through yet. My point is, they left the kid somewhere and we've got to find out where. Somebody must have seen—if the telephone still works at that motel—"

With that he was out of the booth, heading for the pay telephone over in the corner by the restroom.

He came back disgusted. "Some guy answered. He kept asking who I was, and he wouldn't tell me anything except he did say that Ed Bartlett—if I remember right the way I read the signs, Ed Bartlett's the owner or manager or something—he said Ed Bartlett had been taken to the hospital a coupla hours ago."

"Did he tell you who he was?" Ishi asked.

"Nah," Marubyashi said in disgust. "I asked but he wouldn't tell me. And he didn't sound natural. He sounded like some sort of foreigner or something."

"I answered the phone in the lobby," Kerensky reported. "Was that all right?"

Shigata turned to look at him. "What did you do that for?"

"I was going to the car to get some more film, and then I remembered I left my film in Steve's car and Steve is not here, so I thought I would check the lobby and see if there was any film for sale there, and I went in and then I remembered that Ed Bartlett went to the hospital and the phone was ringing so I answered it because there was nobody else to answer it. Was that all right?"

"I guess it has to be all right, since you already did it," Shigata said. "But don't do it again. Who was it?"

"I don't know. He wouldn't tell me who he was. He wanted to talk to the manager. I asked him who he was but he would not tell me and then he asked me who I was and I did not tell him. He sounded," Kerensky added thoughtfully, "as if he might be some kind of foreigner. At least not from around here. He did not sound like a Texan. If he is not a Texan, is he a foreigner?"

"Not necessarily," Shigata said. "What else did he ask?"

"Nothing. He just wanted to talk to the manager."

Now that the bodies were gone, it was a little easier for Shigata to pretend it was only a crime scene. The ache in his throat, though not totally gone, had diminished. He was watching Gentry and Conroe dust for prints, carefully staying a fraction of an inch above the water so they wouldn't ruin their brushes on something they couldn't get prints from, and after they finished with a particular area he began on it. The suitcases, first, the suitcases that Gentry had just photographed and fingerprinted the outside of because there was no indication that the murderers had ever touched them and anyway you generally can't fingerprint clothes even with the most advanced of techniques, and that was all that was in the suitcases, clothes. So the murderers weren't hunting the safe-deposit box key? That could be true only if they did not know the key existed—or if they were certain they could force Rocky to tell them where it was, so they wouldn't have to hunt it.

Would Rocky have told them? With the mental picture of the body in his mind, Shigata wasn't certain—but then he remembered himself, tied to an overhead beam in a garage that now no longer existed, being asked the same question over and over and over, while utterly unbearable pain slammed into him, and he hadn't answered, he wouldn't answer because it was Gail they were asking about, it was his child they were asking about—and Rocky knew that key, the tapes that key protected, were his only hope of keeping his son safe.

There was no way to know for sure. But Shigata didn't think Rocky had told even if he had been asked, was certain he hadn't volunteered the information no matter how many hours it took him to die.

He took every item out of each suitcase individually, felt every seam, every hem, every lining, and then methodically, with Conroe and Gentry watching astonished and Quinn helping without asking questions, he took each suitcase apart. But he found no key.

By that time the fingerprinting in the main room was finished. Conroe was packing up his gear, and Gentry had moved into the little anteroom between the bedroom and bathroom to fingerprint the counter and everything on it. It was hard to work in there because she was between the floodlights and the counter, in the shadow cast by her own body, and considering the extent of flooding it probably wouldn't be safe to try to move the floodlights farther into the room. So she was using her flashlight quite a lot. With it in her hand, she glanced into the small bathroom and said, "Phil?"

"Yo?"

"Have you put the camera away?"

"Yeah, why?"

"I thought you looked in here."

"I thought you did." He was getting the camera back out as he spoke. Entering the bathroom by the light of Gentry's flashlight, he halted. "Shigata!" he said. "Did you look in here?"

"No, should I? You're doing the crime scene." And that was unlike him, foggy from lack of sleep and shock and grief; he always looked at everything no matter who was doing the crime scene.

Conroe backed away from the door. "You better."

For knife murderers to take baths or showers at the scene of the crime is not unheard of; in fact, it is so common that the protocol—that is, the recognized procedure—for searching such a crime scene assumes that the murderer cleaned up, and normally the pipes draining the bathtub or shower and the sink would be taken apart to search for traces of blood.

That wasn't going to be necessary, this time. Which was fortunate, because given the condition of the drains it would be impossible until after the water had gone down, probably taking the evidence along with it.

For murderers—any murderers—to leave their clothes behind is distinctly unusual. But these murderers had done it.

The next question was going to be, what to do about it.

The protocol is that each piece of bloody cloth is packaged separately, in paper rather than plastic, preferably not folded, and taken somewhere to dry flat before being repackaged.

The protocol does not assume that the murder took place in a motel during a flood, and there is blood on both beds.

Phyllis had evidently been killed in the bed she was sleeping in, and the body was there until the EMTs took it away. Rocky had died on the floor, but the preceding fight had involved both beds. Those sheets had to be handled especially carefully, because there was always the hope, slim though it was, that at least one of the murderers might himself have done a little bleeding, and these days, with DNA testing, if they could isolate the suspect's blood from the victim's and find the suspect that matched the blood, they could make a positive match in just about three weeks.

So both sets of bedding had been packaged, each item already out in the lab truck individually, and Gentry and Conroe had been debating, trying to figure out a way to take along the mattress from the bed the men had fought on.

Now there were two complete sets of clothing and no place to lay them out to figure out what size they were, so as to put a lookout on whoever had worn them.

Shigata strode back into the bedroom and looked around. Then he began to unplug the television. "Anybody got a screwdriver?" he asked a moment later.

"Yeah, I'll get you one." Conroe dashed out to the lab truck, then returned a moment later with an entire tool kit.

"All I wanted was one screwdriver," Shigata said, unscrewing the two small screws that had kept the television's plug firmly in the electrical outlet. A moment later he had moved the television onto the table between the windows and was clearing off the few remaining items on the dresser. "Now if I had something to spread them out on individually . . ." he muttered.

Kerensky cleared his throat. "Uh—sir," he said diffidently.

"Yeah?"

"I saw a stack of newspapers in the lobby. They are on the counter, so they are still dry."

"Good. Go get them."

* * *

The clothes belonged to two different men, and one was not far off twice the size of the other. Finally, there was enough for a lookout, and Shigata went back to the Bronco, surprised by the daylight, scarcely noticing that the rain had stopped falling, to radio headquarters himself.

"Notify all units in the area to be on the lookout for two Oriental males. Subject number one is about six feet two inches tall, about two hundred thirty pounds, probably black hair and brown eyes. Subject number two is about five feet five inches tall, about a hundred ten pounds, probably black hair and brown eyes. Both may be heavily tattooed and both may be lacking the tip of the little finger of one hand, but those two items are not certain. Subjects are wanted for murder and both are to be considered armed and extremely dangerous."

For what good that will do, he reflected, reentering the motel room. The world is a melting pot, and there were plenty of Oriental men, large and small, in Galveston and Houston. Unless they were doing something to attract attention to themselves, nobody would even stop and question them, and chances were they would be doing nothing to attract attention to themselves.

Gentry and Conroe were still examining the clothes. There was nothing unusual about them. Two pairs of Levi jeans, two sweatshirts, two sets of Jockey brand underclothes, two pair of sports socks. They'd taken their jackets and shoes with them.

All the clothes had been washed at home or in a laundromat; there were no distinguishing marks about them.

All the clothes were sodden; they'd been lying on the bathroom floor, and besides the water that came in from outside, the drain seemed to have backed up. Gentry was packaging the items carefully, trying to keep the bloodstains on the outside and undistorted, and she and Conroe were discussing which one of them was going to take the evidence on up to Austin today, because clearly the scientists needed to get to this fast.

"Chief?" Quinn's hand rested lightly on Shigata's forearm. "You've got to get some sleep. You're dead on your feet."

"I will," Shigata said. "But first I've got to find—"

"Find what?" Quinn asked patiently. "I'll help."

"The key." Shigata looked around. Gentry and Conroe had taken nearly everything out to the lab truck now, and were just waiting for Shigata to finish up before they loaded the lights. It had been a slapdash job of working the scene, but given the situation, it was the best anybody could do. They might find more when the water went down, and they might not. Nobody could guess about that.

"What key?" Gentry asked, coming back in. "I didn't know we were looking for a key."

"Key to a safe-deposit box," Shigata said. "It should be around here somewhere."

"You should have told me," Gentry muttered and started looking again.

In the end it was Quinn who found it, wrapped in two washcloths and stuffed into the bottom of a fake can of shaving cream. "Now will you go somewhere and get some sleep?" he asked Shigata.

"You got any idea where?"

"We got cots set up at the station. 'Course the feet are in water, but the mattresses aren't."

"Uh-huh," Shigata said, and walked out the door into blazing sunshine.

There was one more thing he had to do before he slept, and he wasn't looking forward to it. But if the telephone in his office was still working . . .

The lines going into the police station were pretty well insulated, and the phone was still working. Seven o'clock Texas would make it five o'clock California, too early to call, but he couldn't stay awake much longer and if he waited until he woke up to call and some smart reporter asked somebody the wrong questions—or the right questions, from their point of view—

"Mom?"

"Mark?" She sounded terribly sleepy. And she was old—it was too early to wake her up. "Mark? So early? What is wrong?"

Her English always a little formal, like Kerensky's English—Shigata knew that with her own family, the Omoris, she still spoke Japanese, even though his father had always required that only English be spoken in their house. "It's—Mom? Do you know Isoruko Omori?"

"He is my nephew. Yes. I know him. He was here, oh, about three weeks ago. He asked me about you. Why—"

"Mom, listen, he's dead, he and Phyllis—"

She responded in Japanese, and he could almost see her as she spoke, her white hair flying as she fumbled on her bedside table for her glasses. He said, "Mom . . . Mom . . . I don't understand that. Mom, you've got to speak English, you know I don't—"

"And you should. Your father was very foolish, not to let you learn—"

"I know that, but—"

"And Isoruko—to die so far away from his home—is so sad. Has anybody called his mother and father?"

"Mom, I don't know who they are and I don't know how to call them. Do you want to give me their phone number, or would you rather—"

"I will telephone. Mark, what about Daniel? Their little boy? Daniel? Was it the Yakuza who killed him? Where is Daniel?"

"Mom—Mom—listen, okay? Lissa has Daniel, she's hiding in a motel in Galveston, and yes, I think it was the Yakuza—"

"I told him he should not—but he did not listen, these young people don't ever listen—"

"Mom—"

"I will tell his parents. I will tell his father to call you. Are you at home, or—?"

"I'm at work. We've got a little bit of a flood down here, the house is flooded out."

"I told you you should have stayed in the Bureau."

"Mom, I didn't want to stay in the Bureau. Do you have the number here at the station?"

"I have it. I will call. But I don't know when I can reach—I don't know what time it is there—my brother Taisuko, he will call you."

"Mom, I've got to go get some sleep now, I worked all night—"

He wasn't sure she heard that. She went on, briskly, "You must have Shinto funeral."

"Mom, I'm not Shinto."

"You should be. *Episcopalian.*" She made the word a curse word. "Your father was very foolish. And you can find—"

"Maybe I can find a Buddhist priest, I think I know some Buddhists—"

"Should be Shinto. But Buddhist is better than *Episcopalian.* All right. You go get some sleep. I will tell Taisuko he must wait to call you until later, his son is dead and his daughter-in-law is dead but his nephew must get some *sleep.*"

The phone slammed down, leaving Shigata saying "Ah, Mom" to a dial tone. He dropped the receiver, said, "Oh, shit," and headed for the storage room where the cots had been set up.

Hansen, who could sleep anywhere after two and a half years in prison, was on another cot in uniform pants and a T-shirt, lying facedown and silent except for an occasional deep breath. Two other officers—from what he could see of them, he guessed they were Susa Gonzales and Paul Ames—were similarly arranged, under the scratchy wool World War II army surplus blankets.

Shigata thought he'd never be able to sleep. But after about four deep breaths, he was out.

▽

4

E. P. HONSHU SMILED, BOWED, clasped his hands over his head like a victorious boxer, smiled again, and hated himself. With every movement he made, the sequins sewn onto his coat glittered and flashed in the spotlights and the safe-deposit key hidden in the old-fashioned watch pocket the tailors had put in his trousers while adjusting them to his size seemed to burn into his skin. *If I had any guts I'd—*

What? he asked himself bitterly. *What would I do? What* could *I do? I warned him, what else—*

*They're probably dead by now—and here I stand playing to the lunchtime trade like a—like a—*he could think of no words vile enough.

And he went on smiling, and bowing, until the applause stopped and he began to sing a dead man's songs, copying a dead man's voice, wearing a dead man's clothes. Because that was his gig. He never admitted he was an impersonator. In interviews—and there were a lot of interviews, because Honshu's, originally bankrolled by the Yamagata family of the American Yakuza, had become a popular night spot, a good legal investment that could launder a considerable quantity of other income—he always insisted he was just singing the songs he liked, he had the haircut he felt comfortable in, he wore clothes he enjoyed, and the E. P. in his stage name didn't mean anything.

He sang, and smiled, and hated himself.

After four hours of daytime sleep in a crowded and wet storeroom, Shigata couldn't decide whether he felt better or worse. By the time he woke, he was alone in the storeroom; everyone else was up and gone. He waded barefoot into the muster room, noting that the water seemed to be receding slightly, and refilled the coffee cup he'd left there last night. He carried the coffee on into the locker room and set it on a counter while he attended to other necessities. For some reason nobody could explain, the toilets in the city government building were still flushing and the shower drains were still working; he wondered how much longer that would last.

In uniform now, although he usually wore civilian clothes, he returned to the coffee, sipping at it while he shaved. It was far too strong; probably it had been made strong to start with, and then it had sat too long. He drank the rest of it anyway, fast, nearly gagging at the taste but hoping it would wake him up, and then brushed his teeth to get rid of the strong acrid bitterness.

Then he removed his socks from the top of the heater vent and got his boots down from the top of a locker where he had stowed them, hoping they'd dry a little in the night. They hadn't, much, but at least the socks were temporarily dry and for the moment his feet were warm.

Try to look at the situation sanely, not colored by emotion, he told himself. Most likely, having missed Daniel, the Yakuza killers were already on their way back to San Francisco. His warning to Lissa had been only a precaution. He could see no logical reason the killers would still be around. If Yamagata wanted possession of his grandson—and most likely he did, most likely Rocky had been right about that—he would assume he could get custody later, legally. Because he wouldn't have any idea that the tapes in the safe-deposit box existed. Shigata was certain of that. If Yamagata had known, the killers, one way or another, wouldn't have left that motel room without the key, even though Yamagata would have seen to it that they had no idea what the key meant.

Therefore, logically, Yamagata had no reason to think he

few days, if all other crime would come to a halt long nough for him to work on the one case that had engaged is mind. But it doesn't work that way. He'd been half-awakned repeatedly during those few hours of restless sleep by he clanging of the door to the small, four-cell, city jail. By he time he had his boots on and was out the locker room door into the hall, he could hear Hansen's voice near the booking desk, drawling, "*Sure* you did." Then Hansen, now in civilian clothes, followed by Max Kerensky, entered the muster room. With them was a burly, unshaven white male—*lout* was the thought that entered Shigata's mind—in khaki pants, a torn T-shirt that said I MAY GROW OLD BUT I'LL NEVER GROW UP, a scruffy denim jacket, and handcuffs.

"Now what?" Shigata asked.

"Have a seat," Hansen said in the general direction of his arrestee. "Chief, I caught Curtis Barnes here down on Bayshore Road and around there. He had twelve televisions and ten VCRs in the back of his pickup—"

"In all this rain?" Shigata interrupted.

"Oh, it's quit raining."

"I knew it quit this morning, but I figured it had started back up by now."

"Nope," Hansen said. "The sun's out, and Curtis here was taking good care of those TVs. He had some of those wooden loading pallets in the bed of the truck, and the televisions and all were up on them. Thing is, he just can't figure out how they got there. He says somebody stole his truck last night and he just now found it with all that stuff in it. But seeing as how he's got a burglary record as long as your arm, I sort of wondered, you know. So I brought him in, and had Max here drive his truck in for me and put it in the compound."

"Hmm." Shigata would remind Hansen later that a civilian, particularly a foreign national, should not be that involved in police business. For now he sat, seemingly casually, on the corner of a table a little closer to Barnes than Barnes was likely to appreciate. The fact was, the move had Barnes

was threatened. So the killers—the knives Yar
wielded across the miles—weren't around to b
And the real killer, Yamagata, would be vulnera
an extremely intelligent and well-planned camp
body was going to convict him by putting out an
couple of his *kabun*.

So—and somehow, in the few minutes since he h
the cup of coffee, Shigata had begun to think like t
he had once been trained to be—Shigata had to first
the will so that he could get the necessary court ord
him open another man's safe deposit box. He was we
he wouldn't be able to look in that box by himself
would be representatives of the IRS there—that wa
dard—and probably, if Rocky's mob connection was k
representatives of the FBI would be there as well. Th
fine with him. In fact, he intended to request that a
agent be present. Preferably several, so that he could i
diately turn the tapes over to the FBI and have some re
to expect the FBI agent to get back to his office safely.

If he could just manage to stop himself from being a
of Buddy Yamagata. He'd done everything right, those ni
mare weeks in San Francisco. He'd done what he was s
posed to do, he hadn't let anybody or anything scare him
he'd followed through. (But that was easier then than
might be now; he had nobody to worry about then, no wi
no child, no—foster child—to worry about. Then, there w
no family for the mob boss to reach him through. Now, the
was.)

And he couldn't forget the sound of Yamagata's voice o
his answering machine ten years ago: "Don't ever cross me
again." No threats. Just five words, in a voice that made
threats superfluous.

And now he was crossing Yamagata again. He had to, and
now as then he would not let the fear stop him.

But the fear was physical, a tight knot somewhere in his
abdomen that wouldn't let go even in sleep.

And it would be terrific if the world would just stand still inside Shigata's comfort zone, and Shigata was uncomfortable too, but Barnes wasn't going to know that. "Very interesting," he said. "Did you give him his rights?"

"Oh, yes," Hansen said. "I always give people their rights."

Kerensky looked extremely interested at that.

"Did he sign a waiver?"

"Nope, he said he didn't want to sign anything. I correct myself. He said he didn't want to sign nothing."

"Then I guess we can't talk to him. Take him on back—"

"Hey, wait a minute," Curtis Barnes protested. "You can't—"

"Can't do what?" Shigata asked, very softly. "Can't arrest you for being in possession of stolen property?"

"Can't lock me up without letting me explain—"

"Curtis, you said you didn't want to talk to us," Hansen pointed out.

"Yeah, but—"

"Well, do you or don't you?" Shigata asked.

"I—uh—"

"Oh, I forgot to tell you," Hansen added, in a tone of voice that indicated he had forgotten accidentally on purpose. "When I spotted him, he was coming out of a house carrying a television. I followed him a couple of blocks before stopping him."

"Whose house was it?"

"Mine," Barnes said hastily. "If you'd just asked—"

"That's funny," Hansen said. "I thought it was my house. And if you'd taken a good look at that television, Curtis, you'd have noticed it had my name and Social Security number engraved on it."

"Oh, shit," Barnes said. "Oh, shit. All the houses in town and I had to pick a—oh, shit."

"Does that mean you want to talk to us?" Shigata said.

"Oh, shit," Barnes said again.

"It'll take a little while to find out who the other stuff belongs to," Hansen said, "but that should be enough to make a burglary charge stick real good."

"Before you book him," Shigata said, "let him put all the 'stuff' as you call it into the property room, in case it starts to rain again."

"Fingerprints?" Hansen asked.

"I don't think we'll worry about them this time," Shigata said. "From what I remember of his record, this will be his third separate felony conviction."

Hansen unlocked Barnes's handcuffs, returned them to his own belt, and said, "Come on, Curtis, you and I have some televisions to move."

"Ah, shit," Barnes repeated monotonously, dolefully, and followed Hansen out the door.

Watching them leave, Kerensky asked, "What is this 'giving him his rights'? What does it mean?"

"According to the United States Constitution," Shigata said, "every person arrested for a crime has the right to be represented by an attorney, and he has the right not to discuss the crime with the police if he doesn't want to. And if he wants to discuss the crime with the police, he's allowed to have an attorney present to represent him, and if he can't afford to pay an attorney then the court will appoint one for him."

"So the court pays for the attorney to defend him as well as for the attorney to prosecute him?"

"That's right. And police are required to tell him his rights in case he doesn't know them. And if he agrees to talk to the police without an attorney present, he signs what's called a waiver to show that he agreed. Unless the waiver is signed the police can't legally question him."

"But you could make him sign the waiver—"

Shigata grinned. "It doesn't work that way. If he's not willing to sign it then he doesn't have to."

"But how can you investigate a crime if you cannot ask questions?" Kerensky demanded. "I mean, yes, this time I understand, I was with Steve Hansen and we both saw him coming out of Steve Hansen's house, but if you didn't know for sure—or if you needed a confession—"

"Then we have to find out other ways," Shigata said. "A forced confession is no good at all in court or any other way. Look at it this way, Kerensky. You go to slamming somebody around and you don't get the truth, what you get is somebody so scared he'll say whatever he thinks you want him to say, whether it's true or not."

"Or so angry he will say nothing at all," Kerensky said softly, and Shigata looked hard at him for a moment, wondering whether Kerensky, as young as he was, was speaking from his father's experience or from his own. But he decided not to ask.

"Or so angry he will say nothing at all," Shigata agreed. "Either way, that doesn't help investigations; it impedes them. And it's indecent behavior. If the police go around breaking the law—and something like that is completely illegal—how can they expect anybody else to obey the law? Even putting all that aside, if a police officer forces somebody to sign a confession or even a rights waiver, then the police officer is likely to be in very serious trouble and could even go to jail himself."

"But—"

"Trust me. That's the way it is."

"But when I first arrived in this country I saw on television, a case in Los Angeles—police had stopped a man and they were hitting him with clubs—"

"It happens," Shigata said. "It shouldn't, but it does. If you followed that case, you know the aftermath of it. And if it ever happens in this department, the officers involved better be prepared for more trouble than they'll know what to do with."

Kerensky half shrugged and then asked, "What is this about a third felony conviction?"

"The legal assumption is that if a person has been convicted of three separate felonies, then he's probably incorrigible—"

"What does that mean?"

"It means that probably he can't be rehabilitated, taught

not to be a criminal. If he's been convicted of three separate felonies, then he's probably incorrigible and should be imprisoned for life."

"Then—"

"Except, of course," Shigata added, "that usually somebody who's been imprisoned for life is paroled after seven or so years."

"Why?"

Talking with Kerensky is like talking with an intelligent three-year-old stuck on the 'why' stage, Shigata thought. *But he has real reasons for asking, a real need to know. I've got to remember that and stay patient.*

"Because," he answered, "for some reason which I do not understand, a so-called life sentence is actually considered to last about twenty-one years, and a person begins to be considered for parole after he's served a third of his sentence. As overcrowded as the prison systems are, if he's not likely to be an extreme danger to the community usually he'll be paroled at that time."

"Then what if you *really* want him imprisoned for life?"

"I have no say-so at all," Shigata said. "The courts—the judges and juries—decide that, not the police. If the courts really want him imprisoned for life they may sentence him to life plus ninety-nine years, on the theory that by doing it that way he won't be eligible for parole until he's served seven years for the life sentence and thirty-three years as one-third of the ninety-nine-year sentence. And sometimes the courts in Texas get really harsh and sentence him to life plus nine hundred years."

"And then he will really stay in jail for all his life."

"Probably."

"Only probably?"

"He might appeal to a higher court and get the sentence reduced."

"But if this—Barnes—has, as Steve Hansen put it, a burglary record longer than your arm—"

"A person might be arrested at one time and charged with

many burglaries," Shigata said. "Like when we find out who all those televisions belong to, we might charge him with a separate count of burglary for each one of them. But since the charges were grouped together, it would still—for the purpose of determining number of felony convictions—usually be taken by the courts to count as only one, because they all came at the same time. Also, a person isn't necessarily sentenced to life for a third conviction. It's up to the district attorney to ask for it, and maybe he hasn't before, or maybe the court decided not to grant it."

"What about political criminals?"

"We don't have political criminals. We might not like for people to be Nazis, or Ku Klux Klan members, or skinheads, or Communists, or whatever, but it's not illegal. The person has to commit a real crime to be arrested."

"Steve Hansen said he is not politically correct. And then one time he said something about being in jail and then he stopped and started to talk about something else."

"He wasn't in jail for not being politically correct," Shigata said. "Being politically incorrect—so called—might keep him from being able to get a faculty position at a major university, but that's about the worst that can happen to anybody for that. And I wish Hansen had never mentioned political correctness to you."

"But it is important for me to know. If we are going to find a way to make my country function—we have to know how other countries function. And the idea of political correctness, that frightens me. I am not ashamed to say that frightens me. If even in this country a man may not think what he wants to think—"

"There aren't any thought police," Shigata said patiently. "I'm not what they would consider politically correct either. Hardly any police are. And hardly anybody really cares."

"Then what was Steve Hansen in jail for?"

"He was in jail because a former police chief here convinced a jury that Steve had killed his wife."

"Whose wife? The police chief's, or—"

"Hansen's wife," Shigata clarified.

"Did he?"

"No."

"How do you know?"

"I examined the evidence."

"Then the former police chief—couldn't he examine the evidence too?"

"He wanted Hansen to be guilty. To start with I think he really thought Hansen was guilty, but by the time he knew different he also knew who was guilty, and he was covering up for that person. I think Hansen would rather not talk about that right now."

"Then you have crooked public officials in America also," Kerensky said.

"We do, yes. We try to get rid of them, but we can't get rid of all of them."

"What happened to the crooked police chief?"

"He died in a car wreck."

"Ah. And if he hadn't—?"

"If he hadn't he'd now be in prison himself."

"I want to write series—*a* series—of articles for my newspaper at home about the police department here. Maybe even a whole book. Is that all right with you?"

"I suppose—"

"To get the information for the book I want to ride with Steve Hansen for a month or two. And I want to take very many pictures."

"Oh, shit." Shigata ran his hand over his chin musingly. "What did Hansen say about that?"

"He said it was okay with him if it was okay with you. Is it okay?"

Kerensky, Shigata thought, seemed fond of the word *okay*. "I'll have to check with the mayor," he said. "But unless she says no, consider it approved."

"The mayor is a woman?"

"Yes. Any problems with that?"

"Nothing. I just had heard—are there any colored police?"

Shigata winced. "That word is so politically incorrect that even Hansen and I don't like it. We say black, or African-American. And yes, there are many black officers on other departments. As small as this department is, I don't have but four. I'd like to have more, but the salary is higher in Galveston. We have a real retention problem here."

"The Party told us," Kerensky said, "that in America the women and the colored people—excuse me, the African-American people—were mistreated and abused."

"We try not to mistreat and abuse anybody," Shigata said, "but I suppose no country can succeed completely with that goal. At least not so far as I know."

"But—"

"You're an intern now, right?" Shigata interrupted. "A journalism intern?"

"That is correct."

"From the University of Texas in Austin?"

"Yes."

"When do you return to classes?"

"Probably in September."

"When you get back there," Shigata said, "take a few American history courses, okay? And maybe a few courses in ethnic relations and gender studies? Because I've got work to do, and as much as I'd like to, I don't have time to stand here and teach you history."

"Is it all right if I ask Steve Hansen while I am riding with him?"

"Ask me what?" Hansen said, coming back into the muster room with Barnes still tagging morosely behind him.

"About American history. And political correctness."

"Ask Hansen whatever you want to ask him," Shigata said. "Now I've got to—"

"And I can go with Steve Hansen to look at the city jail and the county jail?"

"Look at whatever you want to, wherever you want to," Shigata said.

"And I can take pictures wherever I want to?"

"I don't have any say-so about the county jail," Shigata said. "That's county. But other than that, yes, take pictures wherever you want to. I've got a feeling I'm going to get very tired of you before September."

Kerensky stared at him, then apparently decided that was a joke and produced a grin.

Without further words, Shigata went into his own office (which had only about a quarter of an inch of water on the floor, hardly enough to worry about), shut the door, and reached for the Galveston telephone book. Finding an attorney who had the necessary background to administer a will written and signed in Texas, by a Japanese national who had most recently lived in Mexico but was murdered in Texas within hours after the will was signed, covering property mostly in California—an attorney who had such a background and who felt secure enough to handle the problem—might take more than two or three telephone calls.

"His name was Bartlett," Marubyashi said, lying on his back on one of the two beds in the Galveston motel room. "The manager of the motel. I think the owner too. He was Ed Bartlett, and they took him to the hospital."

"You've said that about two dozen times," Ishi replied wearily. "Now do something about it, or shut up."

"I've got to get to him," Marubyashi said.

"You said that a couple of dozen times too," Ishi said. "You got any idea *which* hospital?"

"This penny-ante town can't have too many hospitals. It's not like home." Marubyashi could not stay long away from San Francisco without getting homesick.

"Well, if we're going to follow up your dumb idea, we've still got to find out which—"

"Get the phone book," Marubyashi said unnecessarily, because Ishi was already opening it. "And start calling."

"He's in—they call it University of Texas Medical Branch," Ishi said, after several telephone calls. "And they say he can have visitors, for just a few minutes at a time. So what do you want to do, take him flowers?"

"Your brain turned to mush?" Marubyashi asked. "I want to find out where Omori went during the day and early evening. Because the kid's gonna be in one of those places."

"If we'd been following him, like the *oyabun* said—"

"In a town this size?" Marubyashi asked. "Without getting spotted? We couldn't. And since we didn't—"

"So what makes you think he knows? And even if he does know, what makes you think he's going to tell us? You plan to beat it out of him in a hospital?"

Unmoving, his hands clasped under the back of his head, Marubyashi said, "That's why I'm going and you're not. Now look, nice and easy, I tell him that was my—ah—brother died in the motel that night, and I need to know where he went after he checked in, who he went to see, who came to see him, on account of that might help me find out—"

"And the fuzz," Ishi said, "wouldn't have already asked him that?"

"Who cares whether they did or not? So I'm asking too. If he knows, he'll tell us. If he doesn't, well, then we'll think of something else. *I'll* think of something else."

"I say we should just let it drop," Ishi said. Unexpectedly, he added, "*Katagi no shu*—"

"You know I don't understand that crap," Marubyashi said. (Mark Shigata could have told him what that meant because he'd learned, ten years ago in San Francisco, and because more recently Rocky Omori had reminded him. The old code of the Yakuza, the vow never to harm the uninvolved human being.)

Ishi turned. "Neither does the *oyabun*. And that's what's wrong. We've vowed to do what the *oyabun* says but the *oyabun* shouldn't tell us to kill a kid. Okay, you think you're the smart guy, go see what you can find out."

"What are you gonna be doing?"

"Taking a nap," Ishi said peacefully. "I didn't get much sleep last night."

Marubyashi laughed, and after a moment Ishi laughed, too.

"Fairly easy, at least that part of it," Robert Keel, the estate lawyer Shigata had located in Galveston, said. "The probate will be a nightmare, of course—probably take months—but getting you into the safe-deposit box—you should have been able to do that without coming to me."

"Maybe," Shigata said. "But it's been a long time since I studied law. I never actually practiced, and my involvement has been entirely with the criminal end of things. Civil law—well—it's different."

"Anyway, if you'll just take this with you, and get a judge to sign this one—" Keel was handing over papers rapidly. "The thing is, obviously we can't even go into probate without knowing what the estate consists of, and you can't possibly know that until you've gotten into that box."

"I'm not sure you've understood me," Shigata said. "The contents of those boxes will not be part of the estate. They're almost certainly evidence of criminal activity, and they've got to be turned over to the United States Justice Department immediately."

"Well, they don't have to be," Keel said. "Not unless they're subpoenaed. Of course a representative of the IRS must be present, but—"

"I'm not waiting for a subpoena," Shigata said. "I want those tapes out of my hands, and into appropriate ones, as quickly as possible. Mr. Keel, it's dynamite, can't you understand that? Two people have already been murdered—never mind, never mind." He picked up the papers and turned to depart.

"I never did understand criminal procedures," Keel said plaintively as the office door slammed.

"I'm not believing this," Marubyashi said an hour later.

Ishi sat up, yawning. "They wouldn't let you in?"

"Oh, they let me in all right," he said wrathfully.

"Well, then what—?"

"Bartlett says he only saw one person with Omori."

"So who was it?"

"*The chief of police,*" Marubyashi yelled.

"Shut up," Ishi said, glancing at the door.

Marubyashi sat down on a bed that gave heavily to his weight. "Don't worry, this time of day who's in a motel room to hear me? But I figure, this one I better call the boss about." He got up again and walked over to the desk–dressing table combination where the telephone was, adding, "You'd never in a dozen years guess who the chief of police here is."

One floor away, Melissa and Gail Shigata were trying to soothe Daniel Omori, who had been crying for his mother for the last two hours.

The glittering white suit E. P. Honshu—who had been born Wataru Yamagata—had paid far too much for when he bought it from a dead man's estate hung on a rack in his dressing room. Facing the wall of mirrors, cleaning off the stage makeup with a lot of cold cream, Honshu—now in faded denim jeans and a white T-shirt stained around the neck with bronze makeup and greasepaint—saw the door behind him open. "What are you doing here?" he asked, his voice muffled by facial tissue.

"I own the place," Buddy Yamagata replied, seating himself casually on the second chair and facing Honshu's reflected image.

"Not on paper you don't. And that doesn't answer my question."

"I own this place and I own you."

Honshu threw another wad of facial tissue in the general direction of a trash can and turned. "Like hell you do."

"I own this place and I own you. I hear you've been in contact with Isoruko Omori."

Honshu turned back to the mirror and methodically spread cold cream all over his face again to get the makeup he'd missed. "Where'd you hear that?"

"I hear a lot of things. All that glop on your face, you look like a fucking whore. What did you tell him?"

Methodically, Honshu began to wipe the cream off. "I told him you were going to kill him."

"He already knew that."

"So now he knows it twice."

"Now he knows it three times. He's dead."

"And Phyllis?"

"Her too."

"She's your own daughter, you son of a bitch." But he didn't shout it. Even now, he didn't shout it. You run a club, you don't make enough noise to disturb the patrons. On paper, Honshu owned the club. On paper, Honshu ran it.

"She left. I didn't throw her out. She made her choice."

"They weren't going to do anything to you," Honshu said around the washcloth and soap he was using to get rid of the last traces of cold cream. "All they wanted was out. You didn't have to kill them. All you had to do was let them alone."

"You ever hear of a guy named Mark Shigata?"

"No. Should I have?"

"Used to be an FBI agent. Stationed here a few years back. Made a little trouble for me."

"No. I never heard of him."

"What did he tell you?"

"Shigata? I told you I never heard of him."

"Omori. What did he tell you?"

"He didn't tell me anything."

"I'm not sure I believe that."

"Oh, you can believe it," Honshu said. "He'd have to have been crazy to trust me. And that one, he wasn't crazy. You called me a whore, Buddy? Well, maybe I am a whore. But if I am I'm your whore. So what does that make you?"

Buddy rose, knocking the chair over.

Honshu walked around him. "You want to kill me too? Go ahead. Kill everybody. That makes you the big man. You know what you are, Buddy? You're a coward. I'm a coward, because I let you own me, I let you run me, but you're a bigger fucking coward than I am. A man fights face-to-face. A man fights men. You killed a woman and even then you did it long distance, by somebody else's hand. Go get fucked, Buddy, if that's all you're fit for anymore, but leave me the hell alone."

Almost to the door, Honshu turned. "Come to think of it, I think maybe I did hear of Shigata. Wasn't he the one you couldn't buy or break or even kill?"

"Get the hell out of here before I break your jaw," Buddy Yamagata said heavily.

Honshu made his way out the back door and across the parking lot to his white Cadillac, the skin between his shoulder blades crawling every step of the way in anticipation of a bullet that didn't come, and the stolen key he'd moved to his jeans pocket continuing to burn into his skin.

▽

5

SHIGATA SPENT THIRTY MINUTES on the telephone with George Clement, the special agent-in-charge of the San Francisco office of the FBI. Once he understood the situation, Clement pointed out that there was no need for Shigata's presence at all; his word as to what Rocky Omori had told him constituted perfectly good probable cause, and the FBI could get into the safe-deposit box with a search warrant.

"I've got the key," Shigata said.

"You could express mail it out here. Or we can always get somebody to drill the lock."

"I've got to be there myself," Shigata maintained.

"Damned if I see why," Clement answered. "But it's your funeral. Look, it's Wednesday afternoon, and I want Harry Fong in on this too."

"Who's Harry Fong?"

"Federal prosecutor. New since you were here. Thing is, he's in court the rest of this week."

"But—"

"Can we plan on Monday?" Clement asked. "You maybe fly in on a red-eye. I'll meet you at the airport."

"I've got a few other people I want to talk to," Shigata said, knowing how evasive—and how infuriating—he must sound to Clement. "Plan on Monday, that's fine, but I'm flying in on Saturday."

"Well, I guess I can—"

"And renting a car," Shigata said.

"Now look—"

"I don't work for the Bureau now," Shigata said softly. He could almost see Clement's exasperation. Clement was a broad-shouldered man with sandy hair and blue eyes who usually dressed in tweeds and bore a distinct resemblance to an actor whose name Shigata couldn't at the moment recall—Brian Keith or Brian Donnelly or something like that; Brian somebody, anyway—and he usually wore his emotions visibly on his face. "Plan on meeting me Monday morning at ten o'clock at the bank. I've still got your home number. I'll call you when I get into town and let you know where I am, in case you need to reschedule."

"Shigata, I don't like this."

"I don't like it so much either."

"Then play it my way."

"I've got to play it my way." Logically, Clement was right. He didn't have to be there. But if he didn't go himself, he'd wonder for the rest of his life whether it was logic that kept him in Texas, or fear. He had every reason to be afraid of Buddy Yamagata, especially after what he'd just seen, but if he surrendered once to fear, he—as Rocky had put it—would never be free again. "Look, if something goes wrong, get that search warrant and go on in. But I've got another thing or two I want to check into in San Francisco between now and Monday." E. P. Honshu, and whatever or whoever Honshu thought worth mentioning. Providing, of course, that he could get Honshu to meet with him at all.

"I can—"

"No, you can't," Shigata said.

"It's your funeral," Clement said again, sounding even more annoyed.

"It might be. But that's how it's going to be."

As soon as he hung up, the dispatcher buzzed. "You've got somebody holding for you. A—a—something like Tesaruko Omori. I asked if somebody else could help him, and he said no."

"Taisuko," Shigata said. "Debbie, if you don't understand somebody's name, ask them to spell it, okay?" At nineteen,

Debbie Bryant was the department's newest dispatcher. Shigata wasn't too happy about already having her on the four-to-twelve shift, which tended to be the most hectic, but she'd wound up there anyway.

"I'll remember next time," she said. "But about this Tes—Tais—"

"Yes, I need to talk to him. Put him through. . . . Shigata here."

"Hello, nephew." A rather deep voice, quite calm, unaccented—but of course he'd had time to get over the first shock, and come to think of it he'd been born in San Francisco, gone at least to elementary school there, probably high school, moved to Japan sometime about 1940, and he'd been in his late teens by then. "Mitsuko let me know."

Shigata mentally blinked only for a second before remembering that Mitsuko was his mother's real name; his father had always called her—and insisted everyone else call her—Sue. "Yes, I hope it wasn't too early—I called her at seven A.M. my time, five A.M. hers, and I never can remember—"

"It was just past ten P.M. when she called here."

"So it's—?" He was too tired. The mental arithmetic eluded him.

"Just past eight now. A.M.. Thursday." Taisuko's voice was patient.

"Okay, it's just past five here—P.M.—Wednesday—so you're, let's see, fifteen hours ahead of me." *And why are we talking about times and dates? Because neither of us wants to be the first to mention what we really have to talk about.*

It was a painful telephone call, one that later he found himself unable to remember in complete detail. Taisuko didn't ask much; he wanted to know only two things about the murders—had Isoruko stuck to his promise to break off with the Yakuza, had Isoruko died honorably? That, and where was Daniel? Reassured on those points, he told Shigata to see to the funerals—there wasn't any use in trying to take the bodies back to Japan—he'd pay whatever it cost.

Shigata tried to tell him that wasn't necessary and was soundly argued down.

"Don't feel bad about not calling me yourself," Taisuko said then. "Your mother doesn't understand what it's like to be so tired you're running on nothing but willpower. You and I do."

"I'm glad you understand," Shigata said. "I would have called anyway, but—"

"But you don't know me," Taisuko said. "And you had every reason to think I could hear it easier from Mitsuko than from you, and of course you were right. I don't know you and you don't know me, and you don't know anything about me or my way of life. Never mind, Mark. I understand the reasons. I knew your father. It wasn't the war that made him a jackass. He always was one; he never could get along with anybody and never was willing to try. The war just gave him an excuse. Marrying him was about the stupidest thing my sister ever did. And I hope you don't mind my saying so."

"I don't mind," Shigata said, though he did, a little. "The truth is the truth. I just—I'm glad you understand." *That's the second time I've said that in about two minutes. I must sound like an idiot. I think my brain is out of gear.*

"He wanted to make you just like him," Taisuko added. "I gather he didn't succeed."

"I hope not. But he left me pretty . . . alienated." Shigata couldn't remember ever putting it quite that way before, wasn't even sure he'd ever thought it quite that way before. This uncle he didn't know was astonishingly easy to talk with.

"Let me know what happens," Taisuko said finally. "And about Daniel, let me know how he is."

"I'll keep you posted," Shigata promised.

"And sometime, you ought to visit me and see what Japan is really like."

"Yeah. Sometime."

Finally off the phone, Shigata closed his eyes for a moment and rested his forehead on his clenched hands. The headache he'd fought off earlier had returned with a vengeance, and emotionally as well as mentally and physically, he was bone weary.

But he didn't have time to be tired.

He walked out to the muster room and refilled his coffee cup, noting somebody had cleaned out the pot and started over, and wondering how Quinn was managing to stay awake on this sort of schedule now that he'd quit drinking coffee. He swallowed three aspirin from a bottle in his desk drawer, tried to think what to do next, and then realized that for a moment he literally could not remember the last time he'd eaten. Then memory swam groggily to the surface. Supper, last night, with Phyllis and Rocky—and now Phyllis and Rocky were dead. He was too tired to feel hungry, but he wouldn't do any good trying to stop their murderer if he went on running on empty. "I'm going to Galveston," he told the dispatcher. "I'll have a radio with me in the car. Once I get into town—" He gave her Lissa's room number at the Holiday Inn, and then he called Lissa and asked her to order from room service so that dinner would arrive not too long after he did.

Then he stood up, car keys in hand, and the telephone rang again.

He thought of letting it ring. But too much was going on. He grabbed for the handset. "Shigata."

"Clement here. Fong called Guicciardini—"

"*Who?*" Shigata interrupted.

"Alberto Guicciardini," Clement said, so easily Shigata wondered if he had it written down on a sheet of paper in front of him—which come to think of it he probably did. "Vice president in charge of the Bank of America branch the box is in. We're going into the box at ten o'clock Saturday morning on a search warrant, with or without you. He'll be there to let us in. We'll have a locksmith there in case we need one."

"I'll be there," Shigata said. "You won't need a locksmith." He slammed the phone down. *I don't know quite how, but I'll be there.*

Then he opened his billfold, got out his somewhat overstretched Visa card, sat back down, grabbed the phone book, and tried to remember which airlines had not gone out of business since the last time he had to fly somewhere.

And I want to talk with Honshu before we go into that box; don't know why but I feel I should—make it a red-eye Friday morning. I won't call Honshu to warn him I'm coming—don't want him to have time to decide he doesn't want to meet me, and from what Rocky told me, he might if he thought he could get away with it. Friday night, he'll be at his club, if I don't reach him sooner than that. I shouldn't have any trouble finding him—

"He's not in the phone book," Ishi said.

"Cops never are," Marubyashi told him. "You ought to know that. But there's this thing called a city directory, most towns have 'em—"

"Right, and you can always find them in a motel at almost six o'clock at night," Ishi said.

"Don't be stupider than you have to be," Marubyashi said. "Galveston is big enough it ought to have a library. And most libraries are open like eight, nine o'clock at night. Give me the phone book . . . You coming with me?" he asked ten minutes later.

"No," Ishi said, "You're the brainy dude that knows about libraries and stuff like that. I'm calling the boss to let him know why we're taking longer than we planned on."

Marubyashi grinned wolfishly. "I already told him once," he said. "You tell him again. And get instructions, who else he wants deleted and how." He strode out and pushed the down button for the elevator.

It went up one floor past him, stopped briefly, and came back down again.

Shigata stepped off the elevator and heard it start again, heading down. Glancing at room numbers, he headed down the hall and knocked on the right door. Lissa's voice inside, quick, frightened. "Who is it?"

"Me."

She opened the door so quickly she must have been standing beside it. "Mark, you look tired to death," she said. "Did you get any sleep at all?" From her face, he'd guess she hadn't done much sleeping herself. She stepped back from the door, her feet silent on the thick carpeting.

"A few hours. Not much." He shut the door behind him and looked around. Unusually, she was spending some of her first husband's money; this was a suite, not the room he'd reserved over the phone. A startling but rather attractive—at least for a short time—orange and turquoise color scheme, Impressionistic seascapes in frames on the walls. Two bedrooms and a living room–dining room combination with a table and chairs, a small fridge, two couches, each of which would fold out into a queen-size bed, and two armchairs, each of which would fold out into a single bed. The suite, intended for a large family come to play on the beach, provided plenty of room for a woman, teenager, child, and cat. Gail must have gone out to the library or to a bookstore and done a little more shopping besides: Lissa wouldn't have left Daniel or taken him out of the room, but *The Cat in the Hat* was open on the floor in front of the twenty-three-inch television, along with several coloring books and a box of crayons; and a skein of yarn and a crochet hook lay on a table beside one of the chairs.

"They said dinner would be up in about fifteen more minutes," Lissa told him.

Gail's cat dashed out of one of the bedrooms, closely followed by Daniel, who, probably with Gail's help, had fashioned a small hat out of newspaper, colored it red, and now seemed to be attempting to fit it on the cat and tie it on with a piece of yarn. Seeing Shigata, Daniel stopped short, and the cat seized the opportunity to escape into the other bedroom. "Is my mom coming pretty soon?"

"I'm afraid not," Shigata said, feeling about as helpless as he'd ever felt in his life. He supposed it was possible that at some time in his adult life he might have talked with a four-year-old, but at the moment he couldn't remember when it could have been, and he had no clear memory of being a four-year-old himself.

"Then is my daddy—?"

"No," Shigata said. "Daniel—"

"Did the bad men get them?"

"What?"

"My mom told me there were some bad men who were trying to get them," Daniel said with astonishing composure. "She told me that if the bad men got them then I'd have to have a different mom and dad. She told me not to tell Daddy because he'd be upset that she knew. She told me she and Daddy were trying to find somebody that would be a good 'nother mom and dad for me and she wanted me to know so I'd be a good boy and 'member she loves me. But I don't want another mom and dad, I want my mommy—" The composure suddenly abandoned him, and he burst into tears. "Did the bad men get my mom and dad?"

Shigata picked him up, sat down rather hard in the closest chair, and said bleakly, "Yes."

"Where did the bad men take them? Will they ever come back?"

"The bad men killed them," Shigata said. "No. They won't ever come back. I'm sorry, Daniel. I'm sorry."

How much does a four-year-old understand? he wondered, as Daniel sobbed in his arms. *How much* can *he understand, even as smart as he seems? Just that he's been abandoned—I wish he'd had more time to get to know us before—*

After a while Daniel asked, "Are you my daddy now?"

Shigata didn't know how to answer that; he looked, helplessly, at Lissa, who looked just as helplessly back at him. The cat walked back in, sat down directly in front of Shigata, and began to take a bath.

And he'd been silent too long, Shigata realized. He said, "Kinda looks that way, doesn't it? I hope that's okay with you."

"Am I s'posed to call you Daddy?"

"If you want to. Or you can call me Mark if you'd rather."

Daniel sniffled a couple of times more, then got down and resumed trying to put the hat on the cat. Lissa, after a puzzled look in his direction that reminded Shigata she was as unused to four-year-olds as he was, turned on the television. "It's about too late for the national," she said, "but I'm keeping an eye on the local, for the weather."

"School starting back up on *Friday*?" Gail yelled.

"Quiet down, we're in a hotel," Lissa said quickly. She'd returned to her crocheting, working without a pattern. Probably another afghan, Shigata figured. She was always making afghans and giving them to the homeless shelter. No reason, she'd answered when Shigata asked. It was just a thing she liked to do.

"But that's crummy!" Gail seated herself with a loud thump firmly on the carpeted floor in front of the television set. "They ought to wait till Monday! Starting on Friday is so dumb—I'll bet they give us a ton of homework—"

"May I remind you," Shigata pointed out, "that the state has set a minimum number of days for school to be in session in each district, and every day you miss now you'll have to make up in June?"

"But *Friday*—"

A knock on the door. "Room service."

In an obviously practiced routine, Gail scooped up Daniel and the cat and headed for a bedroom; only after the door was shut behind them did Lissa open the door. But room service was all it was; although the choice was limited and expensive, as it usually is for room service, what there was looked good—steak, salad, baked potato, pie—only three of each thing, but Daniel wouldn't eat much, and Lissa never ate pie.

The small fridge, he shortly discovered, contained a couple of quarts of milk.

"Are we going to be able to get back into the house tomorrow?" Lissa asked over dinner.

"I don't know," Shigata said. "I haven't had a chance to check on it. It depends on how high the water got and how far back down it's gone. I'll have a look tonight or first thing tomorrow and let you know."

"I guess if we can't I can drive Gail from Galveston for a few days."

"Maybe," Shigata said.

Neither of them added, *if we know by then that the killers are gone, that Daniel is safe*. But Shigata thought it, and knew Lissa was thinking the same. They had to figure a way to get Gail back to school on time, but they couldn't endanger Daniel—or anybody else—to do it.

And after dinner it wouldn't hurt for Shigata just to take off his shoes and lie down for a few minutes—dispatch knew where he was.

"Mark? I'm sorry to wake you." Lissa was standing in the doorway of the darkened room. "It's the department."

"Huh?" Shigata sat up, groggy from deep sleep, shoving tousled hair back with his left hand, momentarily confused as to where he was, why he was sleeping in his clothes, on top of the covers. "What time is it?"

"Just eight-thirty. You haven't slept near long enough—"

"Can't be helped." He stood up, blinking against the light from the front room. "Where's the phone? . . . Shigata."

"Chief?" The voice on the phone was small, frightened.

"Yeah, what is it, Debbie?"

"If, you know that Russian reporter—" There she stuck.

"Kerensky, yes, what about him?" Shigata tried not to sound impatient. Debbie might yet work out as a decent dispatcher, if she could quit being in awe of just about everybody.

"Well, if—um—if his tires got slashed, is that an international incident?" The words fell out in a bundle, almost too fast, too run together, for him to understand.

"No reason why it should be, unless he wants to make it one," Shigata said. "Why? Did somebody slash—"

(In the background now, he could hear Hansen yelling, "Debbie, what in the hell did you call the chief for? I told you—")

"—Kerensky's tires?"

"Yes, and—"

"Debbie, give me the phone!" Hansen sounded furious. "Sorry, Chief, I told her not to wake you. Yeah, somebody slashed Kerensky's tires, all four of 'em."

"Steve, don't you ever sleep?"

"I *was* asleep, that was the problem. So was Kerensky. He's been sticking to me like a limpet, and he's been through about ten rolls of film. So when I went back to the storage room to get some sleep he wanted to go back there too and I figured what the hell. So then Gere Phillips came in and woke me up and said there was a Scout out in front with its tires slashed and did I know anything about it."

"And Kerensky drives a Scout?" Shigata was trying to remember how long it had been since the Scout had been manufactured—at least fifteen years, the best he could remember.

"Yeah, an orange and white one, looks like a slab of unsliced bacon. That oil company loaned it to him. I think they bought it originally for their geologists. It's about twenty years old."

"Let me talk to Kerensky."

In a moment Max Kerensky, clearly still fuming but working at being polite, was on the phone, consciously or unconsciously imitating Hansen. "Hi, Chief, I'm sorry they woke you up."

"Well, I'm awake now. Any idea who might have wanted to do this? Anybody who dislikes you, maybe somebody who's said something to you?"

"No. There was this Mexican, I think he was a Mexican, who was yelling at me today and yesterday, but I did not pay any attention. And if it was him, I do not know how he could have found the car."

"Well, a Scout is pretty distinctive," Shigata pointed out.

"Especially one that looks like a side of bacon. There aren't any in town that I can think of. So if he noticed what your car looked like—"

"Oh. Yes. I see what you mean. But of course it might not have been him. I cannot think of any reason—"

"Will your insurance cover it?"

"I don't think—"

"Do you have comprehensive coverage?" Shigata asked patiently.

"I have comprehensive coverage, yes," Kerensky said. "But I have a deductible of two hundred and fifty dollars, and the tires, I think they cost two hundred dollars. So it would not be covered, would it?"

" 'Fraid not. I don't know, though, it might, because sometimes deductibles apply to accident but not to comprehensive. Well, we'll see what we can do. Let Hansen or me have a look at your policy, and see to it there's an official report made. Can Hansen get you wherever you need to go tonight?"

"We were going to my new apartment. So, yes."

"Let me talk to Debbie again."

"Chief?" Still Kerensky. "What is a limpet?"

"Ask Hansen to explain. Now let me—"

"Debbie, yes. Here is Debbie."

He could hear the thumpings and rustlings that indicated the phone was being handed back to the dispatcher. Then Debbie said, "I'm sorry I called—"

"Don't apologize," Shigata said wearily. "Deciding whether I need to be notified at once about something is a judgment call. You made it. Whether it was the right decision or not, you made it, so stick to it. I'd rather be called unnecessarily than not be called when I should be."

"All right. Thanks."

"You have the number here. I'll be here the rest of the night, so be sure you let Eve know."

"Yes. I will."

Shigata hung up and turned to Lissa. "I've had it," he said and headed back toward the bedroom.

Following him, she said, "You shouldn't have to cope with—"

"It's my job. I asked for it. The kids down?"

"Daniel's asleep. Gail's still up, but she's reading. I told her she couldn't turn the boom box on while you were sleeping."

"Thanks." He shucked off his pants and shirt while Lissa pulled the covers back. Then he asked, "Where did she get something to read? I didn't see her bringing any books with her."

"I sent her to the mall today. In a taxi. With my Visa card. She loved that."

"I'll bet she did." What Lissa described as *her* Visa card, as opposed to the family's Visa card, was the one she paid for with her first husband's money. She rarely used it—almost never, unless it was for something for Gail, because she considered that as her birth father, Sam owed Gail something. "Well, if she's buying books, I guess that's okay." In his underwear, Shigata slid under the sheets; it felt like a hundred years since he'd slept in a real bed with sheets rather than a cot with horse blankets. "Join me," he said, but he was asleep before she could.

"You didn't ask what else she bought," Lissa said into the darkness.

"I don't like this," Marubyashi said.

"Then you should have stayed to argue with the boss, instead of leaving me to do it."

"Look, I can't do everything, lunkhead. I had to go to the library, if we were going to find out where that son of a bitch Shigata lives. Anyway, I never could argue with the boss."

"Neither can I," Ishi said. "So forget it, will you? And let's go."

"It's still too early," Marubyashi said. "Barely nine. They won't be—"

"We still have to buy some gasoline and a couple of cans," Ishi said. "I don't know what time gas stations close around here. And neither do you."

"But this is a resort town, they shouldn't—"

"A resort town in the off season. I didn't see anybody freezing their ass out on the beach today. Come on."

"I still say it's too early."

"Then we'll get the gasoline and then come back here and make plans," Ishi said impatiently. "Or take another nap, if you want to. You can, anyway, I can't sleep before something like this. Too keyed up. Damn, man, sometimes I think you've got sleeping sickness. But right now you don't sleep. Get up off your can, Boat, and come on. I'm not going to do it all myself."

It was past eleven when they approached the house. The garage door was shut; no lights were on. "No sign of a dog," Marubyashi said.

"I scouted that out an hour ago, last time you were asleep," Ishi said. "No doghouse. No dog door. No dog shit in the yard. No dog. Let's get in and get it done and get out—fast."

"I still don't like this. Attacking somebody that's asleep—it doesn't feel right. They ought to at least have a *chance* to fight back."

"Right, as much chance as Omori had. And he was awake."

"That was different."

"Not much," Ishi said. "And nobody asked you to like it. The *oyabun* just said do it, he didn't say like it."

"Awright, awright, awright."

There was a lot of mud in the front yard and in the back, but no standing water. There were only two doors to the house, and three windows that looked big enough for anybody to get out of; Ishi had scouted all that, too. So it was a quick job, really. Snip the phone cord first, so nobody could call for help. Then splash the gasoline silently; nobody would notice that unless somebody was awake to smell it, and nobody was, because all the lights were out. And just in case somebody did wake and try to come out when he found out he couldn't use the phone, Marubyashi watched with a throwing knife in his hand, because this had to be a silent job, while Ishi threw the gasoline around. Then go around the house once, with a cigar lighter because that throws the flame farther than a cigarette lighter does. It didn't take long. Two trips around a small house, once with a couple of gas cans and once with a lighter, don't take long.

Ishi dropped the cigar lighter in the middle of the front door and ran for the car that Marubyashi already had running. Neither of them looked back at the scarlet and yellow lighting up the dark sky.

The telephone shrilled into the night. Shigata had no idea how long it had been ringing before he heard it, sat up, said "Damn," and tried to remember where the telephone was. Then he stumbled into the living room, nearly falling over the cat. "Shigata," he said somnolently.

"Chief?"

And instantly he was awake, because it was Quinn, and Quinn wasn't supposed to be on duty, and there was an odd tone in his voice. "What's wrong, Al?"

"Arson. A hundred percent sure. They left the gas cans in the front yard. And no fingerprints on 'em, looked like they had wrapped towels around their hands or something like that."

"Whose front yard?" But he had a hunch he knew.

"Yours. Sorry."

▽

6

"HOW BAD IS IT?" Lissa asked over what remained of a room service breakfast. Shigata's, ordered after everyone else was through, still hadn't arrived, but he was sitting at the small table with her, drinking what was left of the coffee. Her eyes looked strained, he thought; most likely she had not gone back to sleep after Shigata departed.

"Not total," he said, putting the empty cup down. "The foundation and floors are still there, and part of the walls. It was still pretty wet, and the fire didn't have time to get hold there before the fire department reached it. But the roof and most of the walls are gone, and everything inside—"

"All my clothes," Gail mourned from the chair where she was reading, having been forbidden TV at that hour. But then she brightened, looking at Lissa. "I guess that means—" She looked rather pointedly at her watch.

"Nine-thirty," Shigata said, reading the signal and grinning wearily. "The mall stores will be open by the time you can get over there."

Lissa stood up long enough to get to her purse and hand over a credit card and some cash. "Take a taxi both ways; don't try to walk or take the bus this time. This ought to cover that and lunch, if you stay that long. But don't overdo it," she warned. "Not everything has to be chartreuse and purple, and you don't need fourteen pairs of shoes."

"Mom, *really,*" Gail said. "I *am* sixteen."

"I know," Lissa said.

Gail laughed and headed for the door. But then she turned,

the grin gone. "Daddy?" she said, her voice suddenly a little thin. "This means I don't have anything at all left about my other mom. And—"

"No, it doesn't," Lissa said quickly. Shigata's first wife Wendy, Gail's "other mom" and Lissa's half-sister, had taken Gail at birth to protect her from the savagery and sadism of her birth father, Henry Samford, the man Lissa was then married to, and until she was thirteen Gail had possessed no knowledge at all of any other mother. "Don't you remember? We put all the scrapbooks in the boxes we took to storage, where they wouldn't get wet."

"But I didn't put my school annuals there. And my barracuda. And—"

"I'm sorry," Shigata said. That wasn't much good. But it was all he could think of to say—and personally he couldn't understand how anybody, even someone whose high school mascot was the barracuda, could be so fond of a large plush fish. Fish, in his mind, are neither furry nor cuddly—and barracudas especially are not furry and cuddly. Nor, for that matter, are they pink, blue, chartreuse, and purple.

The barracuda, of course, was replaceable. But Gail had been given it by a boyfriend. That made it a special barracuda that no other barracuda, no matter how cuddly and colorful, could adequately replace.

"This is shitty," Gail said, her voice breaking in a half-sob. "And where are we gonna live? I don't want to change schools now, not when I'm almost a senior!"

"Two months into your junior year scarcely adds up to being almost a senior," Lissa remarked.

"And don't borrow trouble," Shigata added. "We've got enough as it is. You won't have to change schools. I don't know where we're going to live. But I promise you it will be inside the city limits of Bayport. I know it's shitty, babe. But, right now, go buy clothes. Let your mom and me worry about where we're going to live."

Gail stood a moment longer looking forlorn, then shrugged and said, "Okay."

After the door shut behind her, Lissa said slowly, "Sam's house is on high ground. And—I still own it."

Shigata sat quite still for a moment. Then he said, "You know I've never even been through that house?"

"Haven't you? I thought you had. I've never been inside it since I walked out that day—and—and—"

"And saw me. And thought I was Sam."

"If I had looked closer I would have known—"

"Melissa, surely you don't think I blame you for not looking closer."

"No. I know. But, I thought you had been in it. The house, I mean."

"Oh, I was in it, that day. Quinn called me from inside, and I went into a couple of rooms. But not all the way through. I—didn't exactly feel like going up the stairs." He thought about it. "I didn't exactly feel like doing anything, actually. I felt like shit."

"And I didn't help much."

"We aren't going to talk about that."

"No," Lissa said. The bullet wound she'd put in Shigata's arm was, now, the smallest of the scars he'd collected that week. "All right. But I thought later you went—"

"No. Every time you wanted something from the house, I sent somebody else to get it."

"Quinn?"

Shigata looked at her, and she answered her own question. "No. Not Quinn. He wouldn't want to go there any more than you would. His son died in that house. His son and—and Lucie."

Shigata reached across the table and took her hand but didn't say anything because there wasn't anything he could think of to say.

"You know, I never think much about Lucie anymore, she said, glancing at the bedroom, where Daniel was alte nately coloring and playing with the cat. "She never got be four. She never got to be Daniel's age. Sam—killed h before she would have been four. And it didn't matter th

he didn't quite mean to. She was just as dead. Just like the boy was. But—" She took a deep breath. "The house didn't do it. The house didn't do any of it. Sam did it. The house is innocent. And the house is still there."

"You don't have to go back and live in it just because it's there. Considering all the evil done in it, that house ought to be pulled down and the ground sowed with salt."

"No," Lissa said. "No, I don't think so. Because—Mark—let's face it. There aren't very many houses for rent or for sale in Bayport right now, and most of the ones that might be available are on low ground so they're still flooded, and they're pretty small besides. Because of your job, we've got to live in Bayport. And—it's a big house, and it's there, and it's empty. And—and maybe us living there will exorcise a few—ghosts—for me. And maybe for you too."

"Lissa, if we have to we can get a mobile home until we can rebuild."

"No. Not a mobile home. It would be too little, especially with Daniel. And I have to have a garden and so do you; I need my flowers and you need your—"

"Green beans," he agreed wryly. "And tomatoes. That's the Omori in me."

"There isn't a garden there now," she went on, "because Sam didn't want one, but we can make a garden. It's got to be that house. It's there and it's empty. It's empty, Mark. Sam isn't there. And—we remember it, you and I, but Gail's never been there, or Daniel. The yard's probably a mess, after it's sat empty so long, but it's a big yard, and a swimming pool—we'd have to have it cleaned out, and maybe patched—but we could get Daniel a puppy, there's room for one and he'd like that. Kids talk to dogs and cats, especially when they're feeling crummy, and he's going to feel crummy for a while no matter what we do. And besides, maybe if we'd had a dog they couldn't have burned the house, at least not as easily."

"Okay," Shigata said. "If you really want—"

"I don't know if I want to or not. I may—if we get there

and find out we can't handle it we can always move back out, but for now—I never even turned off the utilities. I've just gone on paying them. It wasn't much, nothing was running except I guess the freezer and the fridge—and it was easier to pay it than to call the utility people and identify myself as somebody who had the right to turn the utilities on and off there."

"You want me to get somebody over there to clean it up, then?"

"No," Lissa said.

"Honey, it's been closed up for years, it'll be dusty and—"

"I know," Lissa said. "But I want to clean it myself. Maybe that'll exorcise a few demons, too."

"You sure?" he asked softly.

After a moment, she nodded. "I'm sure." A sudden smile dimpled her face. "I guess nobody ever even cleaned out the fridge. What a mess *that's* going to be! It might be easier to get a new one. No, just kidding. And the freezer—I'll have to throw out everything in it. And . . ."

"And what?"

"Never mind." But then she said, "If we decide to, you know, stay there, I want to completely redecorate it."

"Maybe you'd better plan on doing that anyway."

"You really won't mind?"

"You'll have to spend your money on it," Shigata said. "Because I haven't got it. But—"

The knock on the door signaled room service, and Shigata went to the door.

Marubyashi, who also had ordered from room service, slammed his coffee cup down on the table and stared at the television newscaster. Then he jumped to his feet and headed for the occupied bed. "Fish! Hey, Fish, wake up!"

"Hunh?" Ishi, with his head aching from the celebration after the night's work was finished, rolled over facedown and pulled a pillow over his head. "Lea' me alone."

"Fish, wake up! The son of a bitch escaped!"

Ishi turned over again and picked up one corner of the pillow. "What are you babbling about?"

"Shigata! The son of a bitch—" Marubyashi sat down hard on his own bed, glaring at Ishi.

Ishi sat up. "You're telling me somebody got out of that house? Man, don't make me laugh. That's imposs—"

"I'm telling you," Marubyashi said carefully, "that they weren't *in* the house."

Ishi stood up, then headed with rather wobbly steps toward the counter where the aspirin was. "Then whose house was it?"

"Oh, it was his all right," Marubyashi said wrathfully. "But he wasn't in it. Nobody was. They've been having a flood around here. He and his family—and that's got to mean the kid too—have been staying in a motel in Galveston."

"Shi-i-it," Ishi said, folding a dripping washcloth and holding it to his forehead. "You mean we've got to go after them again?"

"That's what it looks like," Marubyashi said. He picked up the Galveston telephone book and looked at it. "You know how many fucking motels there *are* in this town?"

"Yeah," Ishi said, turning to face Marubyashi, "and I know which one of them I saw this brown van at that said 'Bayport Police Department' on the side of it. I didn't pay any attention, then. I guess I should have."

"So what are we gonna do? We can't hit 'em in a motel like this one. That other one, it was little and spread out, but this one—I got to think."

"You think," Ishi said. "And I'll eat. I think. You got any more aspirin? What in the *hell* did I drink last night?"

"I've got to go back to work," Shigata said. "Not necessarily at the office—I don't think anybody expects me to be in the office today—but I should at least be in town. So I'll check on the house. Do you have the keys? Or do I need to get a locksmith?" A set of keys had been in the police property room once, probably still was. But there wasn't time to look for them now.

Lissa hesitated, frowning. "Mine were in a drawer," she said. "I never got them out. So I guess you'll have to get a locksmith."

"Okay. And Lissa, don't try to head that way yourself. Not yet. I want to make sure it's safe first. I'll have a look at the situation, once the locksmith gets the place open, and then I'll take you there myself. I'll have somebody bring your car back later. Probably—Lissa, I've got to go to San Francisco."

Unlike Clement, she didn't have to ask why. She just nodded.

"I'll get somebody to stay there with you until I get back. Hansen, if that's all right with you."

"What about his son?"

"Todd's out of town; he's in Tyler with his aunt. I know you don't much like Hansen, but—"

"He's tough," Lissa agreed. "You've said that before. And—I do want a dog, Mark. A big dog."

"A big dog or a loud dog?"

"What?"

"Most big dogs are fairly quiet, and little dogs just yap. It's the middle-sized dogs that make the most noise."

"What dogs are the most protective?" Lissa asked. "I've heard pit bulls—"

"Uh-uh," Shigata said. "They're protective, yes, and they're nice dogs to the people they perceive as their pack, but they're too unpredictable. No pit bulls. Let me see . . . German shepherds make good guard dogs."

"I don't like them. They look too official. Like you ought to salute when you see them. I think that's why they're not used much as guide dogs anymore."

"Been replaced, for the most part, by golden retrievers," Shigata agreed. "Want a golden retriever?"

"No. You can't make them bite if you try to, and they don't even bark very much. I want a dog that will bark if there are prowlers around, that will bite if it needs to, just not unnecessarily."

"How about an Akita?"

"I don't know what that is."

Shigata grinned. "They're Japanese dogs, at least I think they are. Very pretty. They look a lot like Siberian huskies. They are pussycats around their family, but let somebody threaten their family and they'll eat the person. Properly trained—and we'd be crazy not to have the dog properly trained, whatever kind of dog we get—they're no risk to the general public."

"Do they bark a lot?"

"Now that I don't know," Shigata said. "I have the impression they're pretty quiet most of the time. But they're smart dogs. They'd let us know if a stranger came around." He stood up. "But we can decide on that later, after we've both had a chance to look at some different kinds of dogs. Right now I've got to get on. Promise you won't try to leave here without—"

"I promise," she said.

In San Francisco, it was not much past dawn. For E. P. Honshu, it felt much earlier or much later, he wasn't sure which. He hadn't slept well—thinking about Rocky, thinking about Phyllis—their wedding a mixture of Japanese and Western style, Phyllis radiant in a heavy white satin dress, Rocky laughing, *sake* in a champagne glass with a white satin bow around the stem, Rocky and Phyllis drinking together—and later the baby, Daniel, how proud everybody had been of him—*did Buddy really intend to kill Daniel too?*

Honshu had tried until yesterday to make himself believe that Buddy wouldn't do that—that even Buddy, as much of a stranger as he seemed to be to the code of the Yakuza, wouldn't really order the death of a child, the death of his own grandson—but the sheets on Honshu's king-size bed that sat in the middle of a room the size of most people's houses, the sheets that were tangled, wet with sweat, told even Honshu what he really believed.

And the key taped to the inside of the toe of a pair of running shoes under the other shoes in his closet, where he was never too tired or too drunk to remember to put it when he got home, burned a hole in his mind. . . .

But if Buddy put a tail on him. . . .

And then logic, coldly, told him that Buddy wouldn't put a tail on him. To Buddy he was a whore; he was Buddy's whore; and Buddy didn't have enough respect for him to feel a need to put a tail on him . . . even now, even now.

Mildly giddy with sleeplessness, he stood up, walked the half a block or so it sometimes felt like from the bed to the bathroom, and turned on the shower. It was too early, yet, to do anything, even assuming he could figure out what to do, but at least he could get some breakfast and some coffee, a lot of coffee, to get rid of this feeling that his head was twice its usual size and stuffed with cotton—no, not cotton, that has too much substance to it, cotton candy, something that you see but almost, almost, it isn't there at all.

"Mister, these are good locks," Gene Martin said, sitting on the front step with what looked to Shigata like a somewhat overfull tool kit beside him. He'd been all the way around the house, examining the front door, the back door, the windows. That was after the fifteen minutes he took to succeed in picking the lock to the twelve-foot-wide gate. Because the gate was open the first time Shigata saw the house, because Sam had been about to back out of the driveway, Shigata had succeeded in completely forgetting the six-foot-tall chain-link fence that completely surrounded the house and lot.

"I know they're good locks," Shigata said patiently. "How long will it take you to make a key?"

Martin shook his head. "Mister, these are Medeco locks."

"Meaning?"

"Meaning I can't pick them. I can't get them open without a key."

"Then who can?"

"That's what I'm telling you," Martin said. "Nobody can. Even the factory can't. These are top security locks. They're made so they can't be picked by anybody."

"Are you telling me I've got to have the door taken apart?"

Martin shook his head again. "Nothing like that. Just the lock apart, that's all. It won't be fixable when I get through. I'll have to replace it. Could be, after I get in I can dismantle the back door lock from the inside without breaking it, so I can find out its key—"

"Can you rekey it?" Shigata interrupted.

"Oh, sure, after I get it apart, but—"

"Do whatever you've got to do to get inside the house."

"Might be easier to break a window," Martin said, "though I'm not even sure of that. This place has security like a fortress, but then—"

"But then somebody would have to climb in the window, past the broken glass, and I'd have to get somebody else out here to replace the glass," Shigata said. "Never mind, just take the lock apart. Replace it with the same kind of lock, and rekey the back so that the same key opens the front and back. Can you put the gate on the same key?"

"Nope," Martin said. "Different kind of lock. Unless you want me to change the lock on the gate."

"How good is the one there?"

"It's good. It's not in the class with Medeco, but no amateur is going to get it open."

"Then just make keys for the lock that's there." He paused. "Uh—how much is this going to cost?"

"Depends on what all I wind up having to do," Martin said. "I figure two, three hundred dollars, four hundred max but probably not that much."

"Ouch," Shigata said. "You take Visa?"

"Yep."

"Uh—my daughter is at the mall with the Visa card. Can I go over to your store sometime this afternoon and pay you then?" Because this was something else that a dead man was going to pay for, as little as Shigata liked the idea. But the money was there. It was Lissa's. And right now it would be stupid not to use it.

Martin looked at him. "Most times I'd say no," he said, "but you being the chief of police and all that—yeah, I guess so."

That settled, Shigata watched as Martin set to work. A moment later, he asked, "How long you figure it'll take?"

"All of it, or just getting the house open?"

"Both, I guess."

"Call it fifteen to thirty minutes to get the house open," Martin said. "Maybe another hour after that to get it all done. Mister, these are good locks."

Shigata was still watching when his radio, which had been busy only with routine traffic, addressed him. "Car One, call your wife."

"Ten-four," he said absently, continuing to watch.

Something snapped, and Martin said, "That's got it." He pulled on the door, and it swung open.

"Let me go in first," Shigata said and stepped in.

It stank. That was the first thing he noticed. It stank—and why shouldn't it? Blood had been shed at that house, both inside and outside, within the last two hours before it was closed up, and it had been closed up for years, ever since the last time Shigata sent Claire Barndt in to get something Lissa decided she needed. Lissa and Gail—and Daniel, he had to start remembering Daniel now—weren't going to sleep here tonight, or any other night until it had been thoroughly cleaned, not if he had any say about it.

The radio spoke again. "Car One? She says it's urgent."

"Ten-four," Shigata said, and mechanically he reached for the telephone on a table in the living room, before realizing that of course it would be dead.

But it wasn't. He had a dial tone. When Lissa said she went on paying for the utilities, obviously she meant *all* the utilities.

He said, "Hi," listened for a few minutes, and then said,

"I'll be there in twenty minutes. If anybody tries to get in, you know what to do."

To Martin, he said, "When you get through, lock up and drop the keys—we'll want three sets, no, make that four—and the bill by the police station. I'll get back to you this afternoon."

"Gail, get back here," Lissa said to herself, then realized the near hysteria in her mind and mechanically made herself breathe deeply and resume her crocheting. It wasn't even noon yet; Gail would be nowhere near through shopping, and getting hysterical wouldn't solve anything. And there was no reason the Yakuza would be looking for her—was there? There was no way the Yakuza would recognize Gail—was there?—unless they had been watching the house, and if they had been watching the house they would have known the house was empty before they torched it—wouldn't they? Unless they did know it was empty, and they torched it out of spite? Most likely they didn't even know Gail existed.

They were just hunting Daniel. Hunting a four-year-old. And hunting the people who had tried to provide a safe harbor for that four-year-old.

Until she heard about the house she'd tried to make herself believe nobody was hunting anybody, they had gone away, back to wherever they came from. Even after she heard about the house—because the house *could* have burned because the flood shorted electrical wires—but she knew that wasn't true, Quinn had told Mark about the gasoline—but there had been a can of gasoline in the garage, for the lawn mower and the Rototiller, it could have burst from the heat of an electrical fire, that could have been the reason for the smell of gasoline. . . .

But she couldn't keep lying to herself. She couldn't make herself believe that, not since twenty minutes ago, not since the voice on the phone said, "Mrs. Shigata?"

And she said, "Yes?"

And the voice didn't say anything. Just the click of a telephone handset being laid back in its cradle, just a dial tone.

She had the pistol with her. But she'd never had a pistol and a small child at the same time before, and until now she hadn't had to realize that there was no place she could put the pistol where she could reach it instantly that was not a place Daniel also could get to, if she was inattentive for a second, maybe going to the bathroom, maybe turning on the television.

But she had the pistol anyway, had it beside her in the bottom of the shopping bag the yarn was in, and if she went to the bathroom she would take the bag with her, and if she walked across the room to turn on the television she would take the bag with her.

And if she went to sleep—

But she wouldn't go to sleep. Not until Gail was back. Not until Mark was back. Not until—not until—

She would have started crying, from fear and frustration, but she didn't want to cry in front of Daniel because Daniel had enough to be afraid of, to be upset about.

How did they know she was here?

In the past, she knew, Mark had hidden children with the Quinn children, or even at Hoa's house in Galveston, or on Hoa's boat, with the Hoa children. Normally those were good hiding places because there were always so many children there, because all the Quinn children and all the Hoa children had a lot of friends and the friends were over there all the time because where there were that many children, to other children it felt like a party all the time.

And if this were a normal situation Daniel would be even safer there, because he was Oriental and the Quinn children and the Hoa children were Oriental and you have to be knowledgeable, to look closely, to tell the difference between Chinese children and Japanese children and Vietnamese children, though of course the differences are there if you know what to look for. Daniel would blend right in. . . .

But because of the flood, the Quinn children were scattered. And yes, some of them were on the boat with some of

Hoa's children—but these people, these Yakuza, knew where Lissa was. That meant there was at least a chance they had been followed, and would be followed if they left the motel—when they left the motel. And that meant she couldn't take Daniel to be with the Quinn children and the Hoa children, because people like this, yes, they would be able to tell the difference between Daniel and the Quinn children, the Hoa children, but they wouldn't care enough to look, they wouldn't mind mowing down twenty children to be sure of getting one child—one small child—one four-year-old boy who had done nothing, nothing, nothing at all.

The mall is on the left, after you get off the bridge they call the Causeway but before you get into the main part of Galveston. About to pass it, Shigata suddenly found himself thinking, *If I'm going to change clothes any time soon I'm going to have to get some clothes. Lissa and Gail took some with them into Galveston, but I didn't. All I've got is what was in my locker at the station.*

But that could wait a little while longer, even if he was in his last—literally last—set of clean underclothes. Then he thought, "Gail is in that mall. . . . At least I hope Gail is in that mall, because if she isn't. . . ."

He turned left, circled around onto the frontage road, and parked almost directly in front of the mall entrance where the pay phones were. Lissa answered so quickly she must have had her hand on the phone. "Any more trouble?" he asked her.

"No, nothing, they haven't called back, but Mark, where are you calling from?"

"The mall, I thought maybe—"

"Thank God!" That was half a sob. "Mark, find Gail, after I talked with you I got to worrying, I don't know where she is."

"Yes, I thought that too."

"Was I being silly?"

"No, I don't think you were. I'll find—"

"And Mark—"

"Yeah?"

"I think you'd better buy something to wear."

"It'll take a few minutes."

"That's okay. You've got to have something, especially if you're going to San Francisco."

"I've been thinking, maybe I'd better not leave you here alone."

"Don't be silly," she said briskly, far more briskly than she felt, because unlike George Clement she realized that Shigata's pride, his ego, were involved with that trip to San Francisco. "I won't be alone, not with Gail and Daniel, and you said you'd have Hansen stay with us. Go on, now, find Gail and then get yourself something—"

"Okay."

"And Mark, get a lot of cleaning supplies, Pine Sol and stuff like that. I mean a *whole* lot."

She didn't have to specify a whole lot, Shigata thought. He was the one who had smelled the house. She hadn't. Unless—and this was impossible—it had always smelled that way.

Gail wasn't too hard to find, and she didn't object too much to being hauled away from The Gap to go to Sears, but that may have been because she had already bought everything in The Gap that seemed likely to fit her and she hadn't been to Sears yet. In fact, she seemed reasonably pleased that Shigata had come along. He could, after all, help to carry. And it was easier to throw the bags she already had into the back of the Bronco and go back into Sears empty-handed than it would have been to haul everything from one store into another.

Besides, the clerks were already eyeing her quantity of purchases suspiciously and calling to check on the credit card. Maybe they'd be less suspicious with an adult along.

"Lissa, it stinks," he said again. "What else can I say to persuade you?"

"Nothing," she said tranquilly. "The sooner I can get

started on it with Pine Sol the sooner it'll stop stinking. The washer and dryer ought to still work, and I've got a carpet scrubber there. If I get started on it now I can have all the carpets scrubbed and all the sheets and towels and stuff washed and dried by bedtime."

And you expect me to sleep in the bed Henry Samford used to sleep in? he thought but did not say. *The bed of the man I killed?*

But it was as if she had read his mind. "I'm not going to open Sam's room yet at all," she said, "except to dump some Pine Sol in a dish on the floor in there to get rid of smells. I'll leave that for later; we'll want to completely remodel it before we even think about using it. There's another room about as big that I used to use when he wasn't there. It was my room, always my room, he never used it, and I had a place in it I could even hide from him, if I didn't hide too long so he started tearing things up, and I knew not to do that. You did get a lot of Pine Sol, didn't you?"

"Yes," he said briefly. "All right, if I can't persuade you, we might as well get started. But listen, I don't want you to check out of the motel yet. You might get there and find out it's just not going to be livable for a while, or at all. Keep the room here a couple of days more, in case you need it. We can always drive back and forth for a few days."

She thought about it a moment and then nodded. "Okay. I might as well leave the dirty clothes here, then, and come back and get them later. I'll call down to the desk—"

"You don't have to call down to the desk," he said patiently. "We aren't checking out."

"But going out with the cat and the suitcases—"

"We don't have to go past the desk. Lissa, if the desk doesn't know we're leaving then—"

"Oh. Yes. Somebody else might not know."

Shigata nodded. He knew Gail had understood just as Melissa did, and there was no reason yet for Daniel to understand.

Not yet.

But despite being called a motel, this was built like a hotel. There was no way to carry things down to a car and keep both the room and the car in sight at all times. So Gail made a lot of trips, carrying everything—suitcases, cat carrier—with Shigata walking with her every trip, keeping his hands completely free and very near his holster, locking the car each time before leaving it and unlocking it when returning to it, while Lissa sat up in the suite in a bedroom, with Daniel, with the pistol near at hand, and every time Gail and Shigata came back in the door Shigata signaled with the doorbell, not the dah-da-da-dah-dah signal everybody used but a different one he'd devised from memory, from a long time ago when he played drums in a high school band.

Then, finally, the car was loaded and they all went down together, Gail carrying Daniel in case they had to move faster than a confused four-year-old could be counted on to move, Lissa carrying the sack of yarn that had the pistol in it.

"You drive," Shigata told Lissa. But before he got in, he removed the shotgun from its rack on the floor of the car. He climbed in on the passenger's side, the shotgun at his knee making him feel like an orchestra violinist formally resting out a measure not to be played by violins. "Gail, you and Daniel lie down on the seats."

"No seat belts?" she asked impishly.

"Fasten seat belts and then lie down on the seats. I don't want either one of you to be visible from the street."

Most likely the whole set of preparations would be unnecessary. Most likely nothing was going to happen. Most likely they'd make the twenty-minute trip from Galveston to Bayport comfortably, easily.

But most likely wasn't certainly. Maybe he should have asked for a highway patrol escort. But he'd have felt like a complete idiot doing that, and then nothing happening, as probably would be the case.

They passed the mall on his right, and drove across the Causeway. He'd been debating with himself—stay on I-45 as long as possible, or cut off on one of the little country roads that would bring him to Bayport without having to drive through downtown at all.

Probably either would be safe.

If they had set up an ambush, they would have put it on I-45, because they—especially if they didn't know the area—would have no idea which little road he might take off on. So if they had set up an ambush the Shigatas would be safer to take a side road.

But if they were following the Bronco, it would be easier for him to get backups—fast—if they were on I-45.

If they attacked at all—whether it was by ambush or by following him—he'd want backups. He didn't tell Lissa to turn off, and automatically she stayed on I-45.

And they were ten minutes out of Bayport, almost exactly halfway between Galveston and Bayport, when the shotgun blast from the small white Subaru nearly drove the Bronco off the road into a ditch.

▽

7

IN THAT FIRST SECOND, even as he realized the shot had come from the little Subaru that had crept up the passing lane until it was parallel with the Bronco in the slow lane, Shigata thought wildly, *I should have been driving, Lissa can't deal with this.* But after a fraction of a second of blind shock, followed by an aborted hand movement toward the bag where her pistol was, Lissa did deal with it. She steered to the right, down onto the shoulder, and back out onto the pavement in an instant U-turn, taking the driver's side away from the Subaru and the passenger's side toward it so that Shigata was able to turn his shotgun onto the attackers.

In the backseat, Gail screamed once and then was as silent as Daniel, a silence Shigata found utterly terrifying, more so even than that first unexpected shot or his own return fire that he never really quite heard with his brain, even though it must have been loud in his ears, because he was so intent on what he was doing and what he was fearing. But no matter what might have happened, it was impossible to deal with more than one problem at a time. "Duck!" Shigata yelled.

Miraculously Lissa both heard and understood him. She simultaneously hit the brake pedal and ducked so that her head was below the level of the open windows. Not that that was as much protection as she could wish for; shotgun pellets will penetrate a car body. Had already penetrated this car body; he'd heard several from the second shotgun blast rattle off the window just behind him, and felt a couple of them, though by then they'd lost enough momentum that they hadn't hurt him. But when she braked and let go of the steering wheel the car skewed into a fishtail that may have—must have—temporarily baffled the killers in the Subaru. Shigata heard the third blast from the Subaru but did not feel it hit the Bronco at all.

He fired back a second time and saw the windshield of the Subaru shatter. On the passenger's side, not the driver's side. That was what he had hoped for; in the Subaru as in the Bronco, the gunfire was coming from the passenger's side.

But some of the pellets must have gone toward the driver's side, or else the passenger fell toward the driver and knocked him off balance, because the Subaru careened wildly for what seemed to Shigata like a longer time than it probably was and then slammed head-on into the back right side of the Bronco.

A moment that simultaneously seemed instantaneous and timeless, during which both cars were moving to the accompaniment of the grinding, shrieking sound of metal locking, unlocking, crushing. Lissa didn't try to steer, which was just as well, because no attempt would have worked. She just sat still, as Shigata did, except that he kept the shotgun raised, ready to fire if the need and the possibility were there. The sun, overbright after a week of rain, blazed from metal here and there and suddenly died as the metal moved back out of the sun's path, and there was all the time in the world to notice the terrified expression on the face of a gray-haired woman in a neat blue suit whose new Ford pickup truck had been coming up fast behind the Subaru, the woman trying now to steer out of the way of the collision, to notice the grass on the side of the road still dry and brown as hay in January despite the rain, to hear the sound continuing ten times worse than fingernails on a chalkboard. Then both cars were still, in a silence that felt loud, and Shigata, breathing hard in the dust that had shaken loose with the impact and now seemed to fill the car, reached over and turned off the ignition just to be safe, although there didn't seem much likelihood of fire.

"Gail? Daniel?" Lissa cried, turning to peer anxiously into the backseat.

"We're okay." Gail's voice more excited than frightened, although the fear would come later. Daniel was beginning now to cry a little, but it was a frightened crying, not a hurt crying, and he was whining to be allowed to get up and see what had happened. "No, Daniel, you can't look," Gail told him. "We still have to lie down until Mom says we can get up."

Shigata tried to open his door. It was jammed; although the front end of the Subaru had hit farther back, the whole right side of the Bronco was partially caved in. He could probably get it open if he tried long enough, but right now speed was essential. "Backseat, Lissa," he yelled, and Lissa, trying without much success to stay low in case more shooting broke out, snatched her crochet bag (with the pistol in the bottom of it) and scrambled into the backseat as he crawled through the front seat across the space where she had been, opened the left front door, jumped out, and ran for the front of the Subaru, shotgun in hand. By this time cars had stopped on both sides of the highway, and a few people—most of them probably assuming this was no more than a collision—were heading toward them.

"Police!" Shigata yelled. "Stay back!" But they weren't hearing him, despite the fact that he was—as he had been for two days, since showering in the locker room after sleeping fitfully in the storage room—in police uniform, with the gold badge pinned to his shirt front instead of inside his wallet. Of course the shirt, the gold badge, were covered by a gray jacket, but the jacket had BAYPORT POLICE DEPARTMENT lettered on the back, departmental patches sewn on both sleeves, and CHIEF OF POLICE embroidered in gold thread on the front pocket.

The smaller man, the one on the passenger's side of the Subaru, had been thrown clear when his door sprang open, and the shotgun he'd been firing lay a few yards down the road from his inert body, almost parallel with the Bronco. Shigata couldn't see his face and was glad of it, because from the looks of the back of the head, that man was no longer a danger to anybody. It was the other one, the larger one, the driver, that Shigata had to worry about now, because he was conscious if battered and dazed, and he was climbing out of the wreckage, yelling loudly and incoherently—in a way he must have hoped was frightening—brandishing a large knife or small machete that Shigata assumed—hoped—was all he was armed with.

And damn the civilians, they were coming from all directions now, only a few of them staying back even though by now all of them must have seen the shotgun, and although police have the right—and sometimes the duty—to risk their own lives, they don't have the right to risk civilian lives unnecessarily. Shigata had his shotgun in his hand but he didn't dare fire it; he couldn't draw his pistol without dropping the shotgun but he didn't dare drop the shotgun because the big man (or one of the spectators, not knowing what was going on—and there was always the possibility that one of the spectators was a backup for the two men in the Subaru) would go for it, and he couldn't fire the pistol even if he did have it drawn for the same reason he couldn't fire the shotgun: there were too many civilians gathered around, and even if he had what might look like a clear shot—which he didn't—there is always that unpredictable ricochet effect to be remembered and taken into account.

So he did the only thing left to do; he aimed a fast drop-kick at the big man's hands.

And any other time he might not have been fast enough, not for something like that, not against an opponent who outweighed him by sixty or more pounds, was at least ten or fifteen years younger, and probably had better training in unarmed combat than Shigata had gotten from the FBI Academy, but this time the opponent was dazed, had blood streaming from his forehead from where he had hit against the windshield, and was still breathing heavily from where his chest had slammed into the steering wheel, and the knife flew about seven feet and clattered onto the pavement. Now Shigata raised the shotgun into firing position. "Freeze, you son of a bitch!"

And the big man, not yet quite suicidal and certainly unaware of Shigata's attitude toward firing into a crowd, froze.

"Now turn around, slowly. Spread your feet—farther apart." The purpose of that, of course, was to throw the man off balance. It is much harder either to run or to attack when off balance. While he was maneuvering the big man into a better position, Shigata simultaneously maneuvered himself so that he had his back to the Bronco, as a partial protection just in case one of the other cars that had stopped on both sides of the highway contained backups for the would-be assassins, though he was beginning by now to rule out that possibility. "Lissa?"

"Huh?" the big man said.

"We're all right," Lissa said quickly. Shigata hoped she was telling the truth. But at least Daniel had stopped crying.

Speaking again to the big man, Shigata said, "Hands behind your back."

Handcuffs. No leg-irons. No backups. Car phones, portable phones, are readily available to the general public, but they're not in the budget of the police department of a very small town. What to do now? He had the radio in the Bronco, but he knew better than to turn his attention away from a Yakuza-trained assassin, even one who was handcuffed, long enough to try to use it. Lissa had never used the police radio and didn't know how; instructing her, almost as much as using the radio himself, would diffuse his attention. And of course no police department in the area would expect to hear her, would recognize and automatically respond to her voice.

And as he wondered what to do next, a male voice right beside Shigata said, "You a cop?"

"Yes," Shigata said without turning his head.

"I hoped you were. I mean, all this ruckus—"

"I hear you," Shigata said. "Yeah, I'm a cop."

"Anything I can do to help?"

That was the kind of offer any law enforcement officer likes to hear. "Get to a phone and—"

"I'm an insurance investigator. I got a car phone."

"Call nine-one-one and tell them Chief Shigata from Bayport needs backups and an ambulance this location. Tell them what's going on. Can you describe the location well enough?"

"Yeah," the man said and departed.

To his prisoner, Shigata said, "Turn around slow. . . . Now. What's your name?"

No answer. Until an eager voice from the Bronco said, "I know him. He's a friend of my daddy. Mister—Mister—Boat. He used to do magic tricks. Did he hit our car?"

"Yes," Shigata said, and then he said, "Mister Boat?" But that had been enough to tell him that at least one of the men who murdered Rocky Omori, who tortured Rocky Omori to death, had at one time been counted enough of a friend for Rocky's child to recognize him. He wondered what Mister Boat thought of himself, or whether Mister Boat allowed himself to think at all.

But Mister Boat—whoever Mister Boat really was—remained silent, and Shigata had to wait until the first backup, a highway patrol unit, arrived, to get Mister Boat's billfold out of his pocket and find out that his name was Benjamin F. Marubyashi. Then the nickname made sense: even Shigata knew that *maru* is Japanese for "boat," even though the name itself probably meant something far different.

"Who's your friend?" Shigata asked.

Still no answer. "I'll check," the highway patrolman—whose name tag said his last name was Taggart—volunteered. A moment later, with the small man's billfold open in his hands, Taggart said, "It's Ken Ishi. And he's going to be a DOA."

"I figured," Shigata said.

"Ishi Fishie," Daniel said. "I know him, too. But he doesn't do magic tricks. What's a DOA?"

"Never mind," Shigata said, glad that the position of the cars prevented Daniel from getting a look at Ishi. "We'll talk about it later." By now he could hear the Martian yodel of an ambulance siren heading up from Galveston. The ambulance might as well slow down. Shigata felt sick; he'd killed only once before in his life, and that time, like this time, had been unavoidable if he intended to remain alive himself—this time, if he intended to keep his family alive. But that didn't make him any happier with the idea.

He glanced quickly, longingly, at the Subaru; he wanted to search it, and almost certainly the courts would have no objection whether or not he had a warrant, considering the situation. But he didn't want to risk even the slightest chance of Marubyashi getting off on some sort of appeal. "Taggart," he said, "keep him covered. I'll be using your radio for a minute. And be careful; he's smart." The word *smart*, used by cops of criminals, is rarely a compliment.

"Right," Taggart said.

Shigata noted the California license plate number. So it probably wasn't a rental car, it was probably a car belonging either to Ishi or Marubyashi. He wrote down the year, the color, and the model, then headed for the highway patrol car and switched the radio to the intercity frequency.

"Quinn and Hansen are en route to your location already," the dispatcher told him.

"Same car?"

"No, sir, separate cars."

"Tell Quinn to head back in and get a search warrant." He provided the information to go on the warrant, the description of the vehicle to be searched, the probable cause. "And run it on NCIC and find out the registered owner. Tell Quinn that goes on the warrant too."

Logically it would have been better to have Hansen get the search warrant; Hansen was better educated, far less likely to make the kind of minor spelling and punctuation mistakes that sometimes get search warrants thrown out of court. But Quinn had the common sense Hansen lacked.

Affadavit, two copies; warrant, three copies. Sworn to before a judge, signed by the judge who then keeps one copy of the affadavit. It was a time-consuming process; he'd be lucky to be through searching the car by supper time, especially as long as Quinn would take on the writing, the typing. But he'd still rather it was Quinn than Hansen doing it.

Though if he'd stopped to think that Hansen might still have Kerensky with him, and would thoughtlessly bring Kerensky—complete with camera—out to this scene, he might have made a different decision.

Returning to the prisoner—and he still hadn't taken the time to check on Lissa and the kids, all he had was Lissa's word that they were all okay, and they could be very shaken up and Lissa would still say that—he said conversationally, "Benjamin Marubyashi, you are under arrest for aggravated assault and attempted murder. You have the right to remain silent. . . ." After completing the legally required warning, he added, "I've got a search warrant coming. We'll be searching your car. Anything you want to say to me in the meantime?"

"Fuck you," Marubyashi said.

"That's not real informative."

"Look, fuzzball," Marubyashi said, "you don't mess around with Buddy Yamagata."

"You've been watching too many old movies."

"Buddy Yamagata will step on you like a roach."

"Really? Last time he talked to me he was going to step on me like an ant, but he didn't do it. And the last person who was going to step on me like a roach is dead."

"Hey, Chief."

Without turning, Shigata said, "Yeah, Hansen? When did you get here?"

"Couple of minutes ago. I just got to thinking, listening to him talk, did you ever stop to think that maybe all these Japanese monster movies, you know, Godzilla and all that, are metaphors for the Yakuza?"

"No, I never thought about that," Shigata said, "and—"

"Well, think about it—stomping around stepping on everybody, and they're all such ugly muthahs." Hansen grinned at Marubyashi.

Shigata had his mouth open to suggest Hansen get his mind on his business, until behind Shigata, a formal, very slightly accented voice asked, "What is a muthah?"

Hansen, attempting to explain that *muthah* had arrived in the English language as a truncated form of a longer and much ruder phrase, had chosen to begin with the Mexican and Puerto Rican *chinga tu madre,* and Kerensky, who spoke no Spanish at all, was becoming more confused by the second. Shigata supposed he could be grateful for that; at least it kept Kerensky out of the way while Marubyashi, somewhat more thoroughly fettered, was loaded into a sheriff's car for transport to the Galveston County Jail. By this time Galveston ident in the person of Investigator Phil Conroe had arrived to photograph the scene; an ambulance had arrived to take charge of Ishi (who was going nowhere until a medical examiner's investigator also arrived); and a wrecker had turned up to remove the Subaru, which was going nowhere until it had been searched. The ambulance and wrecker were now parked on the side of the road, and after Conroe finished the initial photographs of the wreckage, Shigata went to see whether the Bronco was going to be drivable. It looked all right from the outside. The wheels weren't jammed; nothing seemed to be leaking.

Lissa was still in the backseat with Gail and Daniel. Nobody seemed to be injured, but Shigata felt cold all over at the sight of the hole in the driver's side. The pellets had passed just behind the driver's seat, no more than a foot above the backseat; if both children (and never mind, now, that Gail at sixteen didn't like being called a child) had not been buckled into their seat belts and lying down, one or both of them would have been seriously injured or killed.

He climbed into the driver's seat of the Bronco and looked in the back. Lissa's appraisal seemed accurate; everybody looked all right, though Daniel was the only one who seemed to be enjoying the situation.

He turned the ignition key experimentally. The engine started, and he thought of pulling over to the side of the road to allow a little more room for the traffic that by now was probably stacked up clear to the other side of the Causeway. Several highway patrolmen were letting cars through one at a time on the far left shoulder of the northbound side. He could, he decided, let the wrecker move the Subaru off the road also. That would leave the highway reasonably clear and maybe even cut down on the gawkers driving slowly on the southbound side and piling traffic up there, too.

On second thought, neither the Bronco nor the Subaru could be moved. Nobody from the ME's office had arrived yet, which meant Ishi still wasn't officially dead. As the body was between the two cars, it was protected as long as the cars weren't moved. Move the cars, and it was a body on the highway. Too visible, and too likely to be further damaged.

Hurry up and wait. The theme song anytime several government agencies are involved.

And as usual when a law enforcement officer of any description is the victim or intended victim, there were about ten times as many cops roaming around the scene as there needed to be. "Lissa," Shigata said, "I think these two were alone, which means the danger is probably over for now. I'll be stuck here for hours, but there's no sense in you waiting. If you want, I'll have somebody take you back to Galveston and get your car, so you can head on to the house."

"Do you have the keys to the gate and the house?"

"The dispatcher'll have them. You can pick them up from her."

"Will it be okay if I come back here and get the cleaning supplies out of the Bronco? Or will it be better for me just to get some others?"

He thought about that, then said, "Swing back by here. Stop somewhere and get me a Coke, will you? Diet Coke with a lot of ice?"

"In this weather?"

"I'm thirsty," he said. "And if you brought me coffee it'd be cold by the time it got here."

"Okay." And if she was forcing cheerfulness a little, at least it was better than showing too much distress in front of the children. They'd do some private talking later. "I'm thirsty too," she added.

Gail and Daniel immediately announced that they, too, were thirsty. Shigata figured they probably were. Being shot at and being in a wreck are situations likely to trigger at least mild shock. And shock brings thirst.

Marubyashi was probably thirsty, too. But that was Marubyashi's problem. He could get some water after he was booked.

Shigata went and talked to another Galveston County deputy sheriff, then returned to the Bronco to send Gail and Daniel over to the sheriff's car. "Lissa, you wait a minute," he said. After the children were out of earshot, he said, "I want you to take Daniel over to Hoa—"

"I'm not going to do that," she interrupted.

"But—"

"I'm not going to risk any more children."

"Listen a minute," Shigata said. "There's no reason anybody would be at risk. You can tell Hoa I said to put out to sea immediately, don't come back in until I say it's safe."

"No," Lissa said. "I knew you'd say that, and I've been thinking about it. I'm keeping Daniel with me. I realize it's not quite safe. But I don't know that—those people—wouldn't find a way to chase Hoa at sea. And they'd as soon kill ten children as one child. We know, now, that's what they're trying to do. Rocky was wrong in what he told you; he guessed wrong. That man isn't trying to get Daniel back; he's trying to kill Daniel. I thought it all along. I—know what that kind of man does, when he's thwarted, when somebody dares to defy him. I don't think there's any way they could find us at—at the house. Because it's still listed in the telephone book in Sam's name"—there, she'd finally been able to say the name; she must be getting better, she told herself—"and the city directory probably shows it as empty. Nobody at the station would tell, and none of the neighbors know. And right now there's nobody to follow us, and they know this car but they probably don't know my car, but even if they do as soon as I get there I'll put it in the garage and close the garage. If I just keep Daniel indoors—but I won't risk Hoa's children, and Al and Nguyen's children."

"Okay," Shigata said. "Okay. You're probably right. I just—I'm so used to thinking, if there's a kid at risk we take the kid to Hoa, or to Nguyen."

"I know. And usually that's the best thing to do. But this time—this time I don't think it is. I'll check out of the motel now and get the stuff we left. I think it's safe right now. Not permanently—that kind of man would spend ten million dollars to catch a mouse, if the mouse spat at him—but it'll take him at least a few hours to find out what happened here, and get somebody else here. And by that time—by that time you'll be there. Now what does *she* want?" Gail was back out of the sheriff's car, heading for Shigata and Melissa.

"I've got to get Tiger," Gail explained.

"No you don't have to get Tiger," Shigata said. "Your cat will be just fine here with me."

"But he's thirsty."

"Then bring him a drink of water on the way back. You're not getting the cat now."

A Galveston car left a moment later with Lissa, Gail, and Daniel; with some difficulty, Gail had been convinced that Tiger would be all right until they could come back and get him. Shigata noticed that Lissa took her crochet bag as well as her purse. But that was all right. He didn't feel altogether certain she was safe without the pistol. Logically, he knew it would take at least a few hours, probably at least a day, for Buddy Yamagata to get anybody else to Galveston County. But his emotions didn't believe a word of that.

And there was a county medical examiner car. Finally. "What've you got for me this time?" Bob Mann asked.

Shigata gestured toward the corpse and handed over the corpse's billfold. "We've taken enough photographs," he said.

Mann took a few more anyway and then let the emergency medical technicians turn the body over. "Shotgun," he said. "Oriental, judging from the name and what I can see of the face. Is this connected with that thing at the motel the other night?"

"Yes."

"Who accounted for him?"

"Me," Shigata said.

"How come?"

"Have a look at my car."

Mann looked at the way the two vehicles were locked together, the Subaru straddling the entire northbound side of I-45, rammed into the right side of the Bronco, which was facing south in the northbound lane. "Okay," he said, sounding puzzled.

"Now have a look at the other side."

Mann walked around and looked at the other side of the Bronco. "Great jumping Jehosaphat," he said. "What's going on?"

"I don't want to take the time to tell you all of it," Shigata said. "Just—my wife and daughter and foster son were in that car with me. My wife was driving. I didn't—aim to kill him. Just to stop him. But there didn't seem to be any way to stop him without killing him."

"How was he driving and shooting at the same time?"

"Haven't you had your radio on?" Shigata asked, and then he began to explain.

Mann was gone and the body, along with the ambulance and ambulance drivers, was gone. But Shigata was still waiting for Quinn and the search warrant when Lissa got back in her red Pontiac. He'd seen Quinn headed for Galveston a while back, on the other side of the road on his way to get a judge to sign warrants, but Quinn sensibly hadn't stopped to chat. He'd driven straight past the scene, using his siren once or twice to get past gawkers, and kept going.

Shigata and a couple of state troopers helped to transfer suitcases, cleaning supplies, Gail's clothing purchases, and the cat and its possessions over to the Pontiac; then Lissa headed for Bayport.

Later, he wished he'd taken the time to tell Mann all of it. He might as well have, because an hour later, after driving the Bronco to the side of the road and letting the wrecker move the Subaru, he was still waiting for Quinn and the search warrant.

"Now I see why Daddy got six cans of air freshener," Gail said, wrinkling her nose at the smell. "Mom, you mean we've got to clean all this?" She gazed in some horror at the size of the living room.

"You haven't even seen the rest of the house yet," Lissa replied tranquilly despite the queasiness of her stomach. "Why don't you take a quick look around before we start putting things away?" She began to open draperies and windows to let in fresh air despite the chill of the January afternoon. Sam never would let her open draperies, and the house—no matter the time of year, no matter how brightly the sun burned outside—had always been a little dark. In one part of her mind she could understand that; he was an evil man, he must have been afraid to let the sun see his deeds.

The house would never be like that again; as soon as the present danger was over she'd take down every one of these draperies, take them to be dry-cleaned, and then take them to Goodwill. She'd replace them with curtains. White open-weave curtains, and never mind how often she'd have to wash them because of the black pollution from the oil refineries. She'd wash them and be glad to do it. She would never again have dark, heavy draperies, in this house or any other.

"Oh, wow, can this be my bedroom?" Gail yelled from upstairs.

"Which one?"

"This one at the end of the hall, in the front. Can it be my bedroom?"

"I suppose." Lissa had to stop for a moment to remember what that room looked like; it was supposedly a guest room but they never had guests, and she had been in it only once a month or so to clean. She wondered again why Sam had wanted four more bedrooms than anybody ever used and a swimming pool nobody ever swam in. She supposed they must have been status symbols for him.

"Can Daniel have the room next to me?"

"I'll have to think about that," Lissa said, reluctantly making her way upstairs to inspect. "No, I think not. He needs to be a little closer to Daddy's and my room, and this is going to be it. So I think Daniel had better go—here." It, she thought, standing in the hall, was the room that would have been Gail's at birth if Lissa hadn't given Gail to her sister for protection.

"Wow, Mom, this is *big*! How many rooms does this house have?"

"Why don't you count them and find out?"

"In a minute." She hurried back into the room she had claimed.

Lissa sprayed air freshener, opened the windows in what was now Daniel's room, then checked to be sure the closet was empty (and she would have to send Mark out later to buy some clothes for Daniel to supplement the few things that had been in his parents' suitcases, to hold him until things quieted down and she could take him out and really shop for him). Gail dashed back down the stairs, came back up with the cat carrier, dashed back down, came back up with the litter box, dashed back down, and came back up with cat dishes. "Now I can let Tiger out. But just in my room for a while, until he gets used to things."

"I want Tiger in *my* room," Daniel protested.

"Later," Gail said. "After he gets used to the house. Then he can run all over the house. Come on, Daniel, let's look outside. . . . Wow, Mom, you didn't tell me there was a *swim-*

ming pool! You mean we've been living all the time in that little house, when we could have been living here? Wow! And there's plenty of room—we could get a greenhouse—"

"You've been talking about that greenhouse for almost a year," Lissa said. "I still don't think you'd do anything with one if you had it."

"I don't want a big one," Gail said. "Just one big enough so we can have fresh tomatoes all the year round. . . . Aw, Mom, do I have to get started *now*?"

"If you expect to sleep tonight in sheets that have been changed in the last four years, we have to get started now," Lissa said. "Go upstairs and strip the beds in the rooms we'll be using and bring all the sheets down to me. Then I'll start doing the laundry and you can start rewashing all the dishes."

"They're not dirty. The cupboards have been closed, and—"

"Gail. Dishwasher. Now."

"You said strip the beds—"

"Strip the beds and then get to the dishes. Gail, I can't do it all myself, and as soon as I have the washer running I'm going to start shampooing the carpets. I think that's where a lot of the smell is."

"What about the fridge?— Aw, Mom!" Gail, catching a glimpse of the look on Lissa's face, slapped her hand over her mouth. "If I hadn't said anything—"

"If you hadn't said anything I'd still have asked you to do it. You're in charge of cleaning the kitchen, and that's part of the kitchen. There are two large trash cans in the garage. If you need more space, there are plenty of trash bags. We'll go out to eat tonight, because after you clean the fridge out I want it to air overnight with a couple of boxes of baking soda in it before we put anything in."

Gail opened the refrigerator door, made a face, and closed it. "Can't we just get a new fridge?"

"We might, but we can't today." Lissa opened a closet and got out a carpet machine. Gail, the picture of dejection, trudged up the stairs.

A moment later, hearing water running, Lissa went to the

downstairs bathroom. Daniel had well understood that the entire house had to be cleaned: he was scrubbing the tub. "Good for you," she said. "And when you get through, I'll—uh—mop the floor." It was going to need it.

Shigata was still waiting; he'd sent Hansen back to Bayport to handle anything that came up there. This wasn't Bayport territory anyway; it was county territory or state territory, and he had a couple of deputy sheriffs and a highway patrol unit standing by with him. The judge must have gone to lunch in Houston, he thought. Waiting three hours for a simple search warrant . . .

He got back into the Bronco, turned on the engine, and said, "Car One to headquarters."

"Go ahead, Car One." The dispatcher's voice.

"What's going on there?"

Hansen broke in. "Chief, you know Pete Ybarra?"

"Yes, why?" Pete Ybarra, who owned a downtown one-man barber shop, had arrived in Bayport well before Shigata had. A Cuban émigré, he was now an American citizen.

"I just put him in jail on public intox and affray."

"Where was he intoxicated and where did the affray take place?" *Affray* is a rather more formal and legalistic way of saying somebody got into a fight, usually one that he himself started.

"Uh—police station. He came in here practically foaming at the mouth and complaining that the Communists are taking over Bayport, and then he took a swing at Kerensky. He didn't make any more sense'n a drunken piss-ant. And I think he was the one that cut Kerensky's tires. You want me to keep him here and turn him loose when he sobers up, or make a formal charge and ship him on down to Galveston?"

"Considering a foreign national is involved, you'd better go on and charge him," Shigata said regretfully. *Times I feel like I'm policing in the UN. Talk about the world village.*

And there, finally, was Quinn with the search warrant.

Shigata already had taken custody of the shotgun and the knife and sent them on back to Bayport with Hansen. It didn't take too long to find in the trunk a small white Styrofoam ice chest filled with ice and two small plastic bags.

In each plastic bag was one human ear. One of the ears was still wearing a small, dainty ruby stud earring.

▽

8

JACK SAITO, IN AN OFFICE that was anything but Japanese-style minimalist, sat more still than people normally can sit, watching Buddy Yamagata talk into the phone. "Right," Yamagata was saying. "I'm not quite sure what the situation is, but he does work for me. . . . Right, Asian importing, that's right. . . . He seems to have gotten into some sort of shootout, I have no idea what caused it. . . . Just ascertain the situation, for now, and let me know what happened. And of course, try to get him bonded out. I'll mail you a retainer, ten thousand dollars enough for now? You'll let me know if the bond costs . . . Right. Right."

Saito picked up the cigarette he'd left in an ashtray on his side of the desk, sprinkled ashes off the end, and put it back in the ashtray. He continued to watch Yamagata.

The telephone conversation ended, Yamagata turned his attention back to Saito. "A law firm in Houston," he said. "Oyama and Yoshimura. My secretary got them out of the yellow pages."

"And they've never heard of you."

Yamagata grinned.

Saito picked up the cigarette again, breathed smoke, and put the cigarette back in exactly the same spot in the ashtray. "And they've never heard of the Yakuza. Or if they have, they figure it's still in Japan where it started."

Yamagata continued to grin. Then he crossed his arms on the huge desk and leaned forward. "And you, my tame ninja," he said—

Saito's smile broadened slowly. He knew he looked like a ninja, as much like a ninja as Yamagata looked like a sumo wrestler. And he figured he could outthink and outfight just about any old-style ninja he might happen to meet.

"—are the other string for my bow. I don't want Marubyashi to talk to anybody for any reason about anything. If Dennis Oyama can get him out fast, fine. He jumps bond and comes back here and what happens next isn't Oyama's business. But if he's still in when you get there—"

Yamagata didn't say anything else.

Saito didn't have to hear anything else. He picked up the cigarette, breathed smoke again, and put the cigarette out. "Right," he said, and got up and ambled out the door.

"I can't believe you've gotten so much done so fast," Shigata said. The smell, as well as all the dust, was gone from the living room and kitchen; the draperies were open and the windows shone, and yellow roses that had to have come from the florist were arranged in a vase on a side table.

But he didn't like the overplush beige carpet. He didn't like the carpet at all, or the too-heavy, too-dark draperies, or the walls with no pictures hanging on them, or the furniture that looked like something out of the showcase of an expensive furniture store. In this damp climate, hardwood floors weren't too practical, but he hoped that when Lissa got around to her planned redecorating she'd pull out the carpet and put in bright vinyl flooring. The pictures on the wall at the other house were gone, but as soon as he got back from San Francisco he'd take Lissa around to several stores and they'd find things they liked to put on the walls. As for the furniture—maybe the furniture wouldn't be so bad once the other things were changed. But maybe it still would. He wanted the house—if he had to live in this house—to look like a place where people lived, not a place for photographers to come and take pictures and go away again.

But it wasn't really the carpet, the walls, the draperies, or the furniture that bothered him. It was the associations.

And it remained to be seen whether changing things inside and out could nullify the associations.

"We didn't do it all ourselves," Gail said, preening. "Mom called Janie Quinn and she came and helped us. She would have done it just because, but Mom said this was a paid job. She paid Janie and me both. And she paid Ed and Don to wash all the windows while Janie and I were doing everything else. Except the bathrooms. Daniel scrubbed the tubs and the showers and everything."

Shigata nodded. The Quinns always needed money, and the Quinn children weren't afraid of work.

"And *I*, of course, didn't do anything at all," Lissa said ruefully after Gail's recital.

"Well-ll," Gail said, and smiled. "Mom did all the laundry. About five hundred tons of it. It's still not finished. And mopped the bathrooms after Daniel got through 'cause he sort of splashed. And changed all the beds except in that one room and sprayed the mattresses with Lysol. She just stripped the bed in there and sprayed the mattress because it smelled ikky, I mean it really smelled ikky, I didn't know a water bed could smell that bad, so I'm glad that was the only water bed, and she took everything else from that room and put it in boxes for Goodwill. She did a lot of other stuff too but I wasn't looking 'cause I was busy. What's wrong with that room, anyway? It looks like a real nice room to me. But Mom acts like it's haunted or something. She ordered lots and lots of flowers and put them all over the house and didn't put any in that room, and she locked the door to it with a key."

"We'll talk about that room later," Shigata said. "For now, just stay out of it and assume we have a reason." If nothing else, he wanted to make a thorough search for concealed weapons in there before letting anybody into the room. "I noticed the flowers; they're nice. So what did Tiger do while everybody else was so busy?"

"Tiger ran and fell down the stairs," Daniel yelled. "And then he *ate* the roses! Roses aren't to *eat*!"

"Tiger did *what*?"

"He was upstairs," Gail said, "because Mom said he ought to stay in my room till he'd been here awhile, only I forgot and left the door open, and Tiger came running out of the room and he ran to the stairs and didn't see the stairs and tried to keep on running and sort of fell down the stairs. But he didn't get hurt," she added hastily. "He just fell about two stairs. Then he got up and I grabbed him and put him back in my room. And then he was mad, so he tore up some roses and I think he ate one of them because he barfed and I had to clean it up."

"Sounds like everybody's been busy," Shigata said more heartily than he felt. He still felt like an intruder in this house. Or perhaps, he thought, it might be more accurate to say that this house felt like an intruder in his life.

But it wouldn't do any good to anybody to say so, especially not when Gail was talking excitedly about the swimming pool, and telling how she'd picked out the absolutely perfect place for a greenhouse that she was sure Shigata and Quinn could build in a weekend. "Maybe so," Shigata said. "We'll have to see about that. Meanwhile, as soon as I get a shower and put on some clean clothes, will everybody be ready to go get a pizza?"

Daniel abandoned his coloring book, jumped up and ran around the room three times, and then returned to his coloring book. Apparently this was the appropriate response to a pizza.

"Do you have any clean clothes?" Lissa inquired.

"I have some clean clothes. Fortunately I'm easy to fit." He'd bought jeans and shirts, dark gray chinos, and underclothes. He'd also selected one suit and paid extra to get it altered by Friday morning, and he'd tentatively decided to get more suits while he was in San Francisco. He didn't live in suits, the way he had when he was an FBI agent, but it remained true that as police chief he needed more suits than, say, Quinn or Hansen did.

For now, until the insurance paid off on the house, he'd

had to give up using his own filled-up charge cards and was now using his card from the Visa account Lissa called hers. He didn't like doing it, but given the situation, it would be stupid not to use every resource he had available. Half the house insurance would go to pay off the remaining mortgage. But the house had been half paid for; he'd have some cash eventually, when the fire marshals got through investigating the arson.

Hansen, sitting as any cop sits with his back to the wall and his face to the door, looked rather guilty when the Shigatas entered Pizza Hut, but the nearly empty pitcher of beer between him and Kerensky didn't vanish. Neither did the full one the waitress plopped down before going to get the Shigatas' order, and Kerensky poured both glasses full before going on talking. His English had slipped noticeably (not in clarity, but in grammar; he must have been exposed to a lot more slang than he usually used), and Shigata wondered how many previous pitchers there had been. He was sitting too near them, and Kerensky's voice was too loud, for him to be able to avoid hearing the conversation.

"So anyway, the soldiers and all sealed the front," Kerensky was saying, "but I guess they didn't even know there was an alley back there, so a bunch of us, we snuck in the back door and stole all the equipment."

"Yeah?" Hansen said. He was reminding Shigata of a description Quinn had once given: when Hansen is drunk he says less and less and less, and just sits and studies people as if he had them under a microscope.

(Gail, enjoying the new role of big sister, turned Daniel's place mat over and gave Daniel a pencil. Shigata wasn't sure why; the puzzles required the ability to read, and Daniel, as intelligent as he obviously was, couldn't manage that yet.)

"So here we were driving around Moscow with a truck full of stolen broadcasting equipment, and people kept borrowing—uh—all right, you want the truth, stealing—petrol, I mean gasoline, for us to keep the truck running, and we'd find a place where the electricity was on and there was enough of it for us to hook up the equipment, and we'd mount the antenna on top of the truck and make a real fast news broadcast and then unplug everything and pull the antenna down and hide it and get out of there fast before they could, you know, triangulate and find us. And we had to make the broadcasts at different times because they kept trying to jam us, but they couldn't jam us all the time because they were too busy, and people were keeping their radios on all the time so they could hear—"

"But I thought you were on the barricade," Hansen said.

"I was. Part of the time. Most of the time, actually. Because it wouldn't have helped for the truck not to get caught if we didn't have any news to broadcast. And I'm a reporter. So I'd go to the barricade and find out what was happening there. Other people were finding out what was happening other places. And some of the time we'd take the news back to the truck ourselves and other times we'd give it to somebody else to take back."

"But how'd you take the news, if you didn't know where the truck was going next?"

"Some of us knew," Kerensky said. He chugalugged half a glass of beer and poured again from the pitcher. When he resumed speaking, he sounded completely sober. "Some of us knew. Some of the time. Whoever was going back to the truck knew where it would be the next hour. But no longer. Nobody knew the full plan, not even the people on the truck. The plans had to be made and remade hour by hour. Because—we didn't know who was going to win. And what you don't know, nobody can make you tell."

What you don't know about, you can't tell, E. P. Honshu thought miserably. He was at an expensive health club. He could afford the membership, just like he could afford the fancy condo he was living in, the Cadillac he drove, the clothes he wore; the club was doing well. *Doing well and laundering money. But I'm not supposed to know about that.* He'd left his street clothes in his locker; now, in a new swimsuit he'd bought today while killing time and numbing his mind by buying things he didn't need, he was wading into the shallow end of the heated, double Olympic-size swimming pool.

I didn't want to know any of it. I asked Rocky not to tell me anything. I didn't have to ask Buddy not to tell me anything, he wouldn't anyway, not even how my own club—at least according to city licenses it's mine—is run. But Rocky wouldn't not tell me. Rocky wouldn't not involve me. Now I've got this and I can't give it back and I don't know who to give it to. I want to bring Buddy down, if I knew how, if I just had a way. What kind of a man would order his own child, his own grandchild, murdered? Somebody needs to bring Buddy down and this might do it. If I just knew what to do with it. But I don't, and I don't want to get hurt.

Why me? All I ever wanted to do was sing, sing and have a nightclub. Buddy said he'd let me sing, he'd let me have a nightclub, he'd provide the money, all I had to do was play it his way.

And if I didn't play it his way I couldn't sing and I couldn't have a nightclub and I couldn't do anything else, because he'd kill me.

He'd just have had me shot, then. But then was a long time ago. Then I didn't have a nightclub. Then I didn't have a condo. Then, I didn't have any of this fancy stuff. Or an—unclean—mind and soul.

Then I hadn't met Rocky Omori, hadn't listened to Rocky Omori.

I can't give it back but if Buddy catches me with it on me I'm dead, dead the same way Rocky is dead. I couldn't stand that. I don't know how Rocky could stand it, could go on and do what he did knowing that's what they'd do to him, and I know he knew.

I know they search my place, sometimes. They search all of my places, my condo and my dressing room and my office.

I can't give it back and I can't keep it because I can't let them find it. I can't give it back and I can't keep it and I can't give it away and I can't even throw it away because that might be the day they'd search my trash if I threw it away at home or at the club, or the day Buddy decided to have his whore followed if I tried to drop it into the bay.

I can't give it back and I can't keep it and I can't throw it away and I can't give it to somebody else. Rocky, what the hell did you do to me? I didn't want to be involved in any of this. All I wanted to do was sing.

He struck out strongly, laps across the pool, back and forth, back and forth. Strong lungs make a better singer. He didn't look at who was walking around the pool. He didn't look to see who was in the pool with him. He just went on swimming.

And the key he'd snapped into the locker key pocket of his swimsuit burned into his thigh.

The door opened, and mechanically, Shigata glanced up. Like Hansen, like any cop, he had his back to the wall so that he could easily see anyone who entered. This was one he'd just as soon not see, and under his breath he muttered "Shit!" as Hansen looked up sharply to eye the newcomer.

"Shit!" Daniel echoed happily.

Shigata shook his head. "I've got to start remembering to watch what I say, don't I?"

"I'm afraid so," Lissa said. "But why—?"

"Pete Ybarra," Shigata said. "Cuban barber. Lives in those apartments right up behind the Pizza Hut. Drinks too much. Hansen jailed him earlier today for trying to pick a fight with Kerensky in the police station. Looks like he got out on bond. And he hasn't had time to sober up."

"Who's Kerensky?" Lissa asked, and for the first time Shigata realized how fast things had been moving. Usually he kept her current on what was going on in town.

"That's Kerensky," he said pointing to Hansen's drinking buddy, and then began to explain who Kerensky was while eating his pizza and salad and keeping one eye on Ybarra.

Ybarra was quiet at first; he ordered from the counter and Shigata hoped he'd just take the pizza and leave. But he didn't. He went and sat down at a table—one of the little glass-topped tables that has a Pac-man game built into it—and after a moment a waitress brought him a pitcher of beer.

Ybarra pulled out a couple of quarters and dropped them in the slot and began to push buttons. His muttered expletives got louder, and once he slammed the side of the table with his hand.

Shigata got up and walked over to the counter. "Don't let Ybarra have any more beer," he said quietly.

He didn't have to identify himself; he was talking to manager Sheila Carmichael, who looked in Ybarra's direction and nodded. "I'll tell Celeste."

But he hadn't taken the precaution soon enough. After a moment, Ybarra abandoned the small table, staggered past the salad bar, and approached Hansen and Kerensky. *"Hijo de puta,"* he said a little more loudly than under his breath.

Kerensky didn't speak Spanish, but Hansen did. "Watch it, Ybarra," he said. "You've already been in jail once today. You trying for a second trip?"

"Fucking Russian Communist—"

Kerensky jumped to his feet. "Who are you calling a Communist?"

"Sit down, Max!" Hansen yelled. "Ybarra—"

But Kerensky didn't have time to sit—not that he wanted to—before Ybarra, swearing in Spanish and English, swung at him. Kerensky ducked and then swung back; more by luck than skill, Ybarra staggered back out of the way. Carmichael headed for the telephone. Shigata was out of his seat by then, grabbing Ybarra from behind, and Hansen slammed his hand down on Kerensky's shoulder and shoved him back down. "I said *sit down,* Max! Can't you see the man's drunk?"

Standing right back up, Kerensky began to shout, "He hasn't got any right to call me a—"

"Sit down and shut up, Kerensky!" Shigata yelled from behind Ybarra. "Unless you want to be taken in too."

Kerensky sat abruptly. Ybarra continued to struggle. And a siren sounded outside. Susa Gonzales came in fast, took in the situation, and spoke in Spanish to Ybarra, too fast for Hansen to understand. Shigata didn't understand Spanish anyway, except for a little of the more popular profanity, but he was able to understand Ybarra's reply. So was Gonzales, obviously, because she took the handcuffs off her belt rather briskly and reached under Shigata's hands to attach them to Ybarra's wrists. "Public intox," she said. "Disorderly conduct. Anything else, Chief?"

"Simple assault," Shigata said, stepping back as Ybarra continued to swear rather monotonously. "Transport him back down to Galveston, Susa, and tell them to hold him overnight even if somebody does try to bond him out again. Give him some time to sober up." He rounded angrily on Kerensky. "As for you," he said, "you better get it through your head that even in this country the police have some authority, and you're not going to keep on getting away with flouting it. Failure to obey the lawful orders of a police officer is a statute crime. The next time a cop tells you to sit down and shut up, you damn well better do it, is that clear?"

"Yes, sir," Kerensky said, his blue eyes looking somewhat round and widely open.

"Good. Where are you living now?"

"Those apartments right over there," Kerensky said, gesturing in the direction of the same small complex where Ybarra lived. "Steve Hansen helped me find it and has been helping me move, because my tires—I still have no new tires."

"You couldn't have picked a worse place," Shigata said.

"But it is very close to Pizza Hut, and that is my favorite store because they sent us pizzas to the barricades."

"Right. It is very close to Pizza Hut. And it is very close to Pete Ybarra. Hansen, why did you let him pick that place?"

"I wasn't thinking about Ybarra," Hansen said. "Just, it's a cheap place and Kerensky can afford it on his scholarship. Hey, Chief, I've been meaning to ask you, can the department do something about Kerensky's tires?"

"Certainly not," Shigata said. "But if you want to try to find a service station that'll do it cheap, be my guest. Just make sure they understand it's not an official request."

"Okay," Hansen said.

"And Kerensky," Shigata said, "stay out of trouble."

"How's Daniel?" Shigata asked when Lissa slid back into bed beside him. He could feel her trembling, very slightly, and knew it was not just the cold.

"He's asleep now," she answered. "Poor little fellow, he'll probably be crying at night for quite a while yet."

"Probably," Shigata said. "And we need to let him cry. It'd be worse to make him think he had to bottle it up." After a moment of silence, he asked, "Why the flowers?"

She didn't answer at first; she turned over and laid her head on his shoulder, and he put his arm around her and pulled her tighter to him. "It's okay, Lissa," he told her, and he could feel her nod and could feel the wet warmth of tears on his forearm.

Finally she said, "Sam didn't much like flowers. It wasn't that he hated them, he didn't care if I grew them, but he didn't like them himself, and he got mad if I bought some for the house, even if, you know, all his parties had reasons, they were all meant to accomplish things, he never really *liked* anybody, but he thought flowers were dumb. Even for parties."

"If we did go ahead with this greenhouse Gail keeps asking for, we could have flowers all year-round without buying them from a florist. But anytime you want to buy them—"

"What do you think about the greenhouse?"

He stared into the darkness. "A few hundred dollars worth of supplies. Al and I probably could put it together in a couple of weekends. But—if we got it, that would be telling Gail we're staying here, and I'm not ready to do that yet."

"But she'll be upset if we move back out. She's so excited about the swimming pool. And I checked it. It's filthy, of course—nothing in it now but rainwater and algae—but I don't think it's leaking. We'll have to get it cleaned and refilled. I put the cover back over it, so nobody could fall in easily."

"Do you know if Daniel knows how to swim?"

"That's another thing to think about, isn't it?" Lissa said.

"Tomorrow morning," Shigata told her, "I'd like you to call a fencing contractor. The fence around the yard isn't enough. Tell him we want a complete enclosure around the swimming pool—ten-foot fence and a top on it like the top of a cage. Until we get that, we'd probably better keep Daniel indoors or one of us had better be with him outdoors."

"Okay. . . . Mark," she said after a moment, "if we've got to live here, even just for a while, I'm glad we've got Daniel. If—I mean, with Daniel to think about, I don't have so much time to think about—other things."

She might have gone to sleep then. He didn't know. He lay on his back, listening to her breathe, trying to make himself relax enough to go to sleep in the house that had belonged to Henry Samford, while the single shot he'd fired years ago in the driveway went on echoing in his mind.

After a while, the telephone rang, and he got up to answer it, finding it by following the sound because he didn't, yet, know where things were in Sam's house.

He'd spoken softly, hoping not to wake her, but when he got back into bed she asked, "What was it?"

"County jail," he murmured. "They got my number from dispatch. They wanted to know what to do about Ybarra. He's sort of flipped out. He's keeping everybody awake yelling about Chinese Communists sneaking into the jail. They've moved him into a padded cell where he can't see out but he's still yelling that he saw them coming in."

"Are padded cells really padded?"

"Oh, yes," he said. "The padding is over the floor, the ceiling, all the walls, even the lower part of the door. It's about as thick as a cot mattress. Anyhow, I told them we'll see about getting him a psychiatric evaluation. In the meantime, all they can do is either call a doctor to sedate him, or let him yell. There's not anything I can do about it. And there are a couple of lawyers trying to bond Marubyashi out, but the judge hasn't set bond yet, so they're just going to have to wait."

"What does anybody expect you to do about it in the middle of the night?"

"It's not quite that middle of the night," he said. "Only ten-thirty. It's not their fault I've been keeping the hours I've been keeping."

"It's Marubyashi's."

"True."

This time he did sleep, and if he thought at all, he assumed Lissa was sleeping also. The next time the phone woke him, it was seven-thirty and beginning to be light outside. He put alarm clocks on his mental shopping list and got up to answer the phone.

Lissa sat up. "Who is it?"

He motioned to her for silence. "Shigata," he said and listened. And said, "*In* the jail?" and listened again. "All right, give me forty-five minutes, it's not going anywhere before I shave and shower. And see if you can get hold of his lawyers. I want them to see it before it's moved. What's their names? . . . Then they probably know about it already, but I don't want to give them a chance to squawk."

Lissa climbed out of bed. "I'll make you some coffee. What happened? Will you have time for breakfast?"

"Maybe a sausage and biscuit or something like that. Nothing else. Marubyashi's dead."

"*In* the jail?" she said just as he had.

"In the jail. A runaround trying to serve breakfast found him with a shuriken in his throat."

"A what?"

"Shuriken. Throwing star. An Oriental commando-style weapon."

"So Ybarra's Chinese Communists—"

"Were probably Yakuza assassins. Damn it, where would Hansen be keeping himself?" He grabbed the phone again and called the dispatcher. "Do you know where Hansen is? . . . That's what I figured. Okay, when he checks in, have him call me—no, wait. Tell him to call me about eight, after the shift hits the streets. I'll be out of the shower by then." Because muster—such as it was in a department this small—should be starting shortly, and it would last until eight o'clock. This was one of the days Hansen was supposed to take care of muster.

"Why Hansen?" Lissa asked.

"I had begun to think it would be safe for me to leave you and the kids alone, while I went to San Francisco. Now I don't. His house is still standing in water anyway, and Todd won't come home until they can get back into it, so asking him to stay here won't be much of an imposition."

At eight-thirty, attorneys Dennis Oyama and Alfred Yoshimura gazed at the remains of their late client, sprawled against the back wall with two razor-sharp points of an eight-pointed carbon-steel star still lodged vertically in his neck, his eyes open and staring at nothing. Looking at their stricken faces, Shigata realized that it smacked of Japan bashing to assume that because of their names they were involved with the Yakuza and knew what was going on, and he of all people knew better than to make such an assumption. "I don't pretend to understand this," Oyama said. "Do we have to stand here and look any longer?"

"No, of course not," Shigata said. "But I'd like to have a talk with you. Over a cup of coffee, maybe?"

"Good," said Yoshimura. "I—uh—we don't know Galveston. Where—?"

Shigata directed them to a downtown café and said, "Why don't you head on over there, and I'll be there soon."

"You're not coming with us?" Oyama asked.

"No, I need to talk with somebody else first. Shouldn't take over five or ten minutes."

Moments later, inside the somewhat unfragrant padded cell, Shigata set a paper cup of coffee aside and prodded Ybarra awake. "Pete, I need to ask you some questions," he said. "I brought you some coffee. How do you feel?"

Ybarra sat up. "*¡Madre de dios!* What did I drink yesterday?"

"I don't know, but whatever it was, it was too much of it. You want some coffee?"

"I want to pee," Ybarra said, and he proceeded to do exactly that. He flushed the stainless steel, lidless toilet and ran water from a push-button faucet to splash on his face and then drink from cupped hands. Then he sat down and grabbed for the coffee. "Who're you?" he asked then.

"Mark Shigata. Chief of police, Bayport."

"You Chicano?"

It wasn't the first time Shigata had been mistaken for a Hispanic. As usual, he replied, "No, Japanese-American."

"Japan? Like World War Two?"

"My people got here a long time before that. My father was in the U.S. Army during World War Two."

"Did I see you last night?"

"Yeah, in the Pizza Hut, just before you jumped Kerensky."

Ybarra swallowed half the coffee in one gulp. "How come they let Russian Communists come here? I don't like Communists. They stole my country. I got away on a boat when I was twelve years old, I been living here for thirty years, but most of my family didn't ever get away. My mother died hoeing sugarcane in Cuba, because Castro, he spent all the money so they couldn't use tractors and they got people out there hoeing in the sun. I hate Communists. They say it means everybody gets what they need; really it means nobody gets what they need. Damn stupid people."

"You don't pay much attention to the news, do you, Ybarra?"

"Who has time?"

"If you'd make a little time, you'd know the Russians got rid of their Communist government. Kerensky's not a Communist. His father spent a lot of time in a Communist prison camp in Siberia. He hates Communism just as much as you do."

Ybarra was silent, digesting that. Then he said, "Well, why didn't he tell me?"

"You didn't give him a chance. Every time you saw him you started trying to punch him out. Was it you cut his tires?"

"You s'posed to tell me I have a right to remain silent."

"I'm not charging you on it. I just want to know."

"Yeah, it was me slashed his tires. Is that what you came to talk to me about?"

"No," Shigata said, "I want to talk about last night. You started saying there were Chinese Communists sneaking into the jail. There weren't, but somebody maybe did sneak into the jail. What did you see?"

"I saw a damned Chinese Communist!"

"Ybarra," Shigata said patiently, "you've already shown that you can't tell a Japanese face from a Hispanic face when you *are* Hispanic, and you certainly can't tell anybody's politics by looking at him. Now, what did you *really* see? Tell me exactly what you saw, without adding your ideas about it."

Ybarra took a deep breath. "You know that window?"

"Yeah, I know that window." Shigata didn't need to ask what window; there was one third-floor window that opened onto an indoor recreation area; below the window the wives, girlfriends, and other friends and relatives of prisoners stood in the street or on a grassy lawn to yell up to their incarcerated loved ones and hear them yell back down. It was barred and covered with heavy mesh so that it would admit nothing but voices and a little fresh air.

"Okay, I was where I could see that window. And this guy—he looked Chinese to me, maybe he wasn't, I don't know—but he come *up* to that window. I mean, man, he come *up* to it. And he got that screen out of the way and he come through the bars like a weasel, man, I wouldn't think anybody bigger'n a two-year-old could get through those bars, but he did, and he was walking up and down between the cells and stopping in the shadows like he was invisible, man, and I tried to tell the guards and it was like they was looking right *at* him and couldn't see him."

"It would have helped," Shigata pointed out, "if you had told the guards what you saw, instead of what you thought you saw."

"I was drunk, man."

"I know you were. All right, the man with an Oriental look to him got through the window and then what?"

"He had this Chinese throwing star, it looked sharper'n a saw blade, man, and he walked up to this one cell and this other Chinese Communist, the one in the cell, stood up and started to say something and this Chinese Communist that come through the bars, he threw the throwing star and the other guy, man, he fell back against the wall and didn't say nothing else. And then the other guy, he went right back through the bars like a shadow, like smoke, and went back down the wall, man, do you think he might've been a vampire? Because I don't see how anything but a vampire could get through there. Are there any Chinese Communist vampires? And I tried to tell the jailers—"

"And the jailers wouldn't listen. I know. If we showed you some pictures in a day or two, do you think you could pick out the man that came through the bars?"

"Man, you can't take pictures of vampires. I seen in the movies—"

"Right," Shigata said wearily. *One witness. One witness, in a whole jail full of people who must have been wide-awake. I've heard about ninjas but I never tangled with one, wonder if this could have been one? That's too corny to think about, but how the* hell *did anybody get through those bars and walk up to the cell Marubyashi was in and kill him with nobody seeing him but one man, and that one's crazy as a loon?*

* * *

"So we went back and checked," Shigata said, "and we could see where a grapple had locked onto the bars. I don't know how he got the grapple onto the bars, because they were inside the mesh, but he managed. Then he climbed up the rope attached to the grapple and used some chemical to cut the rest of the way through the mesh. He had to have been extremely athletic to get through the bars, but it wasn't impossible. The bars were two feet apart—wide enough for me to get my head through—and somebody lean enough and flexible enough can get his whole body through anything he can get his head through."

"Seems like you'd get your ears caught," Oyama objected.

"You would, if you tried to back out," Shigata agreed. "But if you go all the way in and then turn around and go back out headfirst, which he obviously did, you wouldn't get your ears caught."

"And you say it was Yakuza?" Yoshimura asked, continuing to stir his coffee as he'd been doing for at least five minutes.

"It was Yakuza."

"Damn!" Oyama said. "We wouldn't have accepted the case if we'd known that. But the way Mr. Yamagata talked, it was a case of some southern redneck picking on somebody for his name and his face. And we figured—"

"I know what you figured," Shigata said. "Let me tell you about Buddy Yamagata."

He talked for ten minutes and then departed, leaving two very young—and very shaken—lawyers to finish their breakfast.

His plane was leaving at one. And he had to get Hansen in to stay with Lissa and hope like hell even Hansen would be enough. Anybody who could—and would—break *into* the Galveston County Jail to commit murder wasn't going to be stopped by the fences and locks Henry Samford had used to fortify his house.

▽

9

LITTLE SHOPS SELLING SOURDOUGH BREAD. Little shops selling Ghirardelli chocolate. You'd think there was nothing else happening in San Francisco, Shigata thought, striding through the airport toward his rental car. Four-forty-five Friday afternoon. He'd made decent time; this time of year, a plane would not be delayed landing in San Francisco because of fog, as it might in, say, June. He paused briefly beside a pay phone. Should he call Clement? But then he walked past. He'd call Clement later. Right now he had things to do he didn't want the FBI in on.

Honshu's. He knew where the club was, had been in it before. He'd probably seen E. P. Honshu before, though he couldn't really remember. But it wasn't quite time for Honshu yet.

The rental car turned out to be a Subaru. At the moment he wasn't too fond of Subarus; he thought of asking to change, but that would take time, and he reminded himself it wasn't really a Subaru that shot at him yesterday, but a person in a Subaru. He picked up his baggage—not much, he was traveling light, but it was still more than they'd let him carry onto the plane.

He hadn't, of course, worn his pistol on the airplane. Even a fed has to pull a wire or two to get away with that, and he no longer traveled with the authority of a federal agent. But he had put it in his luggage, unloaded, the pistol (tucked into a shoulder holster, rather than the hip holster he usually used) in one bag and a box of ammo in the other bag. He thought about getting it out and arming himself in an airport restroom. But that might get some perfectly innocent citizen unduly excited. He'd wait.

He'd need to find a motel to use as a base before he started prowling. But not one at the airport. Motels at airports always cost three times as much as they do anywhere else, and he wasn't traveling on the Bureau's budget, or even the police department's budget—not that the Bayport Police Department could afford an expensive motel any more than he could himself. Burlingame is wall-to-wall motels; he picked one that looked reasonably decent but wouldn't have mints on the pillows or a choice of forty-seven cable channels, checked in, dropped off everything he wasn't using, and reloaded his pistol. Although he'd never had occasion to be aware of California's firearms laws as they related to visiting lawmen from other states, he had a hunch he couldn't legally carry the pistol. He put it on anyway.

Honshu's was on North Point Street, near the cable-car turnaround. It was on flat land, near Fisherman's Wharf and a dozen or so seafood restaurants. He thought of his shrinking cash and credit card reserves, thought of stopping for a hamburger instead, and then thought the hell with that. No matter what your business, you can't go to San Francisco and not eat seafood at least one night. And he'd been having a nightmare of a week that wasn't over yet; he deserved a decent meal.

But in his recent years of policing in a small town where he could park in front of the police station, in his own reserved spot, and walk anywhere he wanted to go, or drive down to Galveston and nearly always find a parking place within a block of his destination, he'd allowed himself to forget San Francisco's parking problems. He drove around Ghirardelli Square and The Cannery, wishing he wasn't here on business, wishing he had Lissa with him to take her in and show her the self-consciously quaint little shops, treat her to lobster and oyster and clam dinners and chocolate and French bread and anything else he could think of, take Gail—

yes, and Daniel, too—to the zoo, take them up the coast and show all of them the caves that sea lions lived in, show them wild pelicans flying around waterfront restaurants, and the little dark bobbing heads of seals in the water as he'd seen one once rounding a headland by a rural restaurant somewhere an hour or so north of Santa Barbara. . . .

But he was here on business. After a while he found a place to park. He left the Subaru there with nothing at all in it and headed for a restaurant, the Rusty Scupper, that was very near Honshu's. He handed over a dollar in quarters to four different panhandlers, each of whom asked with humble eyes and outstretched hands whether he could spare a little change, and reminded himself to get more change at the restaurant. He didn't know who was and wasn't deserving; there was no way to tell; and whenever possible he handed over something to every beggar who approached him.

Very thick clam chowder. New England, not Manhattan, which he considered a lousy thing to do to a good clam and a good tomato. Broiled halibut with a hot, flaky baked potato that tasted as if it might have been baked on a bed of rock salt. A salad that was crunchy with fresh local vegetables. But he couldn't relax over dinner. Maybe he should have called Clement. At this moment, not one person in the world who knew him knew where he was. And considering the errand he was on, that might not be such a good idea.

Jack Saito hung up the phone. This was going to be a revenge killing. But the first problem was going to be to find the people he was supposed to kill.

Usually that wasn't a problem. You know people's routines. You know where they live, where they work. You wait around, and sooner or later you get them. But this time . . .

He'd reported in, after he finished cleaning up after the killing in the jail (a cleanup that included deep-sixing everything he had used that night, including the grapple and the clothing, so that not even the dust of the jail and the dust on his sleeves could be compared later in a laboratory), and the *oyabun* said get some rest and then go after the Shigatas. All of them. They'd shielded the boy quite long enough, and he was tired of messing around with them. Anyway, the man had stretched his luck—and the *oyabun*'s patience—about three times as far as either of those things ought to be stretched.

So Saito went and got some sleep, then went to the police station to wait outside.

That was the first surprise. In a town this size, there wasn't much of a place where he could wait and be inconspicuous. He finally picked a laundromat kitty-corner across the street. He could be waiting for his laundry to dry. Of course people came and went, but if he had a lot of laundry it would take a long time to dry, and nobody stayed long enough to notice he was staying there too long even for the longest drying time.

He'd gotten there about three-thirty, figuring the chief of police would be leaving sometime between four and five, and he'd just follow him home and take care of the situation. Of course he knew the police chief was FBI trained. He and the *oyabun* had a good laugh about that, the idea that somebody with that little training could even think of tackling Jack Saito. It had to have been sheer luck that Marubyashi didn't get him. Bad luck. Marubyashi's bad luck, which was tough on Marubyashi, but in this business you produce or you die.

He waited. And waited. And waited. And finally, at five-fifteen, he went to a pay phone and looked up the number and called the police station. He had to be calling about something, so he said he wanted to talk with the chief about the killing in the jail. And the dispatcher said, "I'm sorry, sir, but the chief is out of town for a few days. Is there someone else who could help you?"

He hung up.

All right, he'd have to get the chief later, or maybe somebody else would get the chief later. But he could get to the others now, if he could find out where they lived.

Where they lived now. Because it was a cinch they didn't

live where they used to live. Ishi and Marubyashi had taken care of that.

So he'd just go ask some neighbors.

And that was the second setback. Some of the neighbors weren't home. There'd been a flood here, and some of the houses weren't livable right now. What neighbors were home said they didn't know. They were sure Chief Shigata would let them know eventually—he'd been a real good neighbor—but right now, they just didn't know.

The hell with it, Saito thought. This is the wrong time of day to go asking questions anyway. He'd drive back down to Galveston, get a decent supper and a full night's sleep, and tomorrow—tomorrow there'd be a lot of ways to track them down.

Though not, to be sure, as many ways as there would be on a weekday. On Saturday you can't call the public utilities and ask questions, it's harder to get information out of the telephone company. . . .

It might take a few days. That was all right. Saito didn't expect automatic success on the first cast. The thing was to go on and on casting, without your fish getting sight of the bait.

Cover charge. Twenty-five dollars for the privilege of entering, of occupying a small round table not very near the show. It was supposed to be twenty-five dollars a couple, but, the maitre d' pointed out, it was no fault of Honshu's that Shigata didn't have a date. At least one drink, maybe two. He ordered one to start with. Scotch and soda. It was a little branded Scotch and a lot of crisp cold soda over glacially hard ice, and it was seven dollars and fifty cents. Shigata handed over a ten and said "Keep the change." He might need the assistance of this waiter later. Honshu's was in business to make money. It did a good job of it.

In this district, it was safe to assume the primary targeted clientele was the tourist trade. But there would be regulars, local people, who came back again and again. Shigata could see why. There was other entertainment, but E. P. Honshu himself was the primary show this night and, probably, every night. Or at least every night that the place was open. He'd noticed the sign outside: Closed Monday and Tuesday.

But this wasn't Monday or Tuesday. It was Friday, and Honshu's was rocking.

Shigata had come in right in the middle of a show. E. P. Honshu, wearing a glittering white suit with wide lapels and pounding on a glittering acoustic guitar, was singing "Jailhouse Rock." His backup band and backup vocalists were all, without exception, wearing glittering white suits—although with far less glitter than his—and blue suede shoes, and they all, even the women, had sideburns and ducktail haircuts. Honshu followed with "Are You Lonesome Tonight" and then changed to an electric guitar and went into another loud, rocking number Shigata was less familiar with. From that he proceeded to one Shigata couldn't remember having heard before, something about "Night Life." He listened to the lyrics; the theme seemed to be something about not giving up, which he agreed with in general, but he couldn't see exactly how it related to the title.

Honshu had quit singing; he was talking now. "People will tell you I'm an imitator," he said. "Now, that's not true."

The room gusted with laughter; apparently this was an expected, anticipated joke.

"I sing the songs I like," Honshu said. "I dress the way I like to dress. This is the way my hair grows, and this is the color my hair is. And—as for my initials, E. P., why, I'm telling you, they don't mean anything at all. And folks, I like my band to look a lot like me."

He picked the acoustic guitar back up and belted into "Hound Dog," and Shigata grinned. Honshu's voice was pitched fractionally lower than that of Elvis Presley; it had a little more dimension to it; and so, oddly enough, this was the best rendition of any of these songs Shigata had ever heard. But he remembered—he remembered. These songs, their singer, had been so shocking, then, thirty and thirty-five years ago. But now, mentally comparing them with what he used to see and hear before he and Lissa had—over Gail's protests—called the cable company and had them disconnect the cable so that MTV could no longer come into their house, he saw in these songs, in their original singer, an essential innocence that no amount of knowledge of his later life, of the manner of his death, of the thousands of tabloid stories about him, could ever erase from Shigata's mind.

Yes, he'd have to talk to Honshu. And there was someone else he'd just made up his mind he had to talk to, and there was a good possibility that this was going to be the night Mark Shigata died.

But for now, he was going to enjoy the music.

This was the longest Lissa had ever been in the general vicinity of Hansen, and she wasn't at all sure she liked him. He didn't say much. He seemed to be watching everybody and everything all the time. And of course she knew that was the reason he was there, to watch. He'd brought a very odd gun with him that he immediately put up high where Daniel couldn't touch it, and he cautioned Lissa and Gail to leave it alone, too. Beside that he brought along a dog, a brown dog with cocked ears he called Junkyard and wouldn't let Daniel or even Gail touch. He introduced Junkyard to all of them, or perhaps he was introducing all of them to Junkyard, and then he took Junkyard outside and said, "Watch."

He came in then and sat down on the couch, arranged a flashlight and a box of ammunition beside him on an end table, and began to read, but even as he read he watched them. He ate supper without leaving the couch and without seeming to notice what it was he ate, and went on watching. Watched Lissa. Watched Gail, until she went upstairs, still disgruntled about having had school that day, to begin her homework. Watched Daniel. There wasn't anything threatening in his watching, exactly; but there was something alien. As if he came from outer space and wasn't sure what people really were.

"What are you reading?" Lissa asked once.

He looked up, looked at her not as if he were startled but more as if he had forgotten she was there and was not quite sure what she was. Then he said, "*Name of the Rose.* Have you read it?"

"No," she said. "I think I saw the movie."

He looked back down. "The movie sucked," he said and resumed reading.

She went and bathed Daniel and put him to bed and went back downstairs, because it didn't seem polite to leave Hansen by himself even if he wasn't quite a guest.

Once Junkyard started to bark, and Hansen instantly dropped the book and, with a flashlight in one hand and his pistol—which was ivory handled, chrome coated, elaborately filigree carved, and inlaid with something that looked like gold—in the other, charged out the front door, leaving it open. She could hear his voice outside, talking to the dog and then to someone else, and then he came back in looking disgusted and shut the door. "It was a couple of high school kids hunting a place to park. I suggested they find a different place."

And he resumed reading.

She made a fresh pot of coffee and told him about it. He said "Thanks" without looking up from his book.

By then it was almost ten o'clock. She went upstairs to get ready for bed.

Hansen went on reading.

E. P. Honshu had gone backstage for a doubtless much-deserved rest period. Shigata got out one of his business cards, wrote on the front of it, "I'd like to talk with you," and beckoned to a waiter. The waiter arrived promptly, doubtless as a result of the earlier tip, and departed, the card borne regally on a silver (or silver-plated) salver and another ten-dollar bill in his pocket. A couple of minutes later Honshu came out.

Seen close, he was sweaty; the sweat had made runnels

down the greasepaint that almost—but not quite—made him into another man. His eyes were tired and a little puffy. He was sweaty, but more than that, he was frightened. Frightened and angry. Shigata might not be as good at reading emotions as he wished he could be, but those were emotions he could read.

Honshu did not sit. "What makes you think I want to talk to you?" he asked.

"Just hoped you might," Shigata said. "I think we have a mutual friend."

"We do?"

"Your friend, I think. My cousin. Rocky—"

"He's dead," Honshu interrupted quickly. "I don't have anything to say to you. Now or ever. You can have your card back." He slapped it down flat on the table, with one finger under it so that no one any farther away than Shigata could have heard the faint chink of metal under the card, turned, and strode off.

Shigata gazed after his back as he departed. Then he shrugged, picked up the card (and the key that was under it), put the card in his pocket, drained the last few swallows of Scotch and soda, and got up to leave.

He didn't go straight to the car; he went instead to Ghirardelli Square, avoiding a panhandler who demanded, rather than asked for, money. "Get lost, friend," Shigata said softly, hand inside his jacket on his gun butt, and the panhandler looked keenly at him and turned to hunt other prey. There was no use calling the police about this, Shigata thought; the area was patrolled as well as possible, and the panhandler hadn't actually done anything overtly threatening.

Inside the maze of shops and restaurants, Shigata rambled around until he found a boutique and bought a greeting card without paying much attention to what it said. Then he went into a restroom. With the door closed behind him, he looked for the first time at what Honshu had scrawled, in what looked like eyebrow pencil, on the back of Shigata's business card.

"Key to Buddy's box. Don't know bank or name he used. Stole it for Rocky and couldn't get it to him, didn't know what to do with it. Buddy's after you. Careful." The number on the key was 1481. There was no doubt at all that it was to a safe-deposit box.

The greeting card had puppies and kittens on the front and a delectable smell of chocolate clinging to it. On the inside it said, "Happy Birthday from Ghirardelli Square to my favorite five-year-old." There was one square of chocolate taped inside. Shigata removed the chocolate carefully, putting it in his pocket, and used the tape to anchor the two safe deposit box keys. He wrote on the blank page, "Note on the back of my card is from E. P. Honshu. Go as easy on him as you can. 1481 is the key he gave me, the other is Rocky's key. If I'm not at the bank Saturday morning, look for me in the bay. I'm going now to try to talk to Buddy." He signed his name after the message.

After tucking the business card partially behind one of the keys, he sealed the card and wrote on the outside, "George Clement, Special Agent-in-Charge, FBI."

A car with a sticker announcing it was rented from Avis slid into his parking place seconds after he vacated it. This part of town stayed busy this time of night. The bars, the nightclubs, wouldn't close until 2:00 A.M., and many of the restaurants stayed open about that late.

Ten minutes. Ten minutes from Ghirardelli Square to the Phillip Burton Federal Building, 450 Golden Gate Avenue. This time of night it was ten minutes; it might be a lot longer at some times of the day. This time of night traffic was light and there was plenty of parking, here, because there weren't many bars in this neighborhood. Nothing to take up time, to let him delay what he knew he was going to do next.

This time of night the building was locked. He parked on the street and didn't bother to feed the meter; he wouldn't be that long. He didn't try to go to the front door. He went straight to the back and pushed the buzzer. It buzzed, and he waited. And waited, and buzzed again, and after a long time a man in the dark blue uniform of the federal police showed up and opened the door.

This was no minimum-wage night watchman; this man was sharp, well trained, well armed, and very alert. Shigata handed over the envelope and said, "See to it Clement gets it first thing in the morning."

"Tomorrow's Saturday," the guard said. "Mr. Clement usually—"

"He'll be here tomorrow," Shigata interrupted. "And it is essential he see it the moment he walks in."

"He'll get it," the guard said.

And he would. Shigata had no doubt whatever of that.

On his way back to the car he paused briefly, rummaged in his pocket for the chocolate, opened it, and popped it into his mouth. *The condemned man ate a hearty meal.* Why not?

He got back into the car, automatically locked his door again because anybody who drives around San Francisco at night with unlocked car doors is crazy, and leaned his head on the steering wheel for a moment. He didn't exactly remember when the headache had arrived, but it was there now. The night had cooled off, was a little nippy but not quite what he'd call cold, but the sweat on his body was icy. He took several deep breaths and let himself feel the fear.

He'd risked his life before. He'd been in gunfights and didn't like them; he'd been through a hurricane and a couple of earthquakes, one pretty bad. He'd been horsewhipped once by a man who didn't kill him only because a dead man can't give information. He'd been on the kind of raids where you wore a bulletproof vest and wished you had one to cover your head and your genitals. He'd worked undercover a time or two, and his life had been threatened by so many different people that for the most part the threats had gone stale. He knew the taste of fear.

But not the taste of this fear.

He took one more deep breath and started the car.

The next big question was, where was Buddy Yamagata.

He had two houses in the San Francisco area that Shigata knew about, almost certainly one or more that Shigata didn't know about, but there was no telling which he'd be using on Friday night. Or any other night. He avoided creating a pattern.

Common sense suggested trying the closest one first. The other one, the really big one, was at Tiburon. You go north on Golden Gate Bridge and head east and then there's a little peninsula sticking its tongue down south into San Francisco Bay, only about eight miles from San Quentin. You'd think, considering the nearness of the prison, that it would be a bad neighborhood. It wasn't. Shigata had heard people say that poverty was a felony at Tiburon. He'd had only glimpses of Yamagata's beachfront house there, a glimpse from the road that showed him nothing at all except trees and a glimpse from a motorboat that showed him the private beach and cabana but, again, not much of the house. From a helicopter he'd seen a little more, but of course that was only treetops and roofs of buildings. So he hadn't seen enough really to see it at all, but if the house and property together had gone for less than seven million dollars Shigata didn't know real estate in the Bay Area as well as he thought he did.

But that wasn't the closest house. The other, the smaller one, was closer, up on Twin Peaks (and Shigata was vaguely aware there was a television show called "Twin Peaks," but he'd never seen it and hadn't the slightest idea whether it was set on the Twin Peaks he knew). This time of year the weather was excellent—warm, almost sweet air, no fog. He couldn't see much except for cold brilliant stars while he was driving up—"up" in altitude but "down" in direction, because he was driving southwest—because the city was behind him. But driving down, if he lived to drive back down, the cities—San Francisco and Oakland and the dozens of smaller towns that made up the metroplex—would be laid out before him, a sparkling diamond necklace around the neck of San Francisco Bay.

This house, too, he'd seen both from the street and from a helicopter. Not, of course, from a boat, this one, but the helicopter was able to hover at a little better angle and he'd looked through binoculars. He reviewed the memory now. About an acre. Fenced even better than Henry Samford had fenced his house, but Buddy Yamagata would make Henry Samford with his five million dollars of oil money look and feel like a pauper. Not a big house, maybe three bedrooms and they wouldn't be too big. Blue aluminum siding, because in earthquake country, if you're smart and have money you don't use brick construction. It's too vulnerable.

Buddy Yamagata was smart and had money, which was lucky for him, because the house and property, which would have gone for fifty thousand max in Shigata's neck of the woods, probably had cost Yamagata a million plus, and not all of that was paying for the view.

The fence was ten feet high, the best chain-link construction, and it carried a little heavier charge than anybody would put on a livestock fence, and on top of each post was another post leaning out at about a thirty degree angle, and strung on each of those posts were three strands of barbed wire. There was one gate, and sitting about five feet inside that gate was a small guardhouse.

Shigata drove up to the gate, honked his horn, and got out of the car.

A guard—not uniformed, but he'd have no provable link with the mob so that he could legally carry a gun—approached the inside of the gate. "Yeah?"

"I want to see Buddy Yamagata."

"Is he expecting you?"

"I don't know," Shigata said. "He might be."

"It's late at night for an unannounced visit."

"But when you announce me I won't be unannounced."

Another guard had emerged by that time. "What is it?" he called.

"Son of a bitch wants to see the *oyabun*."

"Has he got a name?"

The first guard turned back to Shigata, who handed his card through the locked gate. The guards conferred over it, and one of them laughed. The second one said, "The *oyabun* doesn't see cops except on appointment."

"Call him," Shigata said mildly, persuasively. "You might find out he wants to see me."

One of the guards shrugged, then went back inside the guardhouse. "While he's doing that," Shigata said, "I want you to watch me. I know you can't let me in armed. I'm going to take my coat off, take my pistol out of my holster, and put it in the glove box."

"So why are you telling me?" But this guard was opening the gate as he spoke, coming out of it.

"I don't want you to get all excited when you see the pistol."

Shigata disarmed himself. The guard's pose looked casual, as he leaned against the gatepost, but Shigata didn't kid himself: he'd stand no chance at all of using that pistol.

He didn't bother to lock the glove box. When he got back—if he got back—the pistol would be there. So would everything else in the car.

The other guard came out of the guardhouse. "I'll take you to the house," he said.

He did.

In a golf cart.

Oddly enough, Shigata had never before seen Buddy Yamagata. All their dealings had been over the telephone, or through Yamagata's underlings. The man himself probably stood six feet tall or taller and probably weighed three hundred pounds or more, but anybody who thought that weight meant he'd gone soft didn't know much. He wouldn't, personally, be much of a fighter now. But he didn't have to be. A man who controls half the heroin and cocaine and bootleg amphetamine coming into the West Coast of the United States, who controls whorehouses and gambling and murder for hire, doesn't have to be able to fight with his own fists, his own guns or knives. He fights with his money. And that's the most powerful weapon of all.

He didn't look evil. That was about Shigata's first thought on seeing him. He just looked like an overweight former athlete, combed and groomed and manicured, sitting relaxed and comfortable, with laugh lines around his eyes.

His physical condition was easy to estimate because he had chosen to receive Shigata in a sauna. He was wearing no tattoos at all, certainly not the full-body tattoo favored by the Yakuza. He was sitting on a bench made of light-colored wood, dressed only in a towel. A small towel, draped about his lap. Shigata, in a suit and tie, could feel his clothing wilt from the damp heat.

A few months earlier, the Shigatas had cat-sat for a week. Tiger and the visiting cat had fought steadily the entire time, and Shigata had begun to understand a little of feline rules of combat or, more often, spitting and hissing and avoiding conflict. The most important one seemed to be that whichever cat was sitting on a higher place had the advantage; that is, a cat on the television set was superior to a cat on the floor, but a cat on top of the bookcase was superior to one sitting on the television.

Right now, Shigata felt like the cat on the floor.

Theoretically, a standing man has the advantage over a seated one; a clothed man has the advantage over a naked one.

That was not the case here. Shigata knew it because Yamagata knew it.

Yamagata was looking at him, hadn't spoken. Shigata also hadn't spoken. Usually the first one to speak loses. That probably wasn't going to be the case here either.

It wasn't. Yamagata laughed, a deep-bellied laugh that filled the small, hot room. "You have surprised me," he rumbled then. "It isn't easy to surprise me."

"I know," Shigata said.

"Why did you come?"

Shigata took a deep breath. "Rocky Omori was my cousin," he said. "My mother's brother's son."

"Oh, ho," Yamagata said and laughed again, longer this time.

"I cry blood feud on you," Shigata said. He'd gotten that idea from a fantasy novel Gail had at home several weeks ago, which he'd picked up to read in an idle moment. He hadn't the slightest idea whether such a custom even existed in Japan, but he was fairly certain Yamagata didn't know either.

Yamagata's heavy eyebrows lifted. "You intend to kill me?" His voice was heavy with irony.

"No," Shigata said.

"Of course you don't. Because you can't. I, on the other hand, could kill you very easily. I could have you shot, or I could have you killed very slowly, the same way your—cousin, was it?—died. I could have you killed six weeks from now, in your own living room, or I could have you killed at this moment, in this room, and nobody would ever know. You have told nobody you are here. Your friend George Clement would not have allowed you to come if he knew."

"My friend George Clement doesn't control my behavior."

"You cry blood feud on me, and then you tell me you do not intend to kill me. Knowing the power I have, you deliberately put your life in my hands. How do you intend to carry out this blood feud? You cannot. There is no way. You were at Honshu's Club tonight," he added with no change in tone. "Why?"

"I chose to. How did you know? You can't have had me followed. You didn't know I was in town."

"I have—an observant staff. You paid a waiter ten dollars to take a card to my brother. He came out and spoke with you for a moment. What did he say?"

"That he had nothing to say to me. Then or later. He returned my card."

"Did you expect anything from him? He has no more to say to you, and no more courage to say it, than any little whore my underlings keep on a string. You are a fool, Mark Shigata. I did not think you were that kind of a fool. A fool, yes. When last I spoke to you, you could have had ten year's salary all at once. More, if you'd wanted it. I have room in my organization for the man I thought you were then."

"Then you would have controlled me. I don't choose to be controlled by you *or* George Clement. And I didn't come here to kill you," Shigata said. "Only to destroy you."

The heavy eyebrows raised again. "A little melodramatic today, aren't we?"

"Not at all," Shigata said easily. "I know more about you than you think I do."

"Then it was unfortunate for you that you didn't know these things years ago, when last we met. They could have saved you—trouble." Yamagata chuckled again. "It was almost worth the little problems you made me, to see the Bureau bundling you out of town. But I told you not to get in my way again."

"I didn't have as much trouble as you meant me to have. And I knew these things then. But I had no way of using them. I do now." There would be no use in saying that it was not he who had chosen to get in Yamagata's way again, but Yamagata's *kabun* who had taken trouble to him.

"You know nothing," Yamagata said. "But, I don't intend to kill you yet. I will wait until I get word, and you get word, from my hunters in Texas."

"Hunter, I believe," Shigata said, feeling his heart beat even faster. "Only one now. The one who went into the jail and killed Marubyashi. A little hard on Marubyashi, don't you think?"

"He failed me," Yamagata said. "Three times he failed me. He missed the child, at the motel. He missed you, at your house. And he missed you and the child again, on the highway. I do not allow failure. You should not have sheltered the child. I could have let you live, otherwise. You amuse me, posturing as if you had power over me. But now, no. The child will die."

"Your own grandchild."

Yamagata shrugged.

"Rocky misjudged you there. He thought you'd want Daniel back. He didn't think you'd want to kill Daniel."

"Bad blood. Disobedience. I have no use for disobedience."

"And your daughter, was she disobedient?"

An unidentifiable look flashed across Yamagata's face and as quickly was gone. Perhaps, in one part of himself, he did regret Phyllis's death. "She was disobedient. And you are disobedient. Your wife, your children, and last of all yourself will die for that."

"I owe you no obedience, Yamagata. I didn't take your money. I didn't drink your *sake.* I have sworn no fealty to you."

"No, of course not." The rumble of laughter thundered again. "You have cried blood feud on me. You have sworn to—what was it?—destroy me. How, Mark Shigata?"

"I won't tell you that now," Shigata said. "But there are a few things I will tell you. I won't try to kill you. You're right about that. I couldn't succeed, and I know it. As hard as it probably is for you to believe me, I don't even want to kill you. But even beyond that, being killed wouldn't bother you that much. You expect to die that way. It would—fulfill your self-concept. And that's what I know about you that I have known as long as I have known you exist—that you wouldn't mind being killed." Yamagata laughed at that, as Shigata went on. "And I know what you do mind, what you would—and will—hate and fear above all other things. I tried to make it happen before. I couldn't. That's why you won, last time you and I encountered one another. But not this time. I can prove—what I want to prove, this time. You'll be arrested, sometime in the next few days. The evidence will be too good for you to get away, this time. You're not going to play Teflon Don, this time. You're going to prison. And we're not talking about what you'd see as some little piddling state prison like San Quentin, and since Alcatraz shut down there's no federal prison in San Francisco, where you're close enough that maybe what's left of your machine—not that there's going to be much left—could spring you. My guess is they won't even send you to Atlanta. Marion, Illinois, that's my guess.

A maximum security prison that's just about as hard to get out of as Alcatraz. And you're—what, Buddy? Fifty-nine? Sixty? About ten years older than I am. Buddy, you won't live long enough to get out. You'll be there the rest of your life. And I'll tell you one more thing. All the evidence came from Rocky and his friends. They wouldn't have used it if you'd left them alone. They didn't want to use it. But they put it where I could get it."

"And if I killed you now?"

"That wouldn't stop it. I've put it now where my friends can get it." Somewhere, in the course of the conversation, his fear had vanished. He didn't know where it had gone. But the headache, too, was gone, his breathing was easier now, and the only sweat left on him was from the sauna.

"I don't believe you," Yamagata said. But he wasn't laughing now.

"You don't have to believe me."

"And you still haven't told me why you came here. You could have cried blood feud over the telephone. Or by letter. If you insist on melodrama."

"The only way I could be sure you got the message was to deliver it myself. I came here so that when it happens, you'll know where it came from."

"You could have told me when it happens. If it happens."

"I know."

"So you still haven't told me why you came here."

"Buddy," Shigata said, "if I told you five hundred times you'd never understand why I came here. I'm going to leave, now. Kill me if you want to. I know you can. I knew it when I came here. So did you. So it wouldn't be very—sporting. But no matter what you do to me, you can't stop what's happening."

There was a long silence, then Yamagata began again to laugh. "You want me to kill myself to prevent something you can't cause to start with? Is that it? You can't harm me, so you hope to bluff me into destroying myself? You're a fool. I never thought you were a fool."

"You've said that before," Shigata said. "You're repeating yourself. You're boring, Buddy Yamagata. So think whatever you want to." Shigata turned and heard Yamagata's voice following him.

"Shigata. You think you know what I fear? You're wrong. I don't need to fear what won't happen. You don't know how many federal prosecutors I own. You don't know which ones. You can't touch me. So you'll walk out of here thinking everything is going to work your way, and you're going to be surprised—very damned surprised—when it doesn't. And it won't. Well, I know what you fear. It isn't pain. You would die the same way your cousin died, saying no more than he said. It isn't death. If you feared your own death, you wouldn't have come here tonight. I will never kill a man who comes to me alone, unarmed. I would not even have killed Rocky Omori, if he had come to me that way, because I would have known that was not what he feared. I know what you fear. Don't think that your plan, in the totally unlikely event that it occurs, will protect your family. My hunter has his orders. He will not leave the trail for anyone's orders but mine, and alive or dead, free or in prison, I will not give those orders. Marubyashi was a small hunter. The one I have sent to Texas now is my best hunter. Your wife and your child will die, as will the traitor's child. You will live long enough to know it. And then, you too will die. But—maybe not too soon."

Shigata kept walking and, less to his astonishment than it would have been an hour earlier, was allowed to walk out of the sauna and out of the house and down the hill to his car, to put his pistol back into his holster, and to get into his car and drive away.

He tried to call Lissa from the first pay phone he found. Hansen answered, sounding tired, and said everything was perfectly quiet and he had his pit bull out in the yard. "I borrowed an Uzi from the Secret Service," he added. "Is that okay?"

"I guess it has to be okay, since you already did it," Shigata replied. "But what makes you think you need one?"

"If I'm going to tangle with a ninja—"

"You aren't going to tangle with a ninja," Shigata interrupted.

"What else besides a ninja could break into the Galveston County Jail?"

"Ninjas—nowadays, at least—are like Santa Claus and the tooth fairy," Shigata said.

"If it walks like a duck and quacks like a duck it's a duck. If it climbs like a ninja and kills like a ninja—"

"Steve, don't play games with my wife's life," Shigata said.

"Nobody's going to get to her," Hansen told him. "That, I promise you."

Shigata had to accept that promise because there was nothing else he could do. If he went home now, he might personally stop Yamagata's best hunter. But only by staying here could he be sure Yamagata wasn't in a position to dispatch any others.

He restarted the car, uneasily thinking of Yamagata's laughter and hoping that Yamagata wouldn't still be laughing tomorrow. With that on his mind, he drove back to his motel, deciding what he was going to say when he telephoned George Clement at eleven o'clock at night.

▽

10

"I TRUST HARRY FONG," George Clement said. It was the third time he had said it in approximately three minutes. "I mean even his name—Harry Truman Fong—how patriotic can you get?"

"I'm glad you trust him," Shigata said. "But I don't know him. I don't care whether he's Harry Truman Fong or George Washington Fong. I put Benjamin Franklin Marubyashi in jail two days ago. He was Yakuza, and he was killed there by another Yakuza. Names don't mean jack, not in this situation or any other, and you know that as well as I do."

"But—" Clement tried to interrupt.

Like a juggernaut, Shigata's voice rolled over Clement's. "I'm glad you can trust him. I hope I can trust him. But I don't know. And I've got more to lose than you do." He was simultaneously pacing around in his motel room and talking on the telephone, and the cord was becoming steadily more twisted.

"If you'd just told me sooner, as soon as you got the key, so we could have started looking—"

"The banks were just as closed then as they are now," Shigata said. "And it doesn't matter whether you know what bank it is. Not now. You don't have any probable cause for getting a warrant to get into the box. If you had probable cause you wouldn't need the key. You could have the box drilled."

"I realize—"

"I know you do. Because if you'd had probable cause you

could have already found out what bank he had a box in, and you could already have opened it. You've got to hope Rocky's box gives you probable cause to get into Yamagata's box, and into anything else of Yamagata's. And I've got to hope that too. But on top of that I've got to hope nobody gets rid of the evidence before we have the chance to use it."

"If you hadn't gone over there and maybe spooked him—"

"I didn't spook him," Shigata said. "I wish I knew a way to spook him."

"How do you know you didn't spook him? You should have had better sense than to go over there." Clement was trying to sound patient. He succeeded rather in sounding peeved. "What the hell did you do it for?"

"I had a reason."

"What?"

"You wouldn't understand."

"Try me," Clement said.

"I went over there because ten years ago you yanked me out of San Francisco so fast Buddy couldn't come to any other conclusion than that I was running from him."

"We continued the investigation," Clement said. "He had to know that."

"And no case was ever made," Shigata retorted. "I know that. Why not?"

After a pause that probably wasn't as long as it felt to Shigata, Clement said, "Some of the evidence went missing."

"From the federal prosecutor's office."

"Yes."

"And I have to stake the lives of my family and myself on evidence that's going into that same office. And you expect me not to be worried."

"There've been a lot of personnel changes. That was ten years ago."

"I know how long ago it was," Shigata said. "The fact remains that you let him think I was afraid of him."

"You were afraid of him. You'd have been crazy not to be afraid of him. Mark, do I have to remind you what happened?"

"You don't have to—"

"You were working undercover, trying to infiltrate his mob. You were burned—we still don't know how. Knowing who you were, he tried to bribe you into working as a double agent. When that didn't work, he tried to make it appear that you'd taken the bribe, and when the newspapers notified us instead of printing the story and we got to the bottom of what had really happened, he had you ambushed instead."

"I know—"

"And had you shot."

"Not seriously."

"Because you moved fast. That doesn't alter the fact—"

"All right, yes, I was afraid. I was afraid from before the job started, the minute I knew what you were asking me to do. I was afraid but I did the job anyway. I wasn't afraid enough to run away. But he thought I was."

"What difference does it make what he thought?" Clement said. "Everybody who mattered knew the truth."

"Do you think nobody matters but your friends?" Shigata asked. "Like the old saying, with friends like these who needs enemies? Your enemies matter too. Sometimes, in some ways, your enemies matter more than your friends do."

"You're talking about that good old Oriental idea of saving face."

"No I'm not. At least, if I am I'm talking about it from the practical point of view. If he hadn't had reason to believe that he could jack me around maybe he wouldn't have tried it this time."

"No, he'd just have killed you instead."

"Maybe so," Shigata said, "or maybe he'd have decided that a child with me backing him up was too much trouble to be worth trying to kill. But that wasn't the main thing I was talking about anyway, and you know it."

"Then what were you talking about?"

"Suppose he's telling the truth. Suppose he does own somebody in the federal prosecutor's office. It doesn't even have to be an attorney. Anybody. An attorney—a legal aide—

a secretary. Hell, even a janitor. Any trusted person could 'lose' the evidence in about five minutes and that would be the end of the case. I don't want Yamagata to play Teflon Don, because as long as he is free—"

"The Teflon Don grew Velcro," Clement said. "But on Yamagata, we don't even know yet that we *have* any evidence."

"We'll have evidence."

"All right, we'll have evidence," Clement said. "And yes, one person in the office could get rid of it. What do you suggest I do about it?"

Dead silence. Then Shigata said, "I don't know."

"Well, when you decide, let me know. In the meantime, let's all get some sleep, okay?"

Four o'clock in the morning, San Francisco time. Six o'clock, Texas time. Shigata, in San Francisco with a body still running on Texas time, had finally fallen into an uneasy sleep in which he kept dreaming of shootouts. Shootouts in which he didn't have his gun. Shootouts in which his gun wasn't loaded. Shootouts in which there were twice as many of them as he had bullets in his gun.

Some of his friends were asleep. Clement slept heavily, dreamlessly. Hansen would have to wake soon, but for now he was asleep on the couch, the borrowed Uzi within easy reach and his dog on duty outside.

Lissa Shigata was awake; Daniel had awakened ten minutes earlier and climbed into bed with her, crying and informing her that he had an earache and beavers, and it had taken her five minutes to figure out that *beavers* meant fever and another five minutes to locate a thermometer not used in years and to determine that Daniel did indeed have fever—or beavers, as she suspected they would be saying around the household for the next few months. "Let me go get something," she told Daniel, remembering that children should not be given aspirin, and she went downstairs, trying not to waken Hansen, to see what she had that she could give him.

Jack Saito was not asleep. He'd been awake half an hour, lying on his back with his right arm under his neck and his left hand holding the cigarette he was smoking in bed. He was rearranging his plans.

Because if Shigata was still out of town when he called this morning, he wasn't going to get Shigata this trip. He had to get in, strike fast, get out, and Shigata would keep. He couldn't call the *oyabun* and ask instructions, because the *oyabun* said by now there was at least a chance they would have the phones tapped. They knew Omori had talked to Shigata; they didn't know what he had said; but if he'd mentioned the *oyabun* . . .

Well, there was enough chance that the *oyabun* wasn't going to be using the telephone for a while. Or doing any talking in public places. Anybody with good sense knew what that got you. If you'd watched the news at all for the last couple of years you knew about Gotti. If he'd had sense enough to keep his mouth shut in public . . .

So Saito couldn't call and ask for instructions. But that was okay because he wasn't Ishi or Marubyashi, afraid to scratch his butt without an order. He was Saito, and he could think for himself.

So. Change of plans. Take care of the kid, the woman and her kids now—he wasn't sure how many kids there were—and make tracks. He could come back later for the man. If the man didn't come to him, and that wasn't impossible.

But to take care of the woman he had to find the woman. And, as he already knew, the old address wasn't worth anything. He couldn't follow her from the police station because there was no reason she would be going to the police station. That meant he was going to have to get somebody who knew where she was and could be made to tell it. And that would be somebody in the police department, because after this week, no way was Shigata going out of town leaving his wife unguarded.

If Shigata wasn't back in town already, which wasn't impossible. Saito didn't know where the man had gone or for how long, just that the dispatcher yesterday said he was gone. For a few days, which might not be true.

Of course there was always the possibility that Shigata *wasn't* gone, was merely setting a trap. Saito didn't think that was the case. But if it was, he could handle it.

He stood up, lighter than a cat leaping off the bed, stubbed out the cigarette, walked over to the telephone, and dialed the number he'd already memorized.

"Bayport Police Department."

"Hello," he said, not bothering to disguise his voice. If they got close enough to him to match the voiceprints of his known voice with the voiceprints of the voice on the police department tape recorder, they had him anyway. "I have some information about the killing in the Galveston County Jail the other night. I want to talk to the chief."

"I'm sorry, sir, he's out of town." A light voice, female, not altogether sure of herself yet. Good; that increased the likelihood he could rattle her into telling him more than she should. "If I can have your telephone number—"

"No names. No numbers. Who else can I talk to? Who's next in command?"

"Captain Quinn, sir."

"Then let me talk to him."

"He wouldn't normally be in until seven-thirty, sir, but he's going to be a little later today."

"Why? How much later?"

"There was some sort of accident and he had to take one of his children to the hospital. He said it might be nine-thirty or ten before he got in."

"I can't wait that long," Saito said brusquely. "I'm leaving town myself. I talk to somebody within one hour or I don't talk to anybody."

"I could have Sergeant Hansen call you—"

"No telephone numbers," Saito repeated, making his voice sound edgy. "You call this Sergeant Hansen now. Tell him to figure out a place where I can meet him at—um—

seven A.M. Tell him I'll scout it out and if there's a reception committee I keep going."

"Yes, sir, would you hold the line while I—"

"Trace my call? No, thanks, sister. I'll call you back in ten minutes." He hung up. He had her rattled; he could tell from the way her voice was rising, the last thing she said. She'd call Hansen, whoever Hansen was, and with luck she'd get Hansen rattled, too.

"The chief told me to stay here." Hansen's voice was stubborn.

"Five minutes. Maybe ten. How long does it take to drive to the Seven-Eleven and get some Tylenol? You can leave the Uzi here for me. And the dog."

"You think you can fire an Uzi?"

"Of course. Mark says it's a nice little machine gun, hardly any kick."

Hansen looked doubtfully at Melissa. She was a small woman, so slender she was approaching thin. *A nice little machine gun?* But she had killed once, Quinn had told him, in defense of her child. If she had killed once and thought she could do it again, his guess was she could. And, he could hear Daniel crying upstairs. An earache. Todd had a toothache the night Hansen's wife was murdered. Todd had a toothache and was taking codeine and sleeping on the front porch because it was cooler there. A hideously hot night, and maybe that was part of the reason the quarrel had gotten so out of hand that Hansen had left, gone down to Galveston to sleep on the beach, and never seen his wife and daughter—stepdaughter, legally, but daughter in all the ways that mattered—alive again.

Leave now? Leave the chief's wife and daughter alone, when he knew—as he hadn't known, for his own wife and daughter—that there was a threat?

But the child went on crying upstairs, the thin reedy wail of a sick, feverish child. She was going to have to take him to the doctor later today, no matter what the threat was, and

Hansen would have to go with her to the doctor, which meant leaving the house (and Gail, unless Gail went to the doctor, too) alone, which meant somebody could get into the house—

There aren't enough people in this police department. And we're down one more, since Claire went to the Secret Service. We've got to get some new hires, preferably somebody with experience, except what would anybody with experience want with this small town and its small pay scale?

Unless it was somebody like me, somebody who'd been hassled all his life—you're going to do this, you're going to be that—so that he'd never had a chance to think at all about what he really wanted to do. And it may be that one me is about all any police department could handle.

But that was grim humor. And he'd made up his mind. He was going to go get the Tylenol. Because obviously Lissa couldn't go, or Gail, and the closest 7-Eleven was only four blocks away.

And then the telephone rang.

He'd promised to be gone no more than fifteen minutes. He stopped first to get the Tylenol so he wouldn't forget it even if this informant, whoever the informant was, got him thoroughly upset. A flavored liquid Tylenol for kids. He remembered getting baby aspirin when Tamar (*dead four years now, Tamar with her long black hair)* and, later, Todd were that small, but apparently you didn't give aspirin to kids anymore. He didn't know why, but Lissa was insistent on it.

Then he drove over to the Dairy Queen. It wasn't open yet, not for another couple of hours, so the parking lot outside it would be a decent place to meet with the informant. And the informant—unfamiliar, he said, with the area—could find it, according to dispatch.

Max Kerensky, now residing in one of a strip of eight small furnished apartments behind the Pizza Hut that was across the street from Dairy Queen, sat morosely on the edge of his bed and thought of Siberia, where surely no one would slash the tires of a reporter (although they might steal his windshield wipers; it had taken him a long time to fully realize that here he didn't have to hide his windshield wipers whenever he parked his car). But the fact remained, someone had slashed his tires, and his orange and white van—which Steve Hansen had insisted on naming "Roger" because, he said, it looked like bacon, a joke that Kerensky hadn't had the nerve to ask someone to explain to him—was now at a Texaco station three blocks away getting new—or rather, used, which was the best Steve Hansen could cook up at a price Kerensky could pay—tires.

Presumably the tires were now on, and Kerensky could walk over to the service station and pay the money and get the car and drive it to breakfast, whenever he decided to go and get breakfast.

The thought of having his car back again brightened his mood a little. He pulled his jeans and shirt on over the underwear he'd slept in, sat down again to put on socks and boots, and grabbed a jacket. (But forty-eight degrees American style—about nine degrees Celsius, the way he had learned to think of temperature—would be shirtsleeve weather in Siberia this time of year, the snow would be so deep and pure and white—no snow here, and the flowers went on blooming.)

As he strode past the Dairy Queen (and to be sure, it was easier to walk with no snow, but in Siberia very few people had cars, so he was used to walking or using public transportation everywhere he went—no public transportation at all, in this small town, except for two or three taxis), he noticed two cars pulled up side by side, the way police cars do, facing in opposite directions so that the drivers could talk without either one getting out of his car. Only one of them was a police car, though, and the man in it was Steve Hansen. That was interesting, because Steve Hansen was supposed to be at the chief's house, guarding the chief's wife.

Kerensky didn't think of his friend as Steve, or as Hansen, but always as Steve Hansen, affectionately, the way Hansen if he had Russian manners would call him Max Borisovich. He wasn't sure what kind of a name Han was except he remembered it from *Star Wars,* a character named Han Solo, and he wasn't sure why nobody else around here seemed to have a patronymic, but it was interesting that Steve Hansen, who was fast becoming his closest friend in this sometimes bewilderingly foreign land, had one.

It is a reporter's duty to be curious and to satisfy that curiosity at all possible times. If something was going on—

Kerensky quickened his stride, hurried to the Texaco station, rather distractedly paid for the tires, got into his car, and drove back to the Dairy Queen. He knew not to stop. No man likes to be disturbed if he is talking with an information source, and that other man, the one Kerensky didn't recognize except that he looked a little like the chief and like the two men in the car yesterday, was probably an information source.

He drove into the Pizza Hut parking lot, which also served as the access to his own driveway. He entered his driveway and turned to look back at the Dairy Queen.

Steve Hansen was no longer in his own car. He was in the other man's car. He was *driving* the other man's car, which seemed a little odd.

Kerensky decided it was clearly his duty to follow. At sufficient distance that he wouldn't be spotted, of course.

"Who's your friend?" the man asked.

"What friend?" Hansen spoke rather stiffly. The pistol pointed at his rib cage did not encourage long, or free, discussion.

"The one behind us. In the orange van."

"Damned if I know." Hansen fiddled with the rearview mirror. He hadn't the slightest idea why Kerensky had decided to follow but was glad he had.

"Take a good look," the man said in a rather ironic voice.

"He looks to me like a kid." So he did, Hansen thought, a kid with absolutely nothing in his face to show how he had lived the last few years. "Could be practicing his tailing techniques."

"Do 'kids' "—the man's voice mocked the word—"normally practice tailing techniques?"

"You never know," Hansen said, and looked again at Kerensky. "This one does look familiar. Seems to me he's a reporter. I've seen him around the police station once or twice. Not a full-fledged reporter, a journalism intern if you know what I mean by that."

"I know," the man said.

"You still haven't told me the reason—"

"I'll tell you soon enough," the man said. "Turn right at the next corner."

"You're not from around here," Hansen said. "Even if you hadn't told me that I'd have known from the way you speak. So how do you know—"

"I scouted out the location," the man said. "We're going to a warehouse, presently abandoned. I obtained the key to it, on the grounds that I am considering moving my business here."

"And you wouldn't tell me that if you didn't intend to kill me."

"The woman I obtained the key from can describe me as well as you can. I have no orders to kill you. And no reason, if you do what I tell you to do. I don't kill needlessly. Such a thing would be foolish. Turn left at the next corner."

Hansen turned. "You're no amateur," he said.

"No. I am no amateur. Your reporter friend has followed us."

"I noticed. Do you want me to try to lose him?"

"That will not be necessary. If he continues to be a nuisance I will know how to deal with him. Turn right in the middle of the block."

"That dirt road?"

"Yes."

Hansen turned. Kerensky did not follow, and Hansen didn't know whether to be relieved for Kerensky's sake or even more frightened for his own sake. The dirt road ran only to the warehouse the man had spoken of; Hansen knew that before he turned and did not know whether Kerensky would remember or not. He and Kerensky had taken this road two or three times in the last few days, out patroling, hunting flood victims, later hunting possible looters and checking places looters might have decided to store their goods.

"Get out of the car," the man said. "As soon as you are out of the car, put your hands behind the back of your neck and interlace your fingers. Don't try anything stupid. I would prefer to keep you alive. But doing so is not essential."

I know that road, Kerensky thought. *If he's doing something secret he won't want me to follow him there. So I'd better not. I'll go eat breakfast. Probably by the time I'm through he'll be through with whatever he's doing and I can ask him about it. He'll tell me what he can.*

"My orders are to kill the boy," the man said persuasively, waving the pistol in front of Hansen's face. "I have no interest in anybody else. Just the boy. You don't know the boy; you've never even seen him. Why should you risk your doubtless very interesting life, sacrifice your own comfort, to keep alive a child you've never seen? All you have to do is tell me—"

He doesn't know, Hansen thought, trying to move his wrists, bound with his own handcuffs threaded through the legs of the chair, enough to ease the strain on his shoulders. *He doesn't know I do know Daniel. And I don't believe that Daniel's the only person he's after. Even if I did know, I can't tell—but I don't know if I can manage not to tell.*

"I can make you tell me anything," the man said. "If you saw Omori after he died, you know that. Did you see Omori?"

"Yes," Hansen said. Despite the chill of the empty warehouse, he could feel cold sweat in his armpits, his groin, as well as on his face. "Were you there? I thought it was just—"

"I wasn't there," the man said. "But I didn't have to be there to know. Just like you don't have to see it again to know that I can make you tell me anything I want to know."

Hansen wriggled uncomfortably. "You probably can," he agreed. "But cop killing is generally pretty stupid, you know. I realize Yamagata sent you to wipe out Daniel—the boy. But he might not want you to kill a cop to find out where Daniel is."

"So you know about Yamagata. Did it cross your mind it might not have been wise for you to tell me that?"

"If I know about Yamagata, how many other people do you think know about Yamagata? More than you can rub out. I know—and several hundred other people know—that Yamagata was behind the murder of his daughter and son-in-law. That Yamagata was behind the killing in the jail. That it's Yamagata who wants his grandson murdered. But none of those people are—uh—personally important to cops." (And he was lying about that, but this man might not know it.) "If it gets too hard to prove, the cops might stop trying to prove it. But you kill a cop—especially the way you're talking about killing me—and the other cops will never stop looking. And you know just as well as I do that the first time you touch me with a knife you've committed to killing me."

"Buddy doesn't care about cop killing."

"Maybe not. Not if he's ordered it. Not if he's planned for it. But I'm betting you've been out of contact with him for a few days. So you haven't cleared this one with him. And—you know what, mister? If I were you, I'd check with him. Because if you do what he doesn't want done, the next one to go under the knife is going to be you. And tough as you are, I still don't figure you'd like that one bit more than I would."

Hansen stopped talking and watched the man. *He's thinking about it,* he thought. *I might have caught his attention.*

Not that it'll change anything. Of course if he calls Yamagata, Yamagata'll tell him to go right ahead, and he probably knows that. Because it's not just Daniel he's after, no matter what he says. He's already committed to killing Shigata. And if he's willing to kill Shigata he's willing to kill me. But if I can make him think about it first, I can buy a little more time. Maybe time enough for somebody to start wondering where I am. And if somebody wonders, sooner or later Kerensky will find out somebody's wondering. And Kerensky knows where I am.

The man sat quite still for a moment. Then he stood up, turned, and walked out the door, and Hansen breathed a little easier for a moment. But only for a moment, because the man returned with a briefcase. He set the briefcase down on the chair he had been sitting in, and opened the briefcase. Inside it was the gleam of metal. *Oh, God, no,* Hansen thought, and he tried to turn his face away so that he wouldn't see the knife.

"I'm going to have to seize the cash," Fong said. "I suppose Omori intended it as part of his son's inheritance, but as there's no doubt whatever that it's the proceeds of organized crime—"

"I'm not arguing," Shigata said. "Don't worry about the child. I'll take care of him. It's these that I'm interested in." He was sorting tape recordings, each one carefully labeled with the date, the subject of discussion, the names of those talking, and the place it was recorded.

"Are we going to be able to use them, Harry?" Clement asked. "Considering we couldn't get court orders to tap the phones ourselves—"

"I'll have to hear what's on them," Fong said. "But yes, the law specifically covers this kind of thing. Exactly *how* we're going to use them I won't know, not until we've checked into it a little more—"

"Start with this one," Shigata said, holding out a tape labeled YAMAGATA-KENICHI. STORAGE LOCATIONS. The date on it was six months ago.

"Yamagata-Kenichi," Fong read. "Kenichi, that's Yamagata's head attorney. I've got known tape recordings of both their voices, so we can verify with voiceprints that that's really them. But that's going to be stale information."

Shigata knew the law on stale information. A search warrant could be issued only on fresh information, and most of the time that was defined as within the last two or three days. But if, as he hoped, the taped voices spoke of permanent locations, then perhaps he and Fong and Clement all together could think of a way around that law.

"How long will that take?" Shigata asked. "The voiceprints, I mean? I've never used them."

Fong grinned at him. "I had the voiceprint expert standing by in my office. I hoped for something like this. And just in case not all these tapes are in English, I've got a couple of Japanese interpreters standing by also, not that voiceprints are affected by language. And stenos have been called in to transcribe everything. Mr. Shigata, I understand the need for haste. George explained it to me pretty thoroughly. We'll be ready to move fast."

"Did he also explain the need for secrecy?" Shigata asked bluntly. "From what I hear, the security in your office—"

"Is good," Fong interrupted. "But just in case, did you think George went back to bed last night after you talked with him? He didn't. He called me first. And he and I both did some more telephoning. The voiceprint expert was flown up from Los Angeles. We're using stenos on loan from CIA headquarters; they flew in overnight. They brought the interpreters with them, also from the CIA. The only one of my own people we're using is me. I know you don't know me. But I know me. Later—we've got a few other things planned. You'll see."

Shigata looked at Clement. Clement said, "You'll see."

With that, for the moment, Shigata had to be content.

"You're crying," the man said softly.

"No, I'm not," Hansen said. The sharpness of the pain

had brought tears to his eyes, had started his nose running. But that was an involuntary neurological reaction, he told himself. He wasn't crying. Not yet.

He wasn't even really injured. Not yet. His shivering was from fear and the actual physical cold that came from his jacket and shirt being pulled open to his shoulders, his undershirt slit in front, his jeans unzipped and his undershorts pushed down so that his whole chest and abdomen were bare. The cold was from cold, not from shock. He wasn't into shock, not yet.

Using the flat of the knife blade, the man pushed Hansen's cheek, turning Hansen to face him. For a long moment, the men's eyes met, and to Hansen, it was like staring at a robot, a zombie. But not quite. There was intelligence there, but no emotion whatever. The man literally did not care what he was doing to Hansen. He was not disgusted; he was deriving no pleasure from the torture. What he was doing was completely impersonal. And that perhaps was the most frightening thing of all.

"Well, maybe not," the man said. "Not yet. But you will be."

Hansen didn't answer that. There was no use in answering.

Carefully, with the skill of a craftsman, the man cut a slit in the sensitive skin of Hansen's lower abdomen, toward the left side, and Hansen heard the sobbing of his own loud breath. But he still wasn't quite crying. Not yet.

"Well," the man said in a louder voice, "I'll leave you to think about it for a while. I have a phone call to make." He pulled the pants, shirt, and jacket almost closed, and that hurt, too. "Wouldn't want you to catch cold while I'm gone."

His receding footsteps were loud, and then began to fade away, on the hollow wood of the warehouse floor, and Hansen closed his eyes, let his head slump foward, and tried to turn his mind and his sensations off. It didn't work very well.

"Yes, sir. Yes—just a minute, I'm writing it down, did you want to talk to Mr. Shigata? Damn—" The stenographer hung up, turned. "Is there a Mark Shigata here?"

"Me," Shigata said quickly. "What is it?"

"Telephone message just came in for you."

"Let me have it."

If you want Sergeant Steve Hansen back alive, have somebody take Daniel Omori to Galveston and leave him in the mall. We cannot return Hansen unharmed. He has already been harmed. But the harm so far is superficial, though from the way he feels he cannot tell that. You can prevent permanent damage to him. You have one hour to comply. If there is any attempt to keep surveillance on Daniel Omori, Hansen will not be returned.

He dialed familiar numbers, and a familiar voice answered. "Quinn."

"Al—" Shigata read the message. "Is it a hoax? Hansen is supposed to be with Lissa—"

"It's not a hoax," Quinn said somberly. "Lissa sent him out early this morning to get Tylenol because the boy had an earache. Just before he left, he got a phone call to meet an informant at the Dairy Queen. He told Lissa he'd be gone maybe half an hour, and nobody's seen him since. His car's still at the Dairy Queen."

"Any ideas about the informant?"

"No. Dispatch says they asked first for you, and then for me. I was at the hospital—Joe slashed his finger trying to peel an orange with scissors because Nguyen had the paring knife, and he had to have six stitches. By the time I got home Hansen was missing. We've been—trying to decide what to do next."

"Let me call you back," Shigata said, appalled to find himself thinking, *If it had to be you or Hansen I'm glad it wasn't you.* He hung up and went looking for Clement, to ask for federal help.

"What good would it do?" Clement asked. "I couldn't even have agents down from Houston in an hour. And I don't have any right to. There is no real evidence that this is a federal crime. I don't have any authority either to hunt for your friend or place a guard on your wife."

"What does it take—"

"You were in the Bureau nineteen years," Clement said. "Don't pretend you don't know how things work. I know he's your friend. I'm sorry. But I have to follow the rules."

Shigata suggested something Clement could do with the rules. Then he reached for the telephone book. "Yamagata," he said a couple of minutes later, "give me two hours instead of one."

"What are you talking about?" Yamagata's voice was suave, slightly amused.

"You know what I'm talking about. Hansen. Call your wolf off. Give me two hours. One isn't enough."

"I'm sure I don't know what you're talking about," Yamagata said. "I don't know any Hansen. I have set no deadlines for anything. But if somebody had set me a one-hour deadline, Mr. Shigata, I think I would try to meet it." A click, then the dial tone returned.

Feeling sick, Shigata called Quinn again. "You're on your own," he said. "I couldn't get any federal help. See what you can get from state and county. Al, we can't give them Daniel."

"I know. So does Hansen. Chief, I'll do what I can. In the law and outside it."

"Thanks." And that was all there was to say. Last time Quinn had used all his resources, inside the law and outside it, he'd had outlaw bikers out hunting for a missing child. What would he do this time?

What *could* he do this time?

I have too much imagination, Shigata thought.

I have too much imagination, Hansen thought. The man—his captor—still wasn't back from wherever he'd gone. The pain had let up some, was little more than dull omnipresent throbbing. But Hansen couldn't keep his eyes off the knife, off the briefcase that held other metal he couldn't quite make out.

He hadn't cried before. But like it or not, he was crying now.

11

"MARK!" GEORGE CLEMENT CALLED. "Will you come back here to the law library with me?"

At the moment Shigata had no inclination to do anything Clement wanted him to do. But habit, and the need for cooperation, outweighed emotional impulses. Wondering whether his anger still showed on his face, he followed. The overhead lights were out in the long, book-lined room, and when Shigata reached for the switch Clement caught his hand and said, "No."

As his eyes adjusted to the glow of the one lamp that was on, Shigata could see that Fong and two other men were already present at the far end of the large table away from the door.

Shigata pulled out a chair near the door, and Fong said, "Come this way."

Shigata shoved the chair back in and approached the group, pulling out a chair across from the two strangers beside Clement. Fong was already seated at the head of the table. Now he said, very quietly, "We weren't taking your worries lightly, Mr. Shigata. We already knew there were some leaks in my organization. When I took over several years ago we identified—and disposed of—two leaks. We've still got at least one left. This operation is going to get rid of him."

"Mark, these are Jerry Meyer and Will Long," Clement said.

"Good," Shigata said, eyeing the two men, who to his

educated eye appeared to be FBI agents. "Now you want to tell me which is which?"

"I'm Meyer." Meyer must have barely squeaked by the Bureau's height and weight requirements, because he looked small even to Shigata, himself not a large man. His black hair was curly; his brown eyes and rather prominent nose were set in a face so fair as to seem pale.

"Which makes me Long," the other man said, reaching across the table as Meyer hadn't to shake hands. Long would have looked dark in any company, as his skin approached ebony in coloring, but beside Meyer he looked even darker. Despite his coloring, his features had the extremely sharp angularity Shigata associated with the Nilotic peoples of Africa. "I gather you're Shigata. We've been in here since four o'clock this morning."

"Okay," Shigata said, wondering why he was being told that.

"You should have gotten the idea there was something going on," Fong said, "when I shut out *all* of my own people. Those of us in this room are the only attorneys in this operation. This means nobody else would have any reason to use the law library. Which means Long and Meyer were well hidden. And will remain well hidden when the rest of us all—rather ostentatiously—go out for lunch together in a little while."

"Thing is," Clement took up the tale, "normally he—or she, it could be a woman—could wait and grab the evidence whenever the time looked right. But this time Harry let it be known to his people that although they weren't included in the operation he wanted them to know enough so they wouldn't interfere. 'Stay out of the office on Saturday,' he told them, 'because Saturday morning we're going after the evidence to nail Yamagata, and right after lunch we're using the evidence to take out warrants.' "

"Which means," Fong said, "that the only time whoever it is can grab the evidence is during lunchtime. And even that would be taking a chance. But it's a chance he'll have to take."

"Why are you telling me now?" Shigata asked.

"Because none of the suspects knows you," Clement said. "So—if you decided to skip lunch and take a nap in the lounge—"

"I see."

And he did see. He'd go along with the plan; he wanted to be in on taking whoever came in to steal the evidence. But—he couldn't stop worrying about things at home.

And a little knot of anger was growing in him, so much so that when they stood up to leave he grabbed Clement's arm and asked, not caring who inside the room heard him, "Why did you put just a black and a Jew on it?"

"For security," Clement said. "Nobody will ever accuse either of them of being Yakuza."

"So you couldn't trust any sansei?"

"I don't even know what a sansei is."

"You'd probably say nisei. But of course you wouldn't know the difference. A nisei is an American with Japanese parents. A sansei is the descendant of a nisei."

"So now I know the difference. No. I didn't know the difference. Why should I?"

"No reason. Since you couldn't find any you could trust."

"I trust you," Clement said. "I trust a lot of people. But on this operation, I didn't want anybody to be able to say, later, that I'd maybe stacked the decks."

"So if you'd been moving against the Mafia, you wouldn't have used anybody with an Italian last name? Never mind. If you told me that I wouldn't believe it."

"Mark, what the hell has gotten into you?"

"Never mind," Shigata said again. "If you have to ask me that now, then you never would understand. Go on and get your lunch."

"Right. I'm going."

And behind him, as Shigata headed for the door, he could hear Will Long saying, "Right on, brother."

Shigata turned. "I don't mind either of you. It's just—"

"I know," Meyer said. "Believe me. I know." He watched

as Clement opened the door and let Fong and Shigata precede him out, and he was still watching when Shigata glanced back before the door closed.

Hansen woke with a start and had no idea how long he'd slept—a minute, an hour—because there was no clock and he couldn't see his watch. His hands were still bound behind him with his own handcuffs; his ankles were still bound with wire to the legs of the chair he was sitting in. His clothing was still loosely tucked closed over his bare chest and abdomen; he was still cold, and pain still throbbed through him, more now because the position he was in was cramping the muscles of his shoulders, straining the tendons. However long it had been—and it had been long enough that he was thirsty and needed to pee—his captor was still gone.

He wasn't worried about not being found; sooner or later Kerensky would insinuate himself far enough into whatever was going on that the right things would be said and Kerensky would tell the department where he'd been seen last. That being the case, the longer his captor stayed gone the better it would be for him.

But he'd made up his mind to die, if he had to, to shield Daniel Omori, to shield Melissa and Gail Shigata. In one part of his mind he recognized how cockeyed the reasoning was, but in another part of his mind he couldn't help thinking, *I couldn't save my own wife, I couldn't save my own daughter, but maybe—maybe—I can forgive myself for that, if I can stick this out, if I can—not let—this murderer find Lissa and Daniel and Gail.*

If he could do it. And not for the first time, he wished he had just a little less imagination.

Saito sat comfortably on a bench in the mall, smoking. He didn't expect trouble. He also didn't expect to see the boy. The *oyabun* should have had better sense than to make that offer. People were ridiculously sentimental about children;

almost nobody would be willing to exchange the life of a grown man, already busy and active and involved, for the life of a small child who at best was no more than potential. But most likely the *oyabun* knew that. Most likely the *oyabun*, in giving Shigata the apparent choice, was really only twisting the knife in Shigata.

In his mind, Saito chuckled at that. The *oyabun* really had it in for Shigata. Not for the first time, he wondered just exactly how Shigata had succeeded in pissing off the *oyabun* so thoroughly.

He glanced at his watch. Twenty minutes left of the hour. He'd sit here and wait the entire hour, to play fair. After that—well, there was no hurry getting back to the man. Maybe he'd go get something to eat first. A little late for lunch—it would be after two by the time the hour was up—but his body was still on San Francisco time, and it would be just past noon there. Anyway, he hadn't eaten yet this morning; he'd been busy. If he had Hansen figured right—and he was pretty sure he did, Saito usually figured people right—Hansen was intelligent and imaginative. The more intelligent and imaginative a man was, the more scared he would be likely to get if he had time to think about it. And the more scared he was, the more easily he broke. Usually. Not always. In Saito's work there was no always.

Not that Hansen was going to be scared enough to give him the address the minute he walked in. He'd still have to force it out of him. People were tiresome that way, making him force information out of them when they had to know from the start that they'd give it to him sooner or later. It was boring. But if that was the way they wanted it to be, well, that was the way it was going to be.

The police car was at the Dairy Queen. That had to be the starting point, asking around the neighborhood, were you outside about seven, seven-thirty this morning, if you were what did you see?

Quinn looked around at his pitifully small search group.

Corporal Ted Barlow, just turned twenty-five. Officer Paul Ames and Officer Susa Gonzales, both twenty-four. All three of them dead tired because they'd worked deep night—twelve to eight, and Gonzales had a baby keeping her up the part of the night she *was* at home. But Quinn didn't dare pull any more people off the already pitifully small group on daylight patrol in a still-flooded town. Gere Phillips, that was the best he could do. And he still wasn't too happy about the whole idea of having Gere Phillips on the same police department he was on. Shigata had said when it came to hiring he didn't care if somebody was black, white, or chartreuse; male, female, or indeterminate. They didn't have any chartreuse police yet, but Gere Phillips, though technically male, didn't seem any too sure about his gender.

But he did know how to police, and his aim was deadly. Quinn had sent him over to guard Melissa and told Melissa that he didn't care if Daniel had ten earaches she wasn't to send anybody out to get Tylenol again. Of course, she wouldn't need to, because he'd also told Phillips to stop on the way to get Tylenol.

Anything else she ran out of she could damn well do without until they had Hansen back and the ninja dead or behind bars.

It was true that Quinn could lift a telephone and get twenty or thirty more people up from Galveston County. But he'd decided against that. Whoever had Hansen might, if he saw too large a group coming against him, kill Hansen and slip out and never be caught until he came back to get the Shigata family another way. Or maybe until *after* he came back to get the Shigata family another way.

With this small a group coming after him, he might not spook.

With this small a group, it would take longer to find Hansen, and Hansen wouldn't be enjoying that time. But Quinn had spent several years in a Vietcong prison camp. He knew, coldly, that the human body can endure far more than the person living in that body thinks it can. Hansen wouldn't like the time spent finding him, but he'd survive it. And even at the worst, Quinn profoundly believed, life is worth living.

And once it was over, Hansen—with that cockeyed sense of humor he had—was going to enjoy being able to tell the story of how he was abducted by a ninja.

Quinn began to tell the group what was going on.

"But I don't get it," Ames said, after listening intently. "This guy says to turn the kid loose at the mall—that means he'll be waiting at the mall. So why don't we just go pick him up there?"

"Think about it some more, Paul," said Barlow, who clearly did understand.

"I thought about doing that," Quinn said, "but I decided against it. A, we don't really know that he'll be at the mall. He might plan to go there later, or he might have somebody else—possibly some perfectly innocent citizen—there to pick the boy up. B, if he is at the mall, we wouldn't be able to take him without a firefight, and I am not willing to risk that many lives. And C, if he is at the mall and we do manage to take him alive, there's no chance at all he'll tell us where he's stashed Hansen. Which means we'd still have to look for Hansen, and Hansen could die while we were searching. This way, we start looking for Hansen to begin with, and if there's a firefight no civilians are involved. Make sense now?"

"Yeah, but—" Ames began, his tone of voice suggesting he didn't quite understand.

"You don't know much about ninjas," Barlow interrupted. "Quinn's right. There's no way in hell we could take him in public, not without him taking out half the mall."

Gonzales hadn't said anything. She was just listening, interestedly, and now she hoisted her basketweave gunbelt—she was still taking it in a notch every now and then, after recent childbirth—and said, "Let's get on with it."

"You're not going to lunch?"

Shigata, establishing his cover by lying down on the red

leather sofa in the lounge, looked up to see Karoku "Cary" Okuma, one of the CIA interpreters and, Shigata strongly suspected, a CIA agent as well. "No," he said, "I didn't get much sleep last night. I'd be better off trying to grab a couple of winks before we start writing search warrants."

"Right," Okuma said, stepping the rest of the way into the room and closing the heavy door behind himself. "Your wife is in danger and you're pretty sure one of your men is being tortured and you're taking a nap. You know, I really believe that. Mole hunting?"

"What?" Shigata said.

"You heard me. You're mole hunting, aren't you?"

Shigata took a deep breath. "Yes. I'm mole hunting. Now leave me with it."

"I thought I'd stay and help you."

"Get lost," Shigata said roughly. "The Company doesn't work inside the United States."

Okuma's quick grin confirmed Shigata's suspicions. "Ah, but I'm on loan," he said. He pulled a heavy red-leather lounge chair over closer to Shigata. "Let me in on this," he said. "You know as well as I do, stuff like this makes us look bad."

"Stuff like what?" Shigata asked carefully.

"Man, what are we working on? Stuff like the Yakuza. And Yakuza moles inside the Justice Department. There's enough—blind prejudice. We don't need anything that's going to fan the flames. Let me in on this."

"I don't know you," Shigata said.

Okuma got out of the chair and sat down on the floor so that his head was close enough to Shigata's he could talk almost soundlessly. "Don't you? But I feel like I know you."

"Why?"

"When I was a kid, I lived in Topaz. You were born there. Weren't you?"

For a moment Shigata felt he'd been kicked in the gut. Finally he said, "Yes. How did you—"

"Know? After a while they set up schools. My mother was

a schoolteacher. They let her teach. So in the daytime, when she was teaching, a neighbor lady baby-sat me. Her name was Sue Shigata. She had a baby, name of Mark. You. Right?"

It took a moment before Shigata could make himself say, "Yes. Me."

"You want them to rebuild Topaz?" Okuma asked in a conversational tone.

"Are you crazy?"

"No. But I'm telling you, the way race hatred is growing in this country—the way it's being fanned—if we don't want them to rebuild Topaz and the other places like it, we've got to clean our own house."

"Who's *we*? Ninety percent of the sansei wouldn't know a Yakuza if they saw one, much less what to do with one."

"Isn't sansei a bad word right now?" Okuma asked. "I'm out of the country so much, I can't keep straight what's politically correct."

"The hell with politically correct," Shigata said. "What I'm saying—"

"I don't mean we the sansei," Okuma said. "I mean you and me. And however many other Japanese-Americans—there, that's usually okay—are in law enforcement. Especially around here and in Hawaii, where the Yakuza are strong."

"I don't know about you people in the Company," Shigata said, "but personally, I prefer to work inside the law. I'm not setting up any private vigilante squads, even against the Yakuza."

"Well, no," Okuma agreed, "but if we can just get the Yamagata family out of business—and I don't want to see Topaz again. Or anything like it."

"The Mafia has been powerful in this country for over fifty years," Shigata said. "I don't see them building any concentration camps for Italians."

"Ah," Okuma said, "but you can't always look at a man and tell he's Italian."

"You can't always look at a man and tell that he's

Japanese," Shigata said. "Or that he's not. Ask Fong how many people have mistaken his racial background."

"That's different," Okuma said. "The Italians are white. We aren't. Not that I'd want to be; I like me just fine. Shigata, I'm not saying I'm prejudiced against people for what they are or aren't. I hope I'm not. I try not to be. But I have to realize how many people have unreasoning prejudice against me. I can't change that. But anything I can do to get rid of anything that might provide real reasons for the prejudice, I want to do. Like do all I can do to get the Yakuza out of the United States."

"Yakuza, go home," Shigata said. "Like Yankee go home. Think it would do any good if we painted it as graffiti?"

"I wish," Okuma said. "But you can understand why I was glad they let me in on this one. Now, I'll say it again. If you're mole hunting, I want to stay and help."

Shigata thought about it. He didn't mind the silence as he thought, and figured Okuma wouldn't either. Finally he said, "The thing is, I'm afraid somebody might notice you didn't go to lunch with the others."

"The way people were milling around out there, even if they were outside counting I don't think they'd notice. Anyway, everybody's gone now. They'd be more likely to notice if I *did* go charging out this late."

"Then I guess you're on it," Shigata said. "We've got two FBI agents in the law library. You and me in here. No more talking. Listen."

Okuma didn't ask what they were listening for. Like Shigata, he just listened.

"Before you start, will you listen to me a minute?" Hansen said, hating the quiver he could hear in his voice.

"Sure," the man said, pausing, the knife in his hand. "I'll hear what you've got to say."

"It's this," Hansen said, then hesitated a moment. The man didn't say anything. He just waited. "I know—" Hansen began, and swallowed hard. "I know what you can do to me. I know you can make me cry. I know you can make me scream. I know you can make me beg for mercy. But—you can't make me tell you where anybody is, for very deep-rooted psychological reasons that make telling you more painful to me than any physical pain you can lay on me. I wouldn't—if you were a sadist I wouldn't bother telling you that because it wouldn't matter, you wouldn't care. But I don't think you are a sadist. I think you—I think you are a professional. And a professional doesn't want to waste his time. And that's what you're doing."

"I'll take my chances on that," the man said, his tone completely matter-of-fact. "See—I'm a real good shrink. I can get past those psychological reasons."

Hansen turned his head again, wondering as he did it what difference it made whether he saw the knife or not, and said hopelessly, "Don't. Please don't—"

"Now you're wasting your time. Don't talk to me again until you have something I want to hear."

But he's forgotten Kerensky, Hansen thought even as he broke into harsh sobbing. He's forgotten Kerensky. *Kerensky, where the hell are you? Kerensky, help me, in the name of God I'm begging, help me, you're the only one that can, except God—God, help me—help me—*

And Kerensky walked into the police station.

"Get lost, Kerensky," said Marshall Tyler, who was serving as both dispatcher and desk officer.

"I just wanted to talk to Steve Hansen," Kerensky said stiffly.

"So do we all."

"Pardon?"

"Look, you stupid Russki, Hansen is *missing,*" Tyler said. "And if you think we've got time to cope with you right now—"

"How long has he been missing?"

"Since early this morning. And—"

"But I saw him just before eight," Kerensky said. "He was

with another man, driving the other man's car."

With that, Tyler would have run into the muster room, except that a motorcycle accident when he was sixteen had ensured that he would never run anywhere again. So instead he dialed the intercom number, and when Quinn—temporarily back checking maps—answered by saying, "What is it, Tyler?" he said, "I've got a guy out here who might know where Hansen is."

"Who is it?" Quinn asked sharply.

"That Russian. Kerensky."

"Call the squad. And send Kerensky back."

And ten minutes later Kerensky was thrilled beyond measure when Quinn, totally illegally, issued him a rifle. A rifle, because nobody on this mission would be carrying shotguns. On the basis of the telephone message Shigata had received, Quinn figured Hansen and the ninja—and even if, as Shigata insisted, the man wasn't really a ninja at all, it was easier to call him the ninja than to call him nothing at all—would be too close together for shotguns to be used. Shotguns aren't called scatterguns for no reason. The pellets spread. And there was no use killing Hansen in the course of rescuing him.

Hansen had stopped crying. He'd tried, futilely, to turn his head far enough to wipe his nose on the shoulder of his jacket, and he had now resigned himself to breathing through an extremely stopped-up nose. He was light-headed now, and startlingly relaxed despite the pain; he guessed he might be well on the road to either losing consciousness or going into shock, and whichever it was, he was going to welcome it. His breathing now was very deep, slightly irregular, and each breath ended in something between a sigh and a sob. But that was all right. That was all right.

He remembered reading, when his constant reading had taken him on a jag of medieval witch trials, about accused witches going to sleep on the rack. He hadn't believed it, then, had assumed that in fact they had gone into shock, or had fainted. He believed it now. The pain wasn't any less. But his utter exhaustion was so great that if he didn't faint first, he'd be going to sleep shortly. In fact, he was already doing it. He woke again, with a small cry of pain, with every cut, then slept for the seconds or fractions of seconds between cuts. His wife, if she had been alive, could have told him that sometimes women who've been in labor a long time sleep like that, between contractions, half waking to dazed suffering whenever a contraction starts, but in her lifetime she'd been too shy to talk to him about things like that, so he didn't know.

He heard the ninja mutter, "Damn it, he shouldn't be like this this fast." The ninja backed away from him, and the knife was no longer touching him.

He meant to say, "It's because I didn't sleep much last night and I was drunk the night before so the sleep wasn't worth much."

He wondered why the ninja was digging through his briefcase. "Looking for something?" he wanted to ask.

But he was too tired to say any of it now. He'd say it later. His head slumped forward. He was asleep.

Once a man begins to escape into his own body, he's beginning to get harder to break. Saito was extremely annoyed. He'd have thought this man was stronger than that. Letting him rest now was not mercy; it was common sense. Give him a little rest, a little water, he'd be stronger, he'd live longer. There were ways of waking him up, but they had to be applied judiciously, or else he'd be gone before he could provide any information.

Give him a little time. Saito would judge how much time.

"Looking for something?" Shigata asked softly.

The man turned quickly, and his fast indrawn breath belied whatever tale he was going to tell.

He was Anglo. That was the first thing Shigata noticed about him. He was Anglo. So he couldn't possibly have been working for the Yakuza out of any sense of ideological loyalty no matter how misguided. He was working for Yamagata for money, or he was working for Yamagata because he'd been blackmailed into it. Either way, he was beneath contempt.

This couldn't have been the person who "lost" the evidence ten years before. Ten years ago, this man would have been in high school. He couldn't be much past twenty-five, twenty-six, even now. He was blond, blue-eyed, very fair-skinned. He didn't get out in the sun much. He was a little too thin, and there was something about him that reminded Shigata a little of a rabbit and a little of a ferret.

He still hadn't answered.

"Looking for something?" Long drawled, and the man turned that way even more quickly.

Then he looked back at Shigata and Okuma. Back at Long and Meyer.

"Got it in one," Okuma said. "Or do you need us to spell it out for you? Guess what. You're surrounded. And now it's my turn to say it. Looking for something?"

"I—uh—I left something up here yesterday. Needed it—came up to get it—" He was gabbling, snatching for words.

"Is that your desk?" Meyer asked, sounding extremely interested.

"Uh—yeah. Yeah. That's my desk."

"So your name must be Fong," Shigata said. "Funny thing, you don't *look* Chinese."

Meyer laughed at that, and the man looked quickly at him. "What is your name?" Meyer asked.

"Uh—Andrews."

"Andrews what? Or what Andrews?"

"Damon Andrews," the man said, sounding a little more confident. "I work in this office. Really. Ask Mr. Fong. I'm a law clerk."

"Poor little boy couldn't pass his exams?" Long inquired.

"I'll—uh—I'll pass them next time. Really."

"Sure you will," Meyer agreed genially. "Provided they give them inside prison."

"Now wait a minute," Andrews began to protest. "I don't like that kind of threat."

"Who's making a threat?" Meyer asked. "Was I making a threat? I was just saying I don't think they give law exams in prison. And now I guess it's my turn to ask. Looking for something? Because whatever you're looking for, I don't think it's on that tape recording."

Andrews looked down at the boxed audiotape, forgotten in his hand, and put it hastily down on the table. "I just picked it up to see what it was."

"Did you see enough to satisfy you?" Shigata asked.

"Well, I—uh—yes. I was just curious. See, I misplaced my pen, and it's a nice one, my girl gave it to me for a graduation present, and I couldn't remember where I left it, and I thought, you know, I might have left it in here on Mr. Fong's desk."

"Right," Long said. "Andrews, I've been watching you for five minutes."

"What?"

"I said I've been watching you for five minutes. I saw you open the vault to look for evidence. I'll find out later how you knew how to get the vault open. For now let me identify myself. I'm Willie Lee Long, Federal Bureau of Investigation, and you're under arrest for evidence tampering. Don't bother taking the tapes back out of your coat pockets. Those aren't the real tapes anyway. The real tapes are safely put away where you won't find them. Those are blank tapes we bought this morning. We just put them in the other boxes. And now, Mr. Andrews, you're coming into the law library with me, like a good little boy."

"I demand the right to call my attorney."

"You'll get it, as soon as questioning starts," Meyer said. "But right now nobody's asking you anything. And nobody's going to ask you anything. I'm just telling you that I'm Gerald Meyer, Federal Bureau of Investigation. And since you're a Justice Department employee just like we are, Mr. Andrews, I'm sure you won't mind that we're just going to sit in the law library, you and me and Mr. Long there, and be nice and friendly and not say a word to each other for about the next ten hours. Maybe not that much. We'll see how long it takes."

"You can't hold me incommunicado—"

"You want to make a bet we can't?" Long asked genially. "The only question is whether it's at gunpoint or not. I don't really like guns, see, and I won't have to draw mine at all if you'll just walk nice and quiet into the law library and sit down and, oh, maybe, find a good book to read. There, a few hours of absolute peace and quiet to study for your exam, isn't that just what you need? And after a while, if you're a good little boy, Mr. Meyer will go out and get you a Coke and a sandwich. But for now, you just keep your mouth shut so I don't have to tape it shut, got me?"

As Andrews headed for the door to the law library, Long turned to look at Shigata. He raised his eyebrows a little at Okuma but didn't say anything to him. He just gestured toward the lounge, and Shigata nodded. He and Okuma returned to the lounge and almost, but not quite, shut the door.

The second mole came in ten minutes later, pushing the heavy front door to the suite open and saying softly, but not too softly, "Hey, Andy, what's taking so long?" He walked on into the front office, letting the door swing shut behind him. "Andy, hurry it up, they'll be back from lunch in another ten minutes. And the boss doesn't like delays."

"The boss doesn't like failure, either," Shigata said, positioning himself between the man—sansei, this one, at a guess, and Shigata felt half sick with disgust—and the front door.

The man whirled to stare at Shigata, his eyes wide. "How'd you get in here?" he demanded. "And who the hell are you?"

"Oh, just a friend of mine," said another voice. "Don't worry, he's not Yakuza."

And the man whirled again to stare at Long who had approached behind him. "What's going on here?"

"Willie Lee Long, Federal Bureau of Investigation. If you're looking for Damon Andrews, he's in the law library. You're invited to join him there."

"Oh, I think I'll just—" The man began edging toward the door.

"You're invited to join him there," Long repeated, displaying an army-style nine-millimeter automatic that seemed to have appeared by accident in his hand. "And do you perhaps have a name?"

"Yamagata's gonna kill me for this!"

"That's your problem," Shigata said. "Now, what's your name?"

Hansen woke with a cry, feeling his heart pounding in his rib cage twice as hard and fast as usual. He looked, as his eyes began to clear, at the ninja, who was standing, holding a hypodermic. "*Shabu,*" the ninja told him. "Amphetamine. You've had enough of a nap. You'll be awake for quite a while now. Think you can drink something?"

"Yeah," Hansen said, realizing with utter astonishment that at some time while he was asleep the ninja must have washed his face and even wiped his nose. His jeans were wet; his overstrained bladder must have surrendered while he was asleep. Now the ninja was holding a cup of water so he could drink.

Maybe if he didn't drink it he'd die faster. He was beginning to give up hope that Kerensky had told anybody where he was; if Kerensky hadn't, then the only release he had left to hope for was death. He was thinking now that maybe the reason the ninja had seemed to ignore Kerensky was that the ninja had a backup. *Because Kerensky's such a blabbermouth, if he could tell them where I am he'd have done it by now. So if he didn't there's a reason why he didn't. And I'm afraid the reason is, he's dead.*

If Kerensky's dead then I've bought the farm, and the faster I can die the better off I am. So I shouldn't drink anything. The amphetamine's straining my heart, add thirst to that—

But thirst was stronger than a desire to die that was mental rather than emotional anyway, and he was drinking even as he thought and groaned in wordless protest when the ninja took the cup away.

"That's enough for now," the ninja said. "Now, listen to me. I want you to understand exactly what's happening. I've shot you full of amphetamines. You can't faint. You can't go into shock. You can't go to sleep. You can't even die, until it wears off. You're going to be fully awake and fully alert. And you're going to hurt, and go on hurting, and hurt more than you ever guessed it was possible to hurt, until you tell me what I want to know. Now, I've been easy on you up to now. I don't get any kick out of this. I'm just like anybody else. All I want to do is finish my work and go home. But you're interfering with my work, and you've got to stop. I'm going to make sure you stop. So easy time is over with. You're wondering what's next. I could just do it. But I'm going to tell you first. There are some things a man doesn't even want to think about, much less to do, if you understand what I'm saying. I've not been ordered to kill you, but I've not been ordered to keep you alive. My orders about you are to do whatever I have to do. You're going to give me the information I want. You get to decide whether you give it to me easy, or whether you give it the hard way. A man-you—can spare one nut and still be perfectly functional. If it comes to that. Or you can spare both nuts and still be functional, if a doctor gives you the right hormones. Or—you can be nonfunctional. For the rest of your life. Think about it real hard. Are you really willing to swap that for the life of a kid you don't even know? Now, I've asked you a question. And I want an answer. I know that Shigata's wife has the boy with her. Where is she? That's all I want to know. Just one address. Give it to me. Where is she?"

"Where none so damned as you will ever find her," Hansen shouted out of a confused memory of several different Shakespearean quotations that had run together in his amphetamine-drunken brain. Then he started crying again.

▽

12

"WAIT A MINUTE," Fong said, leaning forward. "Back that tape up. Did he say what I think he said?"

Shigata pushed stop, rewind, waited a moment and pushed play, and all three men clustered around Fong's desk listening intently.

"He said it," Clement said. "And that clears it. Son of a bitch! I'd never have figured him on that one."

"Clears that one, and puts him where we want him," Fong agreed.

"What did I miss?" Shigata said. "I heard him talking about a bomb, and something about winning, but—"

"Not winning," Clement said, a note of joyous relief in his voice. "Win. The name of the victim. Win Hamilton. We just heard him give the order. A federal judge. Makes it a federal crime. That's solid. That's grounds for arrest right there, *and* for searching everything under his control. Harry, let's go write warrants."

Suddenly abandoned in Fong's office as Fong and Clement headed for the steno pool, Shigata reached for the telephone again, meticulously charging the call to his telephone charge card although he knew nobody in this federal office would have noticed, much less cared, if he had put it on the prosecutor's bill. The dispatcher answered. "Tyler?" Shigata said. "What's going on?"

"Quinn's out on it," Tyler answered. "He's got Ames and Barlow and Gonzales with him. And that Russian. Kerensky."

"Why Kerensky?"

"Kerensky thinks he might know where Hansen is."

"Call me when you know something more," Shigata said. "Let me give you the number here."

"Yes, sir," Tyler said, considerately not pointing out that Shigata had given him the same number five times in the last six hours. "I'll let you know."

Then Shigata called another number, less familiar to him, but it was answered by a voice more familiar. "Lissa?" he said. "Are you okay?"

"Yes, but I'm so worried—"

"About Hansen? Yes, so am I. I practically feel like I set him up, but the fact is if he'd followed orders—because I told him not to leave you for any reason—"

"And then they'd have gotten Quinn instead," Lissa said.

"I know," Shigata answered, thinking of the things that he wasn't saying but that he was certain Lissa knew were in his mind. *I'd rather it be me, than Quinn. I think I'd rather it be me than Hansen. And—I know what information they're trying to get. They want to know where Daniel is. Daniel—and Lissa and Gail.*

I know I don't break under torture. I know Quinn doesn't. But Hansen—you never know about Hansen. He's so unpredictable. Sometimes he's the most intelligent guy you'd ever hope to meet and other times you expect him to stick his hand through a fan to reach the switch on the back. Sometimes he's got enough guts for an army and sometimes—but I think he'll hold out.

I just—hope Quinn gets to him fast. For his own sake, not just so he won't reach his breaking point. Because I don't want to think about what he's going through now, whatever it is, and whatever it is, he can't not think about it. Because for him, it's here and it's now.

Find him, Quinn, find him fast.

"And Daniel," Lissa was saying. "He's just got an earache, but you know how kids are at that age. Well, you don't, do you? And neither do I. But he's miserable and he keeps crying and crying—and Hansen's dog, it's out in the yard, we can't bring it in and it keeps trying to bite Phillips so he's having to stay inside now, and the dog keeps howling like it knows. *Mark, what are they doing to him?"*

"To Hansen? I don't know. I wish Quinn hadn't told you—"

"I think I'd have known anyway, the way his dog keeps howling. There's something bad wrong. The dog knows."

"I wonder how far a dog can hear? They hear better than people do, I know that. I wonder—Lissa, I'm going to call dispatch again, be careful, love—"

"Yes, I will—Gere Phillips is here. And the Uzi, Hansen left me the Uzi. He was afraid I couldn't use it. But I could. If I had to. You know I could."

"I know," Shigata said. "I'm going to call the station now."

When Tyler answered, Shigata said, "Look at the city map. Try to figure out how many abandoned buildings, or fairly isolated outdoor locations, there are within three miles of my—of where I'm living now. From what Lissa tells me, the dog might be hearing Hansen. If Kerensky's wrong about where he is—"

"Stand by," Tyler said. And a moment later he was back. "All I find is that warehouse area off Holbrook Road. Most of that is empty, and it's not but about a mile and a half as the crow flies. If—stand by. Go ahead, Car Two."

The door to the warehouse didn't burst open, the way it would have in the movies; in fact, Hansen found out later, they didn't come in the front door, which the ninja had barred, at all. They climbed up the ladder of the loading dock and came in an overhead garage-style door that had been left partly open. Nobody entered running, dressed in black and carrying an Uzi, and the movie-required shootout in the warehouse didn't take place. Hansen didn't hear them enter, and later, thinking about it, he knew that the ninja hadn't heard them either. And yes, Hansen was making some noise, but not that much right then, because the worst of it hadn't started yet (and wouldn't, now) and for the moment at least the amphetamine had strengthened his resolve not to beg. So most of his noise was fast, shallow breathing that he blamed partly on the amphetamine and partly on his own fear, and an occasional cry he couldn't hold back as the ninja, working gradually toward his announced goal, demonstrated to Hansen exactly how sensitive the skin of his lower abdomen really was, saying occasionally, monotonously, "You know how you can stop this."

They came in quietly. But suddenly there they were, four men, one woman, all of them in soft-soled sneakers, and one of the men—incredibly, it looked like Kerensky—had the muzzle of a rifle jabbed under Saito's chin and was shoving him back away from Hansen. "Drop the knife," he said in a voice of hot rage, in the lightly accented English that told Hansen he wasn't seeing things, it really was Kerensky along with four police officers.

Hansen took a long, deep sighing breath as the knife clattered to the wooden floor. "You were just in time," he said.

"Your chest and belly are bleeding like a stuck pig, and there's blood all over your pants," Quinn said. "How bad is it?"

"I don't know," Hansen said. "It hurts bad. It could have been a lot worse. He was gonna—Al, he was gonna—"

"Okay," Quinn said. He took the radio from his belt and spoke into it. "Get me an ambulance at the old Denson's warehouse off Holbrook Road. Ten-thirty-nine."

"Just ten-eighteen," Hansen said quickly.

Quinn looked at him.

"I'm not hurt bad enough for somebody to risk his life getting to me."

"Make that ambulance ten-eighteen," Quinn said. He glanced at the ninja, who balanced lightly on the balls of his feet with Kerensky's rifle still under his chin and Barlow's rifle at the back of his head, while Susa Gonzales handcuffed him and Paul Ames roamed around checking to see if there was anybody else in the warehouse. "Stay on guard, Barlow, Kerensky," Quinn added. "He hasn't given up yet. You can tell by the way he's standing."

"Nor have I given up," Kerensky said. "I would be glad of a reason to shoot."

Ignoring that, Quinn continued, "Ames, there's leg-irons in my car, go get them. Ninja, you kick, you die."

"I'm not a ninja," the ninja said politely.

Quinn turned to take his first good look at the ninja, who, to be sure, did not look like the popular conception of a ninja. He was lean enough, muscular enough, but he was wearing tan twill trousers, a tan twill jacket zipped shut so his shirt was invisible, and tan Hush Puppies. Except for the knife he'd dropped and the pistol Gonzales had relieved him of, he was not visibly armed, although Gonzales was now efficiently patting him down and he'd be given a complete strip search, including visible body cavities, as soon as he got into the jail.

"What the hell took you so long, Kerensky?" Hansen yelled suddenly. "First time I ever *wanted* you to run your mouth—how long did it take you?"

"He didn't know what was happening," Quinn said, using his own handcuff key efficiently.

"I know it—I'm sorry—" Hansen was rubbing his wrists and crying again, in front of his friends as well as his enemy, and he hated himself for doing it.

"Did he give you some kind of shot?" Quinn asked, spotting the abandoned syringe.

"Yeah."

"Any idea what was in it? Your heart is going like a trip hammer."

"He said *shabu,*" Hansen said, not too distinctly. "He said it was an amphetamine. I don't know. It was some kind of stimulant and it was strong, that's all I know. I feel like I'm bouncing off a wall, and I can't stop crying."

"It was just amphetamine," the ninja said. "Three times the normal dose. That's part of why he's crying. It heightens sensations and emotions. Including pain. Including fear. And reduces inhibitions. Including those against crying. And against—talking. You can tell his doctor. But he'll be all right, unless he's got heart trouble, and I figure a cop, he won't have heart trouble. So he'll be all right. Just won't sleep until it wears off, that's all."

"You had best hope he's all right," Kerensky yelled.

"Shut up, Kerensky," Quinn said automatically. "And you can move the rifle out from under his chin, now he's got leg-irons on. Hold still, Steve. I've got to untie your ankles. I can't cut this wire."

"I know—oh, God, that hurts—that hurts—"

"Circulation was partly cut off. It's going to hurt. We've got an ambulance coming," Quinn said patiently, knowing Hansen already knew it.

"I didn't tell him," Hansen said.

"That's obvious." Quinn didn't ask what Hansen hadn't told.

"I didn't tell him. I didn't tell him—I'm sorry, I can't stop crying now—I ought to be able to stop crying—"

"Don't try," Quinn said. "It's okay to cry. I'll hold you—that help any?"

"Yeah," Hansen choked, his face hidden against Quinn's massive chest, Susa Gonzales's hands kneading away some of the muscle spasms in his shoulders. After a long moment, Hansen tried to sit up. "I'm okay now. Al, Susa, thanks, I'm okay now."

"You're not okay," Quinn told him, "and it'll be a long time before you are okay. But you're no worse hurt than Shigata was the day we shot Samford. Probably not as bad hurt, best as I can tell. And you've stopped shaking. So I'll let go of you."

Hansen got up cautiously, leaning on Quinn as he rose, and began to straighten his clothes. "I wouldn't," Quinn said.

"I would," Hansen said, pulling his undershorts back up to just above his waist and closing his fly. His face, pale and drawn, and the sweat beads standing out on his forehead told what that effort at dignity had cost him, and he leaned heavily for a moment on the chair he'd been bound to before straightening again. Then he walked shakily across the room. He paused by Kerensky, still standing alertly by the ninja. "I'm sorry I yelled at you," he said. "Just—I saw you following me. And I kept waiting. And waiting. And then I was afraid he—one of his friends—had killed you. And I was scared. For me, and for you."

"I would not have stopped at the road if I had known—"

"And then you'd have gotten you and me both killed. You did okay." Hansen turned to face the ninja. "What's your name?" he asked.

"Jack Saito." The voice perfectly calm, no anger, no chagrin.

"Why didn't you kill me when they walked in? You had time, you could have, so why didn't you?"

"There was no reason for it," Saito said. "I told you I didn't want to kill you. I don't kill people without a reason. I try to do my job. If I fail they send somebody else in to do it. But killing you wasn't a part of my job." Then, astonishingly, he asked, "Have you ever heard of transactional analysis?"

"Yes," Hansen said, "but what the hell connection—"

"It's obvious," Saito said. "You and I have been communicating on an adult-to-adult basis. I congratulate you for that, by the way. It took courage on your part. But anyway, you and I had opposite goals. I wanted information. You didn't want to give it to me. You won. That's all. If I'd had more time I would have won."

"Maybe not," Hansen said.

"Maybe not. That's true. But you had backups and I didn't. So you won. That's no reason for me to kill you. Especially not in front of witnesses. They execute killers in Texas."

"But you've already killed in Texas," Hansen said.

"Have I?"

"In the jail. You killed that—Marubyashi."

"Did I?" Saito smiled, slowly. "Did I?"

Behind him, Kerensky asked, "What is transactional analysis?"

"Chief? They've got him. Got them both. Hansen and the ninja."

"How's Hansen?" Shigata asked quickly. He had waited through some anxious moments, hearing Tyler talking to other people, giving orders.

"I don't know. Quinn called an ambulance for him. Asked for ten-thirty-nine, but then he changed it to ten-eighteen."

"Ask Quinn—"

"Ten-four. Stand by." In the quick, clipped voice of a trained dispatcher, it sounded more like "Teh-fo'."

Shigata waited.

"Chief? I got Hansen on the radio. Not just Quinn, Hansen himself. He says he'll be okay. But he sounded—" Tyler hesitated.

"He sounded how?"

"He sounded like me, when I found out I wasn't going to walk again. But he's up walking around now, so that's not it."

"What about the ninja?"

"He gave the name of Jack Saito. Nothing on NCIC under that name. He's—Quinn says he's not giving them any trouble now."

"All right," Shigata said, "listen carefully, because this is critical. Tell Quinn not to question the ninja now at all. Don't let him make a phone call. Don't let him have a lawyer. Keep him in a holding cell under close guard, at least two guards at all times. Now, if anybody tries to question him, then we have to offer the phone call and the lawyer; we can't hold him incommunicado for more than a couple of hours anyway, but at all costs, *keep that ninja away from the telephone for at least the next two hours.* Is that clear?"

"Yes, sir."

"Call me back if there are any problems. If I'm not here, somebody at this number will know where I am."

"You bastard," Yamagata said. "You son-of-a-bitching—" He went on in that vein for several minutes. Nobody said anything to him; Shigata couldn't be involved with making the arrest because it was out of his territory, but Clement

took him along on the raid as—he said—a professional courtesy to a fellow law enforcement officer.

"I told you," Shigata said after the swearing finally stopped. "I told you last night. You didn't believe me."

"If I had—" Yamagata came to his feet and lumbered toward Shigata, and a couple of FBI agents behind him shoved him down into his seat again as the search continued.

Yamagata straightened his tie slowly. "But no one can stop my hunter," he said. "And he will kill your wife—"

"You mean Jack Saito?" Shigata said. "He's in jail."

This time Yamagata moved a little faster than the FBI agents, throwing a blow at Shigata's face. Shigata danced almost, but not quite, out of the way, and before anybody could stop him he struck back with all the force of his whole body against a foe half a foot taller than he and at least double his weight. Shigata then instantly relaxed all his muscles as a federal agent grabbed him from behind. "What the hell do you think you're doing?" the agent snarled in Shigata's ear.

Yamagata sat down, hard, his lip bleeding, and stared dumbfounded at Shigata.

Shigata stayed completely relaxed until the man behind him released him. "You made a little mistake, Yamagata," he said then. "The feds don't hit people. You know that, and you're right. But—thing is—I'm not a fed anymore. I wouldn't have hit first. But you gave me the opening. And you should have known I'd take it." He carefully unfolded his handkerchief and mopped a small amount of blood from his own upper lip, replaced the handkerchief in his pocket, and faked a cheerful grin at Yamagata.

"And you think it's over now?" Yamagata asked, a wide toadlike smile spreading malignly across his face. "You think, now, Buddy Yamagata and his organization are out of business? Think again. I always have more than one string to my bow."

"Rocky asked me to steal the key, if I got a chance," E. P. Honshu said. "I told him I wouldn't. I told him I was scared.

Well—I was. But later, when I found out what Buddy was going to do, I did steal the key." He paused for a moment, then burst out, "He ordered his own daughter murdered! That's—you don't do that! If—if for some reason you must execute a member of your own family, you do it decently, with a sword. But—not that way. Not that way." Honshu looked directly at Shigata. "Does he know you have that key?"

"I don't think so. Not yet."

"I would like to be the one to tell him. I really would like that."

"You know we can't allow that," Clement said, behind Shigata.

"I asked you to stay out of here," Shigata said without turning.

"It's my case," Clement said. "Honshu, we're turning you loose for now, unless you'd rather we held you for your own protection."

"That is not necessary," Honshu said. "But what are you doing with my brother?"

Clement scratched his upper lip. "He's being charged with the bombing assassination of a federal judge. I expect he'll be held without bond."

"Are you taking him to the county jail? I must—it is my duty to get him an attorney."

"You have a cockeyed sense of duty," Clement said. "Eventually he'll be taken to the county jail, yes. For now, he'll be transported to the federal prosecutor's office. Oh, by the way, don't try to get Kenichi to defend him. We're arresting him, too."

"I understand," Honshu said. "So I may go now?"

"Be reasonable, Captain," Saito said, leaning jauntily against the bars of the holding cell. "I'm not asking for a tommy gun or a packet of cyanide. Just my cigarettes. I can scarcely escape, or signal anyone, with a half-package of cigarettes."

"Interesting you should mention cyanide," Quinn answered, standing far enough outside the bars to be just out of Saito's reach.

"No cyanide." Saito seemed remote, vaguely amused. "Just Winstons. Plain old Winstons, that you can get out of a vending machine. I saw a machine in the hall. If you don't want to give me my own package, get some change out of my property and get me a package from the hall."

"I'm afraid not," Quinn said.

"Why?"

"I think you know why."

Saito shrugged, then sat back down on the bench in the holding cell. "It was worth a try," he said.

"Nice try," Quinn agreed. "But no cigar."

Saito grinned at him.

"Why, Captain?" Barlow asked. "You let most people smoke in the holding cell."

"Most people don't know how to commit suicide with a package of cigarettes," Quinn replied. "And most people don't come from a culture that regards suicide as an honorable exit from trouble, or an honorable apology for failure in an assignment." He walked on down the hall and back out the door, and Barlow could hear the clanging as Quinn restored the large jail-cell key to the box where it was kept.

Then Barlow turned to look at Saito. Saito shrugged apologetically, continuing to look remotely amused.

". . . Wataru Itagaki, attorney-at-law, and I demand to see my client at once. You have no right to hold him incommunicado, and I demand—"

"Hold your horses," said the CIA agent who, not being needed as an interpreter, was temporarily acting as receptionist in the federal prosecutor's office. "I'll check. You sit down right here. . . . All right," he said five minutes later, "you can see him in the conference room. I hope you understand I'll have to check your briefcase first."

Itagaki pulled the briefcase toward him indignantly. "It is a breach of client relationships, you will *not* check my briefcase."

"I'm not trying to read anything in it," the agent said. "I just have to look for weapons, that's all."

Itagaki opened the briefcase dramatically, scattering papers on the floor. "I have no firearms. You can tell that. I have no swords, no daggers, no hand grenades."

"I see that," the agent said, stooping to pick up the strewn paper.

"Give me those at once. You have no right to touch them. Where is the conference room?"

"In here. Now, understand the procedures. Mr. Yamagata has been seated at one end of the conference table. You will sit at the other end. I'll be watching from outside. I won't make any attempt to hear what you and he are saying, but there will be no physical contact of any kind between you and him. If you need to hand him anything, slide it to the middle of the table and then sit down, and he will then stand up and get it the rest of the way. He's been given the same instructions. Do you understand these rules?"

"An indignity," Itagaki sputtered, "but yes, I understand."

The agent opened the door for him. Itagaki entered, shut the door with his elbow, seated himself at the end of the table, and sat quite still, staring at Yamagata at the other end of the table and touching nothing but his own briefcase.

"Well?" Yamagata said, after the staring had gone on for several seconds. "So my brother got me an attorney. Who are you?"

"Recognize my voice," Itagaki said, and if the agent had been able to hear through the heavy door, he would have been surprised, because the voice was not that of Wataru Itagaki but rather of E. P. Honshu. "I have acted before. But not like this."

"Bobby," Yamagata said, slumping down into the chair. "What are you doing—"

"Hear me," Wataru "Bobby" Yamagata—E. P. Honshu—Wataru Itagaki—said. "Hear me, and hear me well. You have disgraced our family. You allowed your daughter, my niece, to be murdered dishonorably in a far place. Your *kabun* have been killed following your orders. Your ninja is imprisoned. You have failed."

"I have not failed," Buddy Yamagata said. "I have had—setbacks. That's all. This—Shigata"—his tone made the name a profanity—"will pay for all he has done."

"This is not a setback. This is failure. Rocky Omori and I tape-recorded your telephone calls, but only the most urgent ones, for the last six months. Rocky willed the recordings to Mark Shigata, and Mark Shigata gave them to the federal prosecutor. The key to the safe-deposit box you rented under the name of Toshimichi Karoku is in the hands of the federal prosecutors. Don't interrupt me; hear me out. I gave it to Mark Shigata. I did. I gave it to him myself. You would have been safe; I was too afraid of you to fight you; but no longer. When you ordered Rocky and Phyllis killed the way you did, I knew you had to be destroyed. I will do you one favor. This last thing I do for you. After this I will do nothing for you ever again."

He slid a sheaf of papers to the middle of the table. Then he paused briefly, maneuvered the top and bottom sheet off the sheaf and returned them to the briefcase, and sat still, again touching nothing but his briefcase.

His features frozen, Buddy Yamagata stood up, took the sheaf of papers, felt his way through them without looking, and nodded.

"I will never look at you again," E. P. Honshu said, and once again Buddy Yamagata nodded.

Wataru Itagaki, the fussy attorney, was back; once again there was nothing visible of E. P. Honshu as Itagaki tapped with his knuckles at the door. The CIA agent opened it, and Itagaki, without looking back, proceeded to the front door of the suite. At the door he stopped and waited. "Well?" he said. "Imbecile, do you expect me to open the door for myself? Can't you see my hands are full?"

The CIA agent shrugged and opened the door, and Itagaki strutted out.

* * *

Kerensky turned, dumbfounded, to stare at the door of the Pizza Hut. "Why are you not in hospital?" he demanded.

"I left," Hansen said genially. "Against medical advice. They made me sign a paper saying it was against medical advice before they'd give me back my pants. And Quinn's going to be mad because he wanted my pants as evidence. What are the two of you doing drinking together? Where's my beer? I'd rather have a beer than all the doctor's pills."

Kerensky slid his full glass over to Hansen. "Until we get a third glass."

"We are friends," Ybarra said hoarsely. "Kerensky and me, we are good *amigos,* right, Kerensky? Kerensky, he is *muy simpático.* He does not like *comunistas.* He helped to overthrow *comunistas* in his country. If I had known I would not have slit his tires."

"See," Kerensky said, not quite too drunk to reclaim his now-empty glass and begin to write on the place mat, "Pete knows lots of people in the Cuban resistance. And when the Cubans get rid of Castro, I'm going to be the first Russian journalist into free Cuba. And I'm going to write a book about it."

"Yeah?" Hansen said, appropriating Ybarra's glass because there still was no third glass on the table and pouring beer into it. "You know, I was always going to write a book, but I never have got around to it."

"Perhaps we should write the book together," Kerensky said.

"Yeah," Hansen said. Then he chugalugged the beer, put his head down on the table, and began to snore.

Kerensky eyed him. "I think the amphetamine wore off," he said.

"What amphetamine?" Ybarra asked.

"It's a long story," Kerensky said. "But he's—what was that word you used?—*simpático.* Do you think we can take him home?"

"I don't believe it," Clement said. "After everything that's happened today, he's actually singing tonight?"

"I thought he might," Shigata answered. His attention was not on the sixteen-ounce steak on his plate, but on the man who had walked onto the stage in a glittering white costume and begun to sing into the microphone, singing a song called "Are You Lonesome Tonight?"

"Do you suppose he is?" Fong asked. "Lonesome, I mean? Shigata, I wondered why you wanted to come here tonight, I guess this is why."

Neither Clement nor Shigata answered, and Fong too was silent. E. P. Honshu didn't talk tonight, didn't use his usual introductory patter, didn't sing any rock or rockabilly. He sang steadily for more than an hour, sang every sad ballad in his repertoire, and then walked off the stage without looking back, without ever speaking.

"Your food's getting cold," Clement said.

"It already did," Shigata said. "I can eat it cold." But he didn't, he just sat still, thinking.

A waiter approached the table, leaned over, and whispered something to Clement, and Clement said, "Excuse me. Telephone call."

In his absence, both Fong and Shigata began to eat.

Clement returned and sat down. "We've lost Yamagata," he said abruptly.

"We what?" Fong said sharply. "How did he escape?"

"With a knife blade," Clement said. "He—God knows how he did it. He stabbed himself just below the heart, dragged the blade straight down, laying his belly open all the way, and then made a horizontal cut just below the navel. He was still breathing when they found him, but not for long."

"That's hara-kiri," Shigata said. "Ceremonial suicide. Where'd he get the knife? Wasn't he searched?"

"Of course he was searched," Clement said, jabbing his fork savagely into a slice of beef. "Officially, nobody knows how he got the knife. But you know that attorney who visited him in Fong's office? Wataru Itagaki? There's not any Wataru Itagaki. Oh, there was one, of course. He picked a name—not quite from the phone book, although it was still listed in the phone book under attorneys. Wataru Itagaki was sixty-seven years old, and he died four months ago. They checked on that *before* they called me. And the alleged Wataru Itagaki was very careful not to leave fingerprints."

Shigata stood up, grabbed a waiter for a whispered conversation, and took off, walking fast. "Where's he going?" Fong asked.

"I don't know," Clement said. "Maybe he got sick."

"You wouldn't make a Japanese sick by talking about hara-kiri," Fong said.

"He's not Japanese," Clement said. "He's—he's sansei. He told me. I think I'd better see what he's up to."

"I'm coming with you."

Shigata stopped them both at the door to Honshu's dressing room. "I've called an ambulance," he said. "But it's going to be too late."

The bright lights of the dressing room glittered from the sequins on E. P. Honshu's costume. The sword hilt sticking out of his belly was thickly jeweled. The rubies were almost, but not quite, as red as the blood on the floor.

Epilogue

IT WAS LIKE THE BEST of the Shinto shrines, isolated, surrounded by evergreen trees.

It was unlike all other Shinto shrines because it was in the delta of the Sacramento River in California.

Shigata didn't approach too close. He didn't know what to wear. He didn't know who the priests were, or how to talk to them. He didn't speak the right language. Only his face was right.

"Rocky," he said, "Isoruko Omori, I'm not Shinto. I don't know how to talk to the ancestors. But—if you do, if you hear me—tell them Daniel's safe. And you and Phyllis are avenged." He wiped his eyes. "And—Wataru Yamagata—if you can hear me—you didn't have to do it. But—I think—I realize why you did."

Cary Okuma, who had driven him to the almost-hidden shrine, moved forward and put a gentle hand on his shoulder.

"Oh, God," Shigata said, and then he said, "I don't even know if there is a God. I don't know who God is. But if there is a God—nobody else could possibly make sense of any of this. Cary, there was no reason, no reason at all, for any of it."

Okuma didn't answer.

Shigata leaned forward, suddenly folded his legs to sit down on the ground, and began to cry, harshly at first, unpracticed, but then more easily.

And a slow wind soughed through the evergreen trees.

Wingate, Anne.
Yakuza, go home!

19.95